BEAR ON THE MOUNTAIN

WATCHDOG MOUNTAIN DIVISION: BOOK 1

OLIVIA MICHAELS

FALCON IN HAND PUBLISHING

 Created with Vellum

For Bess and for Becca. Old friendships and new, both gone too soon.

ONE

Ellie Jameson slipped off the Greyhound Bus in the early morning mist and shivered. The bus terminal in Denver smelled of exhaust and grease from a nearby fast-food restaurant and Ellie's stomach rumbled. She hadn't eaten since Kansas, which was...the day before, she thought, or maybe the day before the day before.

The bus driver climbed down the steps behind her and opened the luggage compartment.

"Which is yours, miss?" he asked, tired but not unkindly.

"The big bag right behind that hard case. I've got a bike in there." She hiked her backpack higher on her shoulders. She didn't tell him about the sleeping bag stuffed in the bike bag.

He nodded. "Planning on doing some mountain biking?"

Technically, she was, but probably not in the way he thought, so she nodded and smiled. "I'm headed for a place outside of Lyons."

"Pretty country," she heard him say from inside the bus's compartment as he pushed the hard-sided suitcase aside and grabbed the black bag. "Here you go." He set the bag on the pavement and arched his back, stretching before he got back on the bus.

"Thank you. Drive safely." Ellie dug into her pocket and took out some crumpled bills to give him a tip. She was down to her last fourteen dollars—a lucky number and a good sign, she liked to think. She took the five, then decided to add two dollars more. Seven was lucky too.

He watched her count out the money, then waved her off. "Don't need a tip from you, miss. Take care." He turned and climbed back up the steps. A couple other people had gotten off but only had carry-ons. Ellie watched them head into the terminal. Each person had someone waiting, who greeted them with hugs and took their bags.

Ellie had no one.

No, worse than no one. She had her family behind her. She prayed they'd stay there.

Ellie wheeled the bag away from the bus to a metal bench and sat down. Water dripped from a corner of the roof into a puddle where a couple of sparrows darted around the bigger pigeons for a drink. One ran straight in and threw water over its feathers, reminding Ellie that she was also in desperate need of a shower.

As the bus pulled away, she unzipped the bag and pulled it down from around the folded-up bike and the sleeping bag. Both belonged to her oldest brother. She didn't want to imagine his face when he found his stuff gone. He was bad enough on a good day, let alone on a day when he woke to find her gone with his things. Nope, she couldn't even begin to imagine how red his face must have been, or how loudly he'd yelled, not caring if he woke up everyone else, or how he must have stomped through the house to see what else she'd made off with—a bag of chips, a box of power bars, her own clothing and a few sundry items, and of course the letter, though none of them knew about that.

And here she was, imagining exactly what she didn't want to imagine. Funny how her brain worked that way.

Ellie reached into another jacket pocket and took out a crumpled plastic wrapper. She shook out the few cake crumbs left and watched the birds run for them. It brought a smile to her face.

"Whatcha doin'?"

Ellie turned her head and looked up at a man in a nice suit. He was fairly tall, thin, and he had a ton of gel in his hair. His tie had the tiniest spot of grease on it.

"Just feeding the pigeons," Ellie said. She quickly looked back down and went back to pulling the sleeping back out of the bike bag.

"You need a place to stay?" he asked.

"No-I'm-good-thanks." Her answer came out as one word. She stood and held up one short end of the sleeping bag to roll it up. He stood about a foot taller than her.

"Let me help you." Before she could protest, the man bent down and took the other end.

"I've got it. Please let go."

He straightened and held his hands up, palms out, and took a step back. He was still smiling at her. Her gaze flicked up, then back to her hands as she folded the bag in half to roll it.

"I just don't want to see the end of that nice sleeping bag get all wet and dirty," the man said.

Ellie said nothing. The sleeping bag wasn't new or even particularly nice.

He chuckled. "Of course, if you're sleeping rough, it's going to get dirty, isn't it?"

She already had, and it did. "I'm visiting my cousin," Ellie said.

"Oh," the man said, folding his arms. "Does she make you sleep in the yard?"

Ellie flicked her gaze up to him then back down. She had the bag almost rolled up into a tight cylinder that she could attach to her backpack. The bike was still folded up in the bag. Lightweight and fancy and nicer than anything she'd ever owned.

"I don't think you have an aunt or a place to stay, little girl."

She cringed at those two words. Ellie was in her twenties, not a little girl, though her small size often made people look twice.

"Why don't you come with me?" he coaxed in a cooing voice that put the pigeons to shame. "I have a nice place, a closet full of nice clothes. Hot food." He lowered his voice. "You came out here for the," he pressed his thumb and index finger together and put them up to his pursed lips, then inhaled loudly, "am I right? I have plenty of that too, and other things."

She barely shook her head.

"Don't deny it, sweet face. A lot of kids like you come out here for that. And you know what? They end up sleeping on the street where not so nice things happen to them. That doesn't have to be you."

Ellie bent and reached into the bottom of the bag.

"You're a sweet little thing, so let me help you." The man took a step forward and reached for her, then stumbled as he danced backward.

Oh yeah, she'd taken one more thing from her brother that was sure to really get him mad. Ellie pointed the .38 special as steadily as she could at the tiny grease spot on the man's fancy tie.

"I don't do drugs and I'm not interested in becoming a prostitute." She held his gaze as she added, "Now go away."

He left her alone to unfold the bike and pop the wheels on. She folded up the bag, stuffed it into the top of her back-pack as best she could, and mounted the bike. As she pedaled away, she told herself that the sweat trickling down her back was only from exertion.

I was aiming at a grease spot, not at a man. A grease spot...

TWO

J on "Bear" Behr rolled into Lyons early one afternoon when the aspen leaves were just beginning to turn golden. He'd driven right past the turnoff that led to his old friend's ranch. Sean Volker wasn't there, would never be there again. He'd heard about Sean's death of course, and it wounded him to the soul. Growing up, Sean had always been the funny one in their group of friends. He could make all of them practically piss themselves laughing over the stupidest shit.

Yeah, there was something about the friends you made as a kid. Back when the world was huge and you had yet to find your place in it, it was good to find your people, the ones who always made you laugh and had your back. Maybe that's why Bear had loved being a Ranger so much—a second chance at that deep, good friendship that was so hard to find.

He pulled into the coffee shop parking lot overlooking the St. Vrain. Riversong had been there forever and he missed the taste of their coffee. Or, maybe it was the mountain air that always made it taste better. Probably both.

He stopped in for a to-go cup. The man behind the

counter turned and Bear recognized him as the owner, though he was starting to get on in years. Sonny, yeah, he was pretty sure the man's name was Sonny. Bear started to say hello when he realized Sonny didn't recognize him.

I've been gone that long he thought. When Sonny looked him up and down and frowned, Bear self-consciously ran a hand through his shaggy hair. His beard was hardly better. *Been a long time since I've had a trim, too.*

"Hey, friend," Bear said. "I'd like a large eye-opener, black, to go. Please."

The man's eyebrows rose. "Took that off the menu a while back, but I'm happy to make it for you. But if you don't sleep for three days, that's on you." He turned and grabbed a jar of some high-octane, extra-caffeinated beans. After he ground them and started the espresso machine, he asked, "You from around here, or has it just been a while since you visited?"

Both. "Born here."

Sonny poured black coffee into a large to-go cup and added the fresh triple shot of espresso, then turned to give Bear another look, trying to place him.

"Well, near here." Bear scratched his beard. He didn't really feel like going into details. He pulled a twenty out of his wallet and laid it on the counter instead.

"Mind letting me park my truck here for an hour? I'd like to go and pay my respects to the St. Vrain."

Sonny nodded. "We aren't too busy right now. Parking lot's empty enough." He set the near-lethally caffeinated coffee on the counter and pushed the twenty back toward Bear. "Parking's free."

Bear shook his head. "Keep the change. 'Preciate it."

Sonny grabbed a slice of banana bread and set it next to the coffee. "Welcome home."

Bear took his coffee down to the river where he'd talk to Sean.

He grinned as he remembered the gang of boys he grew up with. They'd all loved the river. It was a place where they could run free like a pack of lost boys or wild animals. In fact, they'd given each other animal nicknames. Sean was Hawk, for the wounded hawk he'd nursed back to health one summer. With his last name, Bear's nick was an obvious choice but his friends told him it fit his personality too—that he was big and quiet, preferring to mull things over before acting. But when roused, well, you didn't want to fuck with him.

Out of all of them, Sean had loved the river the most. No surprise he'd become a Swick in the Navy where he could spend all his time messing around on boats. If Sean wasn't home, you could find him somewhere along the river. So, that's why Bear chose to come down to the St. Vrain before visiting Sean's sister Arden and paying his respects.

Bear got down to the river's edge and sat cross-legged on a wide, flat stone. He sipped his coffee quietly and watched the water. Someone had stacked a pile of smooth rocks one atop the other so he focused on that and tried to bring back the feeling of being a kid, splashing in the water and laughing with his friends. They dared each other to do the craziest things, not a lick of sense among them. Bear grinned even as his heart felt like it was beating inside an iron box. Sean would laugh at him if he admitted to missing him that much.

"Sorry I wasn't here sooner," he whispered to the water, where a small school of minnows darted in the shadow of the big stone. "Sorry we didn't get one last chance to say goodbye."

A crackling noise got his attention and he looked down in

time to see a squirrel attempting to open the plastic wrap around his slice of banana bread.

"Well, you're a brave little cuss, aren't you?"

The squirrel jumped back when Bear picked up the banana bread and watched him unwrap it. Bear broke off a piece and stretched out his hand.

"Here you go."

The squirrel didn't move. Bear laughed. "Oh, now you're gonna be shy, huh? Come on, buddy, you can have it."

Finally, the squirrel darted forward and grabbed the banana bread out of Bear's hand. It quickly disappeared into his mouth and he scampered back onto the rock, begging for more, making Bear laugh again. He broke off another piece and offered it carefully. The squirrel took it, and like so many wild creatures Bear encountered, trusted him enough to let Bear run a careful finger down its fur.

"Holy shit, it *is* you," Bear heard from behind him as the startled squirrel ran up a tree. "St. Francis, friend to the animals."

Without turning, Bear said, "Only assholes who want broken noses call me Francis."

"Only your best friends know that's your middle name, asshole."

Bear turned to see one of those old best friends grinning at him. Shane Foti. Known to their friends as Elk.

Bear uncrossed his legs and stood up smoothly. "Shane."

"Good to see you, Bear." The men hugged, clapping each other on the back. Shane grabbed and yanked a handful of Bear's hair. "But what the hell is this?" He laughed. "And that beard. You a mountain man now? We need to rename you Grizzly Adams?"

"I was always a mountain man," Bear said.

"Not so much now. Good to see you, man. Been a while."

Bear detected a hint of judgment but he let it go since he probably deserved it. It had been a long time since he'd set foot in Colorado. "Yeah. I wanted to come pay my respects to Arden."

"But you came down to the river first?"

Bear shrugged. "You know. Hawk."

Shane nodded as his expression turned serious. "Because you missed scattering his ashes along here this summer?"

Bear tried not to flinch at that. He'd had no idea.

But Shane caught him out. "You didn't know about that, did you?"

He shook his head.

"Arden said she'd tried to get a hold of all Hawk's old friends to tell them. Hard to do that when she doesn't have an address."

"That's because *I* don't have an address."

Now Shane looked surprised. "What, seriously? You doing the van life or something?" His mouth turned down and his brow furrowed. "It's not mon—"

Bear waved him off. No, it wasn't money.

"I'm solid. I just decided to take a vacation, see the country after getting out."

"Bear. It's been years. After a while, that goes from a vacation to a lifestyle, man."

He only shrugged.

"So you haven't been up to the ranch yet." A statement, not a question.

"No."

"Obviously. Shit's changed, my brother."

Damn. I should have come sooner.

"Changed? Arden all right?"

"Arden's fine. But if you wanna go up and see her, I'll have to call you in first."

Now that was a head-scratcher. "Call her first?" A thought came to him. "You guys...close now or something?"

Shame erupted in laughter. "What, you think I broke the pact we all made not to date Arden? Jesus, Bear, Hawk would come back and haunt my ass if I did that."

Bear grinned, remembering the promise Hawk made them all swear to keep. Not that he'd been the least bit interested in dating his friend's little sister. He didn't think any of them had been, not really. As sweet and pretty as she was though, he couldn't blame Hawk for wanting to nip any fights over her in the bud.

"So what's changed then?"

Shane looked away as he considered his words. "I'll explain on the way there."

Puzzled, Bear said, "I have my truck here. You need a ride or something?"

"No, man. It's best you come in with me." He clapped Bear on the shoulder. "It's been a rough summer and we've got a lot to catch you up on."

Bear couldn't believe what Shane was telling him as they drove the shiny new SUV up the road leading to the ranch. At first he thought Shane was pulling his leg. Arden was engaged to a man whose company had bought out the entire neighborhood on the mountain—including the ranch she swore never to sell? No way. But Shane was dead serious. So Bear wasn't sure about this Kyle McGuire guy. Was he engaged to her just for her ranch? Shane wasn't acting like that was the case, and he would sure as hell be just as protective of Arden as Hawk himself. They all would.

"I'm working for Kyle now, as you can see," Shane told

him. "Bodyguard work." But Shane couldn't fool him. He heard something else behind those words. Bear was quiet but he was no dummy. Shane was former military so there were probably some off-the-government-books jobs going on there.

Not Bear's problem.

"Everybody'd love to see you. How long you planning on staying?"

Bear's guard started to creep up. "Depends."

"We could all go out for a beer, you know? Be good to get the whole gang back together."

"Mm."

Shane drove another minute before speaking. "If you're planning on staying a while, Kyle's looking for people he can trust," he said. "If you need work."

Bear grunted.

"Or...we could use you, too. Like in the old days."

Bear cleared his throat and crossed his arms, remembering now why he'd avoided Colorado.

"We're at it again. But it's not the same without you. We were a team, Bear."

"That was a long time ago. We were all kids."

"And we did some good, man. Sometimes, I think we did more good as a group of teenagers than—"

"I didn't come back here to be recruited," Bear said, his voice louder than he'd planned, but maybe it would get the point across.

Shane pulled the SUV over and looked at Bear. "You turnin' yellow? Should I call you Pooh Bear?"

"Fuck you." Bear refused to look at his friend. He stared out the window instead, where a circling hawk suddenly dove for a mouse or some other small creature in the tall grass ringed with trees.

"Same old Bear." Shane pulled back onto the road.

Up ahead, Bear spotted a gate and gatehouse. "That it?"

"Yep. No getting past the gate without an engraved invite."

Bear side-eyed him.

"Told you, rough summer."

"In Lyons?"

"Times change, brother." Shane's voice sounded regretful.

Times may have changed, but Arden hadn't. She was waiting on the porch of the ranch house, bouncing on her toes with the biggest, warmest smile on her face. A tall man stood next to her, wariness obvious on his face. He had a dog on a leash—what looked like a gold and black mottled Lab.

"Bear!" Arden shouted as she ran toward him, barely giving him a chance to get out of the SUV. His fears that she'd hate him for missing Sean's memorial evaporated. Big smile on his face, he opened his arms, picked her up, and swung her around.

"It's so good to see you, Bear!" He put her down and she gave his beard a tug. "At least I think that's you under all that hair. What's that all about?"

"Can't find a barber I like," Bear joked.

The man who'd been standing on the porch beside Arden had made his way to them along with the dog. He offered his hand.

"I'm Kyle McGuire," he said.

"Already heard good things about you," Bear said, shaking his hand as they sized each other up. "Jon Behr."

"But everyone just calls him Bear," Arden said, her silvery-gray eyes shining. "He was one of Sean's best friends."

That hurt, even though he knew she meant nothing malicious by it.

Kyle's expression changed once Arden mentioned her brother. "In that case, you're more than welcome here."

"For as long as you'd like," Arden added, making Bear wonder what Shane had told them when he called up. "I've already got dinner going, and we have plenty of room here, if you'd like to stay for a few days."

"Careful, or Arden will have you moved in," Kyle joked. "Just look at me."

Arden laughed. "And you showed up uninvited at that."

"Uninvited?" Bear asked, frowning.

"Stick around and I'll tell you the story." Arden bent to pet the beautiful Lab. "It all has to do with Camo here. He's the reason we're together."

Bear bent down to scratch the dog's head. Camo looked up at him with soulful eyes. "I'd love to hear the story."

"Then come on in."

And that was how Bear found himself changing his plans and staying a while.

Bear was enjoying the warm Colorado autumn day when the commotion started.

From his vantage point where he was working on the roof, he could see across the entire yard to the Rockies beyond. Everywhere he looked was drenched in forest greens, golden and white aspens, and dotted here and there with red and orange scrub oak. Someone somewhere had a fire going and the air was tinged with woodsmoke winding through the earthy smell of fall leaves. The sky was an overturned blue bowl sheltering it all.

Bear hadn't been sure how he'd feel about returning home after all his wanderings, but now that he was here, it felt good. He'd be sad to leave again, but it was best he did. If he kept on moving, he could maybe outrun whatever it was that chased him inside.

But, Colorado wouldn't be a bad place to hibernate for the winter, either.

He shook that thought away. No, he'd best move on down to Texas for the winter after he finished up work on his old friend's ranch. Well, Arden's ranch, now that her brother and their parents were gone. Bear missed his friend Sean, missed teasing him about becoming a Swick instead of an Army Ranger as Bear had done. And of course, Hawk had teased him right back, calling Bear Smokey the Park Ranger.

Bear took a deep breath. He was sad that he'd missed Sean's memorial. It was only by chance that he'd returned when he did a couple weeks ago and decided to look in on her. Sure, she still grieved, but Arden was thriving, thanks to Kyle. That made Bear happy and he knew Sean would've been happy too. Kyle was a good man—for a SEAL. Bear chuckled.

Once they got to know each other, Kyle offered him a job with his security company but Bear said no thanks, he was out of that game. He just wanted to work with his hands building things now. Sawdust instead of blood, nails instead of bullets. Kyle understood. They had work for him around the ranch and the safehouses that were part of the huge mountain property, so Bear happily took that. It would keep him in pocket money and out of trouble.

But now it looked like trouble was coming his way.

He heard some branches breaking in the woods at the edge of the yard, not random but steady like something was making its way through the woods. It wasn't deer; they were quiet animals. Elk, maybe, but they also tended to be more careful than this. No, this sounded human. And it was headed straight for the house.

There was one big problem with this scene. The roads,

the forest, the house, all the land on top of this foothill belonged to Watchdog. No one was supposed to be able to just tramp through the woods, and no one had told Bear to expect visitors to the safehouse he was working on. Especially ones coming up behind through the woods.

Bear made his way carefully to the edge of the roof and the top of the ladder. He half slid, half climbed down the ladder quickly and turned to face the intruder. His gun was just inside on the counter next to the back door, but he wanted to see who or what he was dealing with first.

And what he saw confused him before it made him chuckle.

At first, he thought a girl was pushing her bike through the underbrush to the safehouse, until he realized that he was looking at a young woman dwarfed by the pack and sleeping bag on her back. The bike was a nice one, sleek and expensive looking, but not one you'd take over rough country. The woman was working hard to wrestle it under the weight of that pack, which kept snagging on low hanging branches like the trees were teasing her. Her face was red and her sweaty hair clung to her cheeks and forehead. She looked like she was about ready to punch the first thing she came across. The thought of Bear being that first thing, and imagining one of her small fists coming at him, was what made him laugh.

She stopped and looked up and something about her face brought back his childhood in a nostalgic rush that made him want to say *Finally, there you are* to this complete stranger. When she caught sight of him, her eyes grew round until she looked like a fox caught in the headlights. She was real pretty, even pissed-off, and the closer Bear ambled toward her, the prettier she got. No—make that gorgeous, in a sweet way. Big brown eyes to go with that reddish-brown hair. Soft-pink lips, slightly parted. An honest, open face that for some reason stirred up vague memories he desperately wanted to remember.

She's the blooming warmth from whiskey spreading in your chest on a bitter cold winter's night.

Bear didn't know where that thought had come from, but he pushed it out of the way. This woman didn't look like a threat, but she really didn't belong here as far as he knew. He needed to be cautious.

Her chin lifted by degrees as he came closer until she was looking up into his face.

"Who are you?" she asked.

"Same question," Bear answered. "You first."

"I'm Walter Sanders' niece. This is his house." She looked around. "Did his daughter sell it already?"

Bear tilted his head. "You're his niece?"

"I am." She nodded. "My family is estranged, so I didn't know he'd passed away, otherwise I would have come to the funeral." She paused and asked, "I'm sorry, did you know my uncle?"

She was a naïve little thing, telling him all that.

"No, not well. Sorry for your loss. But you're trespassing."

She swallowed and took a step back. "I'm sorry, I didn't know, and the road is blocked off, so I took a little path I knew—"

From the road in front of the house, they heard tires crunching on gravel—a big vehicle coming in hot, followed by doors opening and raised voices.

"Sounds like you're in trouble now," Bear said.

Poor thing looked terrified. Her red face paled and she looked around wildly, then down at the bike.

Yup, it was like Bear suspected—she'd stolen it. His heart dropped. He didn't want to think badly of her, but thieves were thieves. He wondered if she'd come to town like so many others, hoping to live rough in the beautiful state with great weather and legal drugs. The backpack and sleeping bag, her old clothes, they all spoke to that.

"Come on. It'll go easier if you don't run. Lemme help you." He reached out as if he were trying to tame a nervous fox, which he'd done when he was younger. Foxes, racoons, even a skunk once. Bear had a way with strays and wild things, and right now, this woman looked like a little of both. She studied his hand like she couldn't quite trust it, like someone who'd been struck, and his heart opened to her.

"Not gonna hurt you, I promise. Gonna help you, but you gotta trust me. They're good men you're hearing—friends—but they're low on trust and patience right now."

"Not the police?"

Bear sighed. "No." He didn't want to add that the police might be a better deal for her, all things considered. "Come on. I got you."

He watched her weigh her options as she looked into his eyes and he realized he ached for her to make the right decision and trust him. The voices were coming closer and they'd soon be around the house. Kyle and Shane shouted Bear's name and he turned his head to face the oncoming men when he felt her hand in his like she'd just laid a live wire across his palm. He turned back to see her gazing up at him—afraid but trusting. He folded his fingers over her hand, swallowing it up.

Kyle and Arden's dog, a retired military working dog named Camo came running around the house first to inspect the newcomer. The yellow-and-black-mottled Lab took one look at Bear and evaluated the situation.

No threats here Bear silently projected. Camo was one of the smartest dogs he'd ever met. Message received, Camo sniffed at the woman with his tail wagging. She let go of Bear's hand to pet Camo as she gave him a smile.

"Camo!" Kyle called the dog back over and Camo looked reluctant to leave her, which tickled Bear. That dog was devoted to Kyle. *Whoever this woman is, she must be someone special* Bear thought to himself. There was a certain spark to her that he saw even through her fear.

Bear turned toward Kyle and Shane. He held up a hand, signaling that all was well. Kyle gave him a look full of suspicion and rightly so. Shane was more at ease, but still holding himself like a man ready for a surprise attack. Bear understood that feeling down to his bones. But in this case, he was positive they were safe from anything harmful.

"Friend of yours?" Kyle asked, eying the woman.

"Just met," Bear answered. "This is," he paused, realizing that he didn't know her name, "Walter's niece." Saying those words, something akin to an old memory stirred and was gone, like a fish stealing a gulp of air from the surface of a lake before diving to the bottom.

"Walter's niece?" Kyle looked at Shane, who squinted at the woman.

"Elinor." she said. "Ellie, like my cousin, Ellen. Walter's daughter?" She looked at Kyle first, but when her eyes landed on Shane they stayed there. Then she looked at Bear again and tilted her head ever so slightly.

"What are you doing here?" Kyle demanded, and she stepped back. Bear reached out on instinct and grabbed her arm to steady her.

"I need to talk to Ellen." She twisted and reached for a pocket on her backpack.

"Stop right there," Kyle said. "Bring your hand back where I can see it."

She froze and Bear felt her tremble. She slowly turned back with one hand in the air and the other still holding the bike up. "I'm not armed." Her voice quavered.

"Maybe, maybe not. But I know you had a gun at one point and I just want to make sure you aren't going for another in your pack."

A gun? Bear's eyes widened as he looked from Kyle to Ellie then back at Kyle.

"We watched her stashing it in the woods on the cameras, right after we caught her sneaking onto the land."

"I'm sorry about that," Ellie said. "I didn't realize...I thought maybe my cousin still lived here, that there was a new road or something up to the houses since there's that gate—"

"The gate for Watchdog, which is my company." Kyle crossed his arms. "This is my land and one of my houses and you're trespassing."

Shane laid his hand on Kyle's arm. "I recognize her, boss." He looked at Bear. "Don't you?"

Bear studied her again. He was sure he'd remember if he'd met Ellie before.

"She was just a little kid though," Shane continued. "Not that I wasn't one too, last time she was here."

Ellie smiled and nodded. "I was five or six last time Mama brought us to visit. Me and my big brothers."

Shane frowned and nodded. "I was fourteen. Your brothers were assholes."

Bear grinned. Shane always told it like it was. No mystery why his nickname was Elk, the way he 'bugled' whatever he felt like saying.

"My brothers are still assholes," Ellie said matter-of-factly. "And they're bigger now."

Bear chuckled—couldn't help himself.

Kyle gave Bear a sharp look. "*You* remember her?"

Bear studied Ellie. That little piece of memory teased just under the surface. "A little, maybe?"

Ellie squinted back. "And maybe you're familiar to me,

but I doubt you had that beard when we were kids, so it's hard to tell."

Chuckling, Bear ran a hand over his thick, black beard. She had a point. It'd been a while since he'd had a trim. His hair was just as shaggy.

Shane stepped forward. "I'm Shane Foti. This is Jon Behr."

Ellie smiled and nodded. "I remember you guys now. I knew Sean better than I knew his friends, but I mostly played with Arden. She was a little older than me."

Kyle lifted his chin. "So Arden would know you too?"

Ellie nodded. "I think so." She looked around like she just remembered where she was. Bear watched all her bravery drain out. "I'm sorry, I didn't know. I thought my cousin still lived here. I need to talk to her."

"Negative," Kyle said. "First, you're coming with us."

Ellie looked up at Bear and there it went—his heart melted a little more. He had her trust.

"Don't think she meant any harm," Bear said at the risk of being fired and escorted off the land.

"Why'd you have a gun and why'd you hide it?" Kyle asked.

"Had it because I was traveling alone from Illinois," she answered. "Hid it because I didn't want to upset Ellen."

Kyle looked her up and down, taking in her shabby clothes. "Why'd you come?"

She glanced at Bear. "I think I'd like to tell her that. If I can."

Kyle crossed his arms. "I want to see some ID."

"That's in my pack. Can I get it?" She started to reach for the same pocket as before.

"Stop. Bear, take that pack off her."

Ellie froze like she was used to being in trouble—maybe

the kind that involved fists. Bear tried not to growl as he took hold of the bike. He gentled his voice instead.

"It's okay. I'm not going to take your things."

Ellie gave him another trusting nod. He laid the bike down, then helped her wiggle out of the pack. It was more bulky than heavy. Felt like it might be full of clothes. He reached into the pocket and found an old wallet. He opened it and saw only a few dollar bills, no credit cards, and a driver's license. He took the license out, glanced at it—Illinois like she said—and handed it to Kyle.

Kyle studied it, then held it up and compared the photo to Ellie's face.

"Did you know your uncle passed away recently?"

Ellie flinched and Bear felt a deep dark stirring of anger. Kyle was a good man, he knew that. But seeing this little woman flinch like that did something to him that he didn't like.

"She knows, Kyle. Why she's here, ain't that right?" He jutted his chin at Ellie. "Just wants to pay her respects is all."

Ellie switched her gaze to Bear and nodded carefully.

"Sure the two of you aren't friends?" Kyle asked.

"We could be," Ellie answered quickly. "We crossed paths as kids, I guess."

Bear's anger eased, and he chuckled again. How did she do that? "Kyle, why don't we take her on up to the ranch and Arden can have a sit-down with her?" He lifted the pack. "I can hang on to this in the meantime."

"Don't want a potential stranger in my home right now," Kyle answered. He turned his attention back to Ellie. "We're gonna take you down to the office. I'll call Arden and she can stop by, get a look at you. If you're who you say you are, *then* we'll contact Ellen." He leaned forward. "Until then, I'll consider you a trespasser." He turned to Shane. "Think you can find that gun?"

He nodded. "Yeah, give me a sec."

Ellie started to say, "I can—" but Kyle cut her off with a sharp shake of his head and her mouth snapped shut like a steel trap. Bear couldn't help feeling protective of her, surrounded as she was by men twice her size who didn't feel like messing around.

Shane disappeared into the woods and reappeared a few minutes later with a gun. Yup, it was a .38 special.

"Fully loaded," Shane said, handing it over to Kyle, who checked it, then eyed Ellie.

"I was traveling alone," she said just above a whisper.

"By bike?"

"Some of the way. Some by bus. I have the ticket." She was trembling again. Bear held back a growl.

Kyle looked at her, then at the bike. His eyebrows lifted then he blew out a breath through his nose. "Let's go." He turned, Shane beside him. Camo dropped back to trot beside Ellie and she bent to give his ears a quick scratch. Bear picked up the bike and wheeled it on her other side.

She slipped her hand into the crook of his arm and smiled up at him. Just a little ghost of a smile, but there all the same.

"Thank you," she whispered.

Bear only nodded, not trusting himself with words. He only hoped she was who she said she was, and meant no trouble.

THREE

Ellie sat silently in the back of the SUV, wondering what was going to happen next and trying not to be afraid. The quick drive back down the road made her feel queasy. She was already lightheaded and the headache that started at the bus station was now a hammer pounding through sloshing water against the inside of her skull. Her appetite had completely disappeared with the nausea and now all she wanted was to find someplace dark and quiet and lie down. Instead, she figured an interrogation was in her near future. Who were these guys? Had she accidentally sneaked into some sort of military installation? They were acting like she was a terrorist.

She remembered Shane from her visit to Uncle Walter's as one of the older boys in a roving pack who wanted nothing to do with a little kid like her, so she and Arden kept to themselves playing dolls and trying to tame the barn cats at Arden's parent's ranch. She didn't quite recognize Bear—not with that big beard—but she did remember one of the boys was named Jonny, and that he was always getting teased for...something. He seemed a lot smaller then, so maybe that was it.

Ellie glanced at the big man who'd been looking out for her to find that he was watching her out of the corner of his eye. He turned his attention to her completely once she caught him.

"Have you eaten?" he asked.

She shook her head quickly. Just the thought of food made her stomach curdle.

"You need water. And salt." He leaned forward. "Kyle. You got any water up there?"

Shane tossed back a bottle and he caught it, took off the top, and handed it to her. "Drink."

"Thank you, Jon," she managed.

"It's Bear."

She took a deep breath and looked at the bottle, hoping she could keep the water down.

"Come on," he said quietly. "I think you got a little altitude sickness." He moved his chin forward and up, two quick nods that said *drink up*.

She took a sip, then another. Bear reached over and laid the back of his hand against her forehead and then her cheek. It felt rough but warm. Comforting.

"Clammy," he said. "Kyle. She's got altitude sickness."

"Roger," Kyle answered, his voice sounding calmer than when they'd been at Uncle Walter's house. She didn't think he was a bad man—none of them struck her that way, especially Bear.

She liked Bear.

No, they weren't bad men. She recognized what they felt because she'd grown up marinating in that feeling—a mixture of wariness and caution. The fear that something bad could happen at any moment.

Her normal.

She wondered again who these men were and what had happened that put these big, tough guys so on edge.

Ellie honestly didn't know that her cousin had sold the house and moved, but she should have checked before she headed out to Colorado. *Stupid, stupid Ellie* her brother's voice yelled in her head, a phrase she heard at least once a day back home. *Stupid Ellie. Never can do anything right.*

When she'd seen the guardhouse and the gate blocking the road leading up to Walter's house, she'd panicked and turned her bike off into the woods. She was running on pure instinct and fear, ever since she'd left home but especially since the bus station. She'd never in her life pointed a gun at another living soul, not even one who had bad intentions.

Maybe they were right to be cautious around her. Maybe—

"All right, we're here," Bear interrupted her thoughts as they turned into a small parking lot in front of a building that she figured must be near the gated entrance. He reached over and felt her forehead again. "Keep drinking that." Kyle parked the SUV. "And stay there. I'll help you out."

Ellie nodded and took another drink. The men exited the SUV and she waited for Bear. He opened the door for her and helped her down. She caught him smiling behind his beard while his eyes sparkled. He made her feel somehow safe. He had her backpack slung over one shoulder and he offered his other arm, which she took. It made her feel steadier, inside and out.

They walked into the reception area where a woman behind the desk watched her carefully but not unkindly. Ellie noticed a dog bobblehead and one of those cardboard boxes full of snacks for charity. *This place and these men can't be all bad* she thought.

Kyle escorted her into a conference room along with

Shane and Bear. As soon as Bear pulled out a chair for her and she sat down, he left the room and she missed his presence immediately. She turned and looked at Kyle who sat across from her. Shane stood by the door.

Kyle pulled out a tablet and laid it on the table. "Arden is on her way. Should only be a couple of minutes."

"I'll be glad to see her."

"That's what she said about you, too." Kyle's voice sounded lighter and his eyes weren't as squinched up. "She remembers you as a cute little girl."

Ellie grinned and took another drink. She was still feeling lightheaded and by now her initial fear had become detachment. She sometimes felt like she floated somewhere near her body when she was stressed and this was one of those times.

The conference door opened and she expected to see Arden but it was Bear instead, carrying several bags of chips she recognized from the charity display. He sat beside her and dumped the chips on the table. He grabbed one of the bags, tore it open, then handed it to her.

"Eat," he said.

Shane started to reach for one of the bags and Bear practically growled at him. "Not for you. She needs the salt."

Shane backed off, palms out.

Ellie thanked him for what felt like the hundredth time that day and bit into a chip. Her mouth flooded with saliva at the saltiness. She crunched down on the best potato chip— no, the best food—she'd ever had. She forced herself not to tilt the bag up and pour every last chip into her mouth at once.

Bear nodded as he watched her. "Altitude sickness." He glared at Kyle.

"Arden will look her over," he said. "But in the meantime." He got up and adjusted the thermostat on the wall. The air conditioner blasted on, sending even cooler air into the room. Ellie felt better.

The next time the door opened, it was Arden. Ellie would have recognized her anywhere. She was still beautiful with her golden hair and her gray eyes that bordered on silver. Ellie stood up and before she could take a single step, Arden had crossed the room and hugged her.

"Goodness, it's been a long time," Arden said as she hugged Ellie. She held her at arm's length, frowning. "You're so pale and your skin is clammy." She noticed the chips and bottle of water on the table and nodded. "Good. Keep eating and drinking that. Headache?"

"Like my head is going to explode."

Arden opened her purse and took out a pill bottle. She shook two pills into Ellie's hand. "Ibuprofen. It'll help." She looked her up and down again. "Sit down, sweetie. When was the last time you ate for real, Ellie?"

"Um. I ate something this morning."

Arden's gaze flicked to Kyle's. She took the seat next to Ellie. Camo nosed Ellie's hand then rested his muzzle on her knee. In the meantime, Kyle had picked the tablet back up and was fiddling with it.

"I'm getting Ellen set up now for a video chat," he said.

Arden placed her hand on Ellie's. "I'm so sorry. You've got to be completely confused right now."

Ellie nodded. "I have no idea what's going on."

"You're safe," Bear said and she turned to look at him. His eyes were full of kindness. Every last trace of the suspicion she first saw in his eyes was gone. Now that she could really look at them, she noticed their unusual color—gold-flecked brown irises circled by dark gray.

Bear had beautiful eyes.

Arden touched her arm. "What were you doing in the woods? Why didn't you come to the gate?"

Ellie turned her attention back to her old friend. "I wasn't sure what the gate was for. It's been so long and my head was pounding. I thought maybe I'd gotten confused and taken the wrong road, or that a company had moved in, or maybe it was a gated community up here now. And then I remembered the shortcut we used to take off the road and up to Uncle Walter's house so I took it." She looked from Arden to Kyle. "I didn't mean to trespass." She looked back at Arden. "I didn't know Ellen had sold Uncle Walter's house. I wanted to talk to her first."

"First? About Walter?" Her eyes went round. "Oh, God, I'm so rude. I'm so sorry about your uncle's passing. He was like an uncle to me, too. He and my dad were good friends."

"Thank you. He was always...kind...to Mom and me and my brothers."

"Your mom was his only sister, right?"

She nodded. Her vision swam and she closed her eyes as her headache worsened. Ellie felt Bear's big hand land gently on her shoulder.

"Arden. Don't mean to be rude, either, but Ellie needs to rehydrate." He squeezed her shoulder gently and her headache took a big step back.

She picked up her water and took a long drink. Bear already had a second bag of potato chips open and ready. She looked at him with gratitude and ate one. Her head was just starting to clear, though her stomach rumbled.

"Did Ellen move somewhere?"

Arden nodded. "To Arizona."

Kyle looked up at her, a warning in his eyes.

"Kyle, she is who she says she is, I promise," Arden said gently. "You can relax."

"Says the woman who had a gun pointed at me the first time I met her," Kyle said with a grin and a wink.

"What was I supposed to do, Mr. California?" she teased back.

"Okay, she's coming online." Kyle turned the tablet around and propped it up so everyone could see. A black rectangle resolved into a woman's face—Ellen Sanders, Ellie's older cousin.

Ellen's mouth opened with surprise and became a big smile. "Ellie! Oh my, how long has it been?"

Ellie was vaguely aware of the men in the room nodding to each other. She'd passed whatever their identity test was.

"It's been too long. I'm so sorry I wasn't here for Uncle Walter's funeral. I didn't know." Not that she would have been able to come. Not until she got the letter that changed everything.

Her cousin wiped her eyes. "It's all right, sweetie. I can imagine."

Ellie felt her cheeks warm with embarrassment. "It still isn't right. None of this is right." She felt another wave of nausea and Bear put his hand on her arm.

"Are you okay?" Ellen asked.

She looked at Bear. "Altitude sickness?"

"Oh." Ellen nodded slowly. "I should let you go. We can talk later, dear."

"No, wait," Ellie said as she actually reached toward the tablet. "I have to talk to you about something important. It's why I'm here."

"Of course. What is it?"

"I..." She looked around the room. "Can I have my stuff back, please?"

Bear jumped up with a surprising amount of grace for

such a big man and grabbed her pack out of the corner where he'd left it.

"Thank you." She gave him a smile and he just nodded. She opened the front pocket and took out the envelope she'd tried to keep nice and neat, but had since become a bit crumpled and stained.

"Uncle Walter's lawyer sent me this." She opened the envelope and took out the pages inside. She unfolded them on the table and smoothed them out as a pit of anxiety opened in her stomach. This was the moment when she'd learn how much trouble she was in, or if she was saved.

"According to what it says here, Uncle Walter left me some property."

"Property?" Ellen cocked her head. Her eyes went round. "The house?"

Everyone in the room straightened up.

Oh! Oh dear.

No wonder they were nervous if they already bought Uncle Walter's house. But there was no need to be.

"No," Ellie said quickly. "Not his house here, but a house up in the mountains farther west." Kyle visibly relaxed and she grinned at him. "Your place is safe."

Her cousin frowned in concentration. "House? Wait. Is it off Calistoga Way?"

"Yes," Ellie said, double-checking the letter even though she'd memorized it. "That's the address. There's a map, too."

"Good, you'll need one if you want to find it. An *actual* map. Internet maps will have you going in circles. Gosh, I haven't been up there in years. The lawyer who sent you the letter, was it Bruce? Bruce Cole?"

"Yes."

"Yeah, he's Dad's executor. Dad didn't want to burden me with executor duties on top of everything else so he set that up when his mind had just started to go and we got the dementia diagnosis. I knew there was a trust set up for someone, but I didn't know the details. So, that's what happened with the Calistoga property." Ellen's smile was sweet and wistful. "I'm glad Dad was thinking about you."

Ellie blinked quickly and took a shaky breath. "You're... okay with me having it?"

"Well, of course," Ellen said. "He left it to you. It's yours."

Her heart pounded and fluttered and the lightheadedness came back.

"What's wrong?" Her cousin leaned forward and her face grew bigger on the screen.

"I just wasn't sure if you'd let me have something big like that." Ellie tried not to cry.

Her cousin laughed lightly though she looked a little confused. "Of course you can have that old fishing cabin, though I don't know what you'd do with it."

Ellie's heart sank. *Fishing cabin?* "It's not a house?"

"Oh, no, sweetheart. It's an old historical cabin on some land Dad bought decades ago. Dad used to go up with his friends when they wanted to fish or hunt or just hide from the world for a while."

Hide from the world. Now that sounded good.

Her cousin went on. "There's a generator that runs on propane but no running water anymore. The well gave out or something years ago. Dad had a caretaker check on the cabin a few times a year to make sure it was still standing. Honestly, I think what you'll probably want to do is sell it and all the land it's on. There's quite a bit of acreage if I recall. You should get a pretty good price, but it might take a while to find a buyer. I remember that it was remote."

"Oh." Ellie felt her hopes dash as if they'd been pushed straight off a cliff.

"What's wrong, sweetie?" Ellen asked her.

Ellie arranged her face into what she hoped looked happy. "Nothing. Just still in shock a little bit."

"I can imagine," Ellen said. "I'm sure you can find a real estate agent who will help you. I'm so sorry I'm not there and that you didn't know I'd moved. I could come out." Her voice sounded just uncertain enough that it gave Ellie pause.

"No, no, that's okay." Ellie smiled brightly. "I would like to see it though, before I make any decisions."

"Of course." Ellen looked around. "Is Arden still there?"

"Yes, I'm here." Arden leaned in so that she was in the frame. "I already know what you're going to say, and the answer is yes, absolutely I'll take care of her." Ellie felt Arden's hand on her shoulder.

"Oh, it's okay, I'll be fine."

Both Ellen and Bear made sounds that told her they weren't so sure.

"No, no." Arden squeezed her shoulder before she let go. "I know Kyle's scared you to death already. Let me make it up to you. We've got plenty of room up at the ranch. Come spend tonight at least. I haven't seen you in ages. It'll be fun."

Ellen smiled on the screen. "Thank you, Arden."

Bear made another sound, one that sounded like a satisfied grunt.

Ellie took another swig of water. "Thank you, everybody." She and Ellen said their goodbyes to each other.

Ellie put the letter back in its envelope, then put the envelope in her backpack. She stood up and hoisted her backpack onto her shoulder. Arden started talking about going to the ranch, but Ellie had other ideas.

"Actually, I'd like to just bike up to the cabin and take a look at it today."

The room erupted in protests, Bear's being the loudest.

"Nope." He stood and crossed his arms.

Ellie looked all the way up into his eyes. "Nope?"

He shook his big, shaggy head. "No way. Not with altitude sickness."

"I'm feeling better." It wasn't a lie. She picked up the potato chip bags. "These helped so much. What do I owe—"

"Uh-uh." Bear shook his head again. "Don't owe me a thing. Unless it'll keep you from doing something that'll land you in the hospital."

Ellie bit the inside skin under her lip. She needed to see the condition of the cabin. Determine if it was habitable. She had no choice. She didn't want to impose on Arden, who after all these years might as well be a stranger—though a really nice one. And she couldn't afford even a single night in a motel. She'd biked as much as she could, spent a night out in the open, then spent almost all her remaining money on the bus ticket that brought her the rest of the way. All she needed was a roof over her head and she could figure out the rest.

So long as her family didn't find her.

"Boy are you stubborn," Bear said. "I can see those gears grinding." He looked over at Kyle. "Mind if I take a half-day today?"

Kyle nodded. "Fine with me." He looked at Ellie. "Sorry about the misunderstanding earlier."

"It's all right." She looked back at Bear. "If you're offering to drive me up there, you really don't have to. It's only a few miles and I'm fine—"

Bear took hold of her backpack and slipped it off her shoulder. "I'll carry this for you. Grab that water bottle. You got the chips all right?"

Ellie snickered—as if she couldn't carry a couple bags of chips on her own. "I *think* I've got them all by myself, Bear."

He just nodded and started out of the conference room. He wasn't even going to leave her room to argue.

"Maybe I'll come with you," Arden said behind her. "I haven't seen that cabin since I was a little girl and Ellen begged Walter to take us up there."

Ellie turned and caught the tail end of a look Arden was giving Kyle.

"Was it nice?" Ellie asked.

Arden considered her answer, then she shrugged. "It was nice by little-kid standards." She smiled. "Let's go see what it's like now. And, we can catch up."

Ellie smiled weakly. "Yeah, that'd be great."

Except she didn't want to tell anyone anything about back home.

FOUR

There was no way in hell Bear was going to let Ellie bike an inch, let go alone up into the higher foothills at the base of the Rockies, not with altitude sickness. And now that the SUV was bumping over a barely-there logging trail, he knew he'd made the right decision driving Ellie and Arden to the cabin. He couldn't imagine Ellie trying to find her way up after the paved road forked and became a gravel trail that soon hugged the steep side of a foothill, before shrinking to nothing but a couple of deep, parallel ruts running through fields full of tall grass turning yellow.

Arden sat up front beside him. Bear kept looking back at Ellie's face in the rearview mirror as they left more and more civilization behind. Bad enough that Arden was looking concerned, but Ellie looked downright anxious as she watched the scenery turn from scattered ranch houses and barns to nothing but the occasional fence trapping a small herd of grazing cattle or a couple of horses. This old fishing cabin really was in the middle of nowhere, even if it was only about twenty miles away from Watchdog, which was also off the beaten path.

Though nothing like this.

Ellie bounced in her seat as Bear bumped over a hidden rock that probably fell and rolled right into the path some time ago. God knew when the last time was that someone had come up here. According to Ellie's map, they were already on Walter's land and still had a ways to go.

"You okay back there?" he asked.

"Yup." She gave him a brave thumbs-up.

"Head?"

"Fine." She smiled at his reflection. Her eyes looked so tired and worried it hurt his heart.

Finally, even the logging trail gave out to nothing but a field of grass overlooking an aspen glen.

"Oh, I remember this," Arden said quietly. "We're at the end of the trail. We have to walk the rest of the way."

Bear parked as he side-eyed Arden. She returned his guarded look.

"Walk?" Ellie said from the back.

"It's...remote." Arden opened her door. "But we aren't far now. Just down the hill."

Bear jumped down from the SUV and then opened Ellie's door and offered his hand. She barely acknowledged him and he understood why. Her head swiveled around, taking in everything—the blue sky, the quaking aspen leaves that made Bear think of gold coins, and the permeating silence when the breeze died down.

Dry grass crunched under their feet as they approached the aspens. Bear could smell the dust they'd kicked up mingling with the hay, but up ahead somewhere he smelled water too, and pine sap, and the sweet tang of aspen bark mingling with dry autumn leaves. They followed what looked like a deer trail down a hill into the aspens. Ellie's head never stopped turning and he couldn't blame her. Walter's land was beautiful.

"The cabin's just past the aspens," Arden said, her soft voice sounding loud against the quiet. Up ahead, a dark shape came into view. Now Bear could hear the water he'd smelled —a fast stream by the sound of it. He figured it must run right next to the cabin. Bear glanced down at Ellie, whose wide eyes were full of anticipation.

And then they were past the aspens and got a good, clear look at the cabin for the first time.

It didn't look too bad—at first glance. But the closer they got, the more dilapidated it appeared. The dark paint was faded in some spots and worn away in others. The roof over the porch sloped. The brick chimney needed repointing before it crumbled. The roof was covered in pine needles and he could almost guarantee it leaked here and there.

But while Bear inspected the cabin with a critical, repair-man's eyes, Ellie's were full of wonder.

"This is mine?" she whispered. "I can't believe it."

Arden must have mistook her tone. "I know it looks bad, but you'll get it sold, just for the land alone."

Ellie stopped and turned her head. "Sell?" She looked back at the cabin, her head tilted slightly, assessing. "I want to keep it."

Arden's eyes widened and she looked at Bear.

"I mean, it needs new paint, but that's okay. I'm not picky," Ellie went on. Uncertainty had crept into her voice.

"I think it's going to need more than that." Arden touched Ellie's arm. "Let's take a look inside. If we can." She looked at Bear again, her expression asking if he thought it was safe enough to enter.

Bear nodded. "Careful on the steps." They sagged in the middle, but the wood was dry. He was sure they would hold the women's weight and he'd be ready to jump if they decided not to hold his. "Let me go first." The wood creaked but held under his weight. He nodded to them once he reached the porch. The wood there was sturdier, protected by the wide overhang. The front lawn sloped down to a narrow creek hidden in the tall grass. On the other side of the creek, the ground rose sharply, shaggy with grasses and brush with the occasional rocky outcropping jutting through. Beyond that, he could see the top of Blue Mountain in the distance. To his left the creek ran on, twisting and widening until it fed into a lake walled in by a cliff.

Beautiful.

The women joined him. They admired the view in silence.

"We went out on that lake with Walter, and I caught my first mackinaw." Arden laughed lightly. "I felt so terrible about hurting it, so Walter took it off my hook for me and set it free. I imagine it's huge by now if no one's caught it."

Ellie nodded, then turned to the door. The screen was long gone from its frame. Ellie opened it and the first thing Bear noted was that there was no lock whatsoever. Ellie turned the knob and opened the door. Dusty air wafted out. The cabin was dim as they stepped inside and back in time. The kitchen was toward the back of the room—an old-fashioned stove, an ancient fridge—make that icebox—wood cabinets, and a sink, all behind an island that separated the kitchen from the rest of the room. A stone fireplace was on their right, flanked by windows—one broken, which had let in the leaves scattered across the floor. A doorway beside the kitchen area led to an empty bedroom. Steep stairs off the short hallway climbed to the attic, which Walter had used for storage, according to a text Ellen had sent Arden on their way up. And that was the entirety of the cabin.

Bear looked around. He spotted two places where water had leaked in. The wood and plaster were in bad shape. The fireplace needed work and he imagined that the chimney could use a good sweeping. The floor was solid enough—wide boards that needed refinishing but otherwise didn't sag or threaten to give. The rest of the cabin though... He sighed. It needed a lot more than just the TLC of new paint.

Ellie walked through the cabin to the hallway and started up the stairs.

"Careful," Bear called after her. He followed up the stairs. The steps were sturdy—in much better shape than he'd thought they'd be—but with the leaks, he worried about the floor above.

"Oh," he heard her say above him. When Bear reached the landing he understood. There was an amazing view out each dirty window. Once they were cleaned, the room would be much lighter than the cabin downstairs. But the roof...all he needed to see were the birds' nests tucked into a couple of corners. Swallows. He wouldn't be surprised if bats roosted here, too.

Bats. A memory threatened to emerge, something from childhood he didn't care to remember, and Bear fought it back down and returned to the here and now. The cabin was not what Ellie had so obviously hoped it would be. *Refuge.* That was the word that crossed his mind. Ellie wanted a refuge, plain as day. And this was not it.

Arden came up behind him. All she needed to do was sigh and he knew she felt the same way.

Ellie turned. She looked so unsure. But she said, "It's not so bad. Not as bad as I thought."

Bear's heart broke for her. There was no way he could imagine her staying in the cabin or even trying to fix it up. Renovations would go into the tens of thousands—and that was if she could even convince someone to come up here in the first place.

"Ellie?" Arden stepped past him. "Why don't you stay with Kyle and me up at the ranch for a few days while you decide what to do? We'd love to have you."

She looked around the attic. "It's okay. I can find a motel in Longmont—"

Arden blinked. "Nope, I insist. Stay with us."

"I don't want to trouble you any more than I already have."

"No, please." Arden put her arm around Ellie's shoulders. "You haven't troubled us at all."

Ellie laughed and even Bear grinned. "Yeah, I think I troubled Kyle big time at least."

Arden smiled gently and shook her head. "It's in his nature to be suspicious, but once you've gotten past that, he's very...sweet."

Now Bear covered his mouth to hide his smile. Sweet? Kyle? He'd just *love* to hear that.

Arden guided Ellie back to the stairs. "Let's head back. You've had a long trip and you've got to be exhausted. In the morning, I can help you find a real estate agent. What do you say?"

Ellie nodded. "All right. Thank you." She looked around the attic one more time. Her gaze rested on the view out the window overlooking the lake. "You're probably right. I should sell this place before it falls down." Smile fixed in place, she walked past Bear and Arden and headed down the steps. Arden again looked at Bear, her expression full of worry. He couldn't blame her—Ellie might have been smiling, but that smile looked like it covered a world of heartbreak.

And Bear couldn't believe how much that hurt his heart.

B ack at the ranch, Bear and Kyle chopped wood while the women got dinner ready inside. Bear was staying in Walter's house as he worked on it, but Arden insisted he join them for dinner every night. He'd never met a better or more eager hostess. They were far out of earshot from the house when Kyle stopped, leaned on his ax, and told Bear what he'd learned about Ellie.

"While you were up at the cabin, I spoke to Ellen again. She filled me in on the family situation. Walter's family was always on the rough side, and his sister married into an even rougher family. Walter's brother-in-law has a temper, and the sister would periodically leave and bring the kids out here to stay with the Sanders when they were little. Her husband would eventually sweet-talk her into going back, and the cycle would start over."

Bear nodded. A common enough story.

"Then there was some sort of big rift between Walter and his sister and she stopped coming out. Which was fine with Ellen. She says that Ellie was always sweet, but that her brothers turned meaner every visit. Could even be that Walter told his sister not to bring the boys next time, that he was protecting his own daughter."

Bear thought that would cause a mighty big rift. "You think Ellie's on the run from her family?"

Kyle nodded. "Ellen suspects that's the case, especially when I told her about the sleeping bag. Walter was no fool and he was a kind man from everything I heard about him. By the time I came along though, he was already pretty far gone with the dementia."

Bear nodded. "He was friendly to us kids. You think he left Ellie that cabin because he knew one day she'd need it?"

"I suspect that's the case. Ellie's mom passed away a few years ago, probably left her vulnerable." Kyle looked back at the house, making sure they still had privacy. "You remember her as a kid?"

"Barely. I wasn't more'n thirteen or fourteen. Mostly, I remember her brothers as being outsized pricks for their age."

They heard the patio door open and turned to look. The sky was turning violet and the windows were shining with yellow light. Welcoming.

Arden stepped outside. "Dinner's ready, guys. Come and get it."

As they started toward the house, Kyle said, "I feel bad about scaring her earlier."

"You had your reasons."

Kyle only shook his head.

"Dinner was good, Arden, thanks," Bear said as they all sat by the fireplace in the great room.

Arden's smile lit her up like a Christmas tree. "Thanks, Bear."

Kyle had poured everyone a whiskey and it was warming Bear up just right. Ellie sat on the big leather couch next to him, and that warmed him up, too. He could see she was already settling in at the ranch. She'd showered and changed after they came back from the fishing cabin. Color had returned to her cheeks and now she smelled like sweet berries. Her hair shown glossy in the firelight. She looked relaxed as she sipped her whiskey.

"It was delicious," Ellie added, smiling.

"Well, your biscuits were amazing," Arden said. "They made the meal."

Bear's eyebrows rose. He hadn't realized Ellie had made those. Arden was right—they were the best part of an already tasty dinner.

"My mom's recipe." Ellie looked into her glass as she quietly spoke the words. "I haven't made them in a while, so I'm glad they turned out."

Bear felt his chest tighten for the hundredth time that day. He fought himself not to stretch his arm along the back of the couch behind her shoulders then slowly drop it down until he was cradling her. He'd known sadness, been around other people's tragedy enough to have become numb to it. Ellie somehow burrowed right past the numbness, waking something up inside.

Arden and Kyle exchanged looks that told him she'd gotten to them, too.

"I'm glad you've taken up our offer to stay here." Arden reached out for Kyle's hand and he took it.

"Me too," Kyle added. "I'm sorry about earlier."

Ellie brightened. "And I told you that you don't need to keep apologizing." She laughed. "I know how fierce and intimidating I look, so I don't blame you." She sat up as straight as she could, lifted her chin, and threw her shoulders back, making everyone laugh with her. Then she grew serious again. "I'm not going to impose for long. Just tonight."

Arden shook her head vehemently. "Oh, no, you're staying until you can figure out what to do with the cabin. I know a couple good real estate agents, and I'm sure Bruce can help with the legal aspects."

"But that might take a long time." Ellie bit her lower lip.

"No problem. We have the room, obviously."

"And Arden loves to have company over," Kyle added. "You'll get the cabin and the land sold, and then you can decide your next move from there."

Ellie looked away and stared into the fire. She nodded absently. "Right. After I sell it."

"It's not worth keeping, Ellie," Arden said gently. "Right, Bear?"

Bear's lips twitched. He wasn't quite annoyed at being brought into this decision, but he also didn't appreciate it. "Lots of work to be done. It'd be tricky getting handymen up there along with materials. Well-digging's tricky too."

Ellie took a deep breath and nodded. "Land's beautiful though, huh?"

"Very," Arden agreed. "Maybe someone out east will buy it as a tax write-off and not touch a thing. That happens around here."

They sat quietly sipping their whiskey after that. Bear felt Ellie withdraw into herself as if she were a snail pulling into her shell. He'd spoken the truth—it'd be a challenge. Not impossible, but expensive and damn near out of reach for her.

He hated that truth.

Ellie stood up. "I think I'm going to bed. Long day."

Arden stood up to take her glass but Ellie insisted on carrying it to the kitchen and washing it. After that, she wished everyone a good night and went off down the hall to one of the bedrooms. Arden looked glum as she sat back down.

"I feel like I kicked a puppy." Camo looked up alarmed at her from his place by the fire as if he understood what she said. She smiled and shook her head at the dog. "Not literally, buddy."

Bear felt like that too. Without Ellie there, the evening wasn't as warm and comfortable. The peace he'd found after dinner evaporated. It was replaced by something that felt like regret. He stood up to leave.

"You can stay," Arden said as she and Kyle also got to their feet. But the spell of the easeful night was broken.

Bear shook his head. "I'll get out of your hair. Early day tomorrow." He watched his friends' faces fall. He hated leaving on this note, but there was nothing to be done about it. They walked him to the door, Camo leading the way, and Arden told him to be careful driving which made him smile. It was a five-minute drive at most, and he could have walked it. Then again, the night was a lot colder than the day had been, right in line with this time of year.

When he got to the safehouse—now 'Walter's house' in his head—he saw a piece of white paper taped to the door. Curious, he took it down, unfolded it, and read it.

Reconsider? We could use you. it read.

Bear snorted and looked around, as if the guy who left the note was waiting somewhere in the dark for his immediate answer. Of course he wasn't out there; he had better things to do, and Bear wanted no part of that, no sir. He crumpled up the paper and went inside.

The next morning, Bear got up early as planned, after a night full of hazy dreams involving Ellie. Some were about her walking around the cabin—little memories of the day before. But others, well, he didn't want to share those with anyone. He wondered how he'd keep from turning red in the face the next time he saw her. He tried to tell himself it was just because he hadn't been with a woman for quite a while, and not because she'd felt nice with his arm draped around her shoulders. Not because her smile was so bright and hopeful in the face of the odds stacked against her. And definitely not because she made him feel something warm and good.

Bear put Ellie out of his mind all day as he went about his repairs. Yup, he put her out of his thoughts over and over every time she crept back in, right along with the note on the door. Nope, he was going to keep his head down, work hard, and leave when the job was done. Maybe before if he could get away with it. Texas was sounding good. Island living. Easy days and restful nights.

And no roots there. Nothing to time him down.

When he got a text from Kyle letting him know what time to come over for dinner, Bear texted back thanks but he was just going to make a quick sandwich and go to bed early instead.

Bear went to bed and all the thoughts he'd suppressed came roaring back in his dreams. Ellie was somehow in bed with him, her body soft and warm under his. Her sweet berry scent filled his nose, her soft hair brushed against his skin and he groaned her name as he brought them both to ecstasy...

When Bear woke in the morning, he told himself that he was going to head for the ranch house first thing because he needed a tool—whatever tool it was, he'd figure that out when he got there—that Kyle had and he didn't. Crucial, really, to his day. Couldn't work without...whatever it was. Yup, he needed to go to the ranch.

The first thing he noticed was that someone had taken Ellie's bike in from leaving it on the porch. The door was unlocked so he went inside. Arden and Kyle were early risers like he was. Camo greeted him at the door, tail wagging but looking agitated. Bear sniffed the air—no breakfast cooking. He frowned as he walked to the kitchen adjacent to the great room, where he heard voices. He expected to see three people, but only Arden and Kyle stood beside the kitchen island separating it from the great room. They looked upset.

"What?" Bear asked.

Arden held up a sheet of paper and Bear's heart stopped

for a moment, remembering the note he'd found on his door. Was Kyle also—

"We were going to tell you at dinner last night but you didn't come over." She handed him the paper, interrupting his thoughts and making his stomach knot.

Bear looked at the note, puzzled. It wasn't what he'd expected. The handwriting was obviously a woman's.

Dear Arden and Kyle,

Thank you so much for your hospitality. It was good seeing you after all these years. After thinking things through, I've decided to go back home, since I don't think there's anything for me here. I'll let the lawyer know I want to sell the cabin.

Tell Bear goodbye for me.

Ellie

Emptiness like a cold, dark cave opened in his belly. Ellie was gone.

Tell Bear goodbye for me.

That hurt more than if she'd said nothing at all.

"When?" he asked.

"Middle of the night," Kyle answered. "She was already gone when we got up around four yesterday. I checked the cameras, both outside the ranch and the front gate. She left just after three." He glanced down at Camo. "Bribed our so-called guard dog here to stay quiet."

Camo hung his head.

"Heard from her?"

"No," Arden said miserably. "And I don't have her cell-phone number, or a home number. Neither does Ellen."

Bear raised his eyebrows at Kyle.

"Yeah, I've got someone on it, but no luck." He shrugged. "Which leads me to believe her family doesn't even have a landline. Probably uses burner phones, too. We've checked bus schedules and passenger manifests. Nothing, unless she's traveling under a different name. But with her bike..." he trailed off. "She could be doing that, sleeping rough all the way back to Illinois."

Bear nodded. He had an idea of his own about where she might be, but he'd need to keep it under his hat for now.

If his suspicions were correct. And God, he hoped they were.

He wanted—no, *needed*—more Ellie in his life.

FIVE

Ellie had gone to bed that night full of hard emotions that left her tossing and turning. She'd come to Colorado in the hopes of a new home, one she could call hers, one that would make her feel safe for the first time in her life. She'd gambled everything—risking the wrath of her oldest brother especially—only to discover she'd been wrong. Again. All her life was nothing but wrong. But she couldn't help it. Ellie was a born optimist, no matter how hard her family had tried to beat it out of her, tell her that she was a fool—uppity, even—to want a better life. Ungrateful for what she had.

But it was hard to feel grateful when you had next to nothing. Nothing, except hurt and betrayal at every turn.

It was her optimism that got her out of bed every morning. The first light of day always promised her a brand new chance at something better, if she could just keep moving forward and hoping.

And then that promise finally seemed fulfilled when she checked the mailbox at the end of the long lane and saw the letter addressed to her. When she'd read that she'd been left an entire house by her sweet, kind uncle, how quickly she'd shoved the letter into her shirt and hoped it wouldn't rustle and give her away because she knew they'd find a way to take her inheritance from her. Her dad would intimidate her first with threats since he wasn't able to do much else anymore. And if that didn't work, her brothers would follow up with their fists.

She rolled over and absently rubbed her jawline on the side that was missing a molar.

How excited she'd been when her plans finally came together and Ellen told her it was true—she'd been left a house. And how those hopes had faded little by little as she learned it wasn't what she'd thought. Despite everything, they rose again as Bear drove her and Arden up to the cabin. Maybe these people were so used to nice things that they couldn't recognize an old cabin as something nice too. Maybe it was just fine. Maybe...

But then when she'd set her eyes on it, saw the place in person, the peeling paint, the holes in the roof, the miserable little kitchen in even worse shape than the one back on the farm, she'd learned the truth.

Hope was just a crutch for an optimist with a broken heart.

She made a soft, despairing sound.

The clicking of nails on hardwood told her Camo was on his way down the hall. She heard him scratch at her door, so she got up to let him in. She'd instantly fallen in love with the smarty of a dog. He nuzzled her hand and she crouched to pet him, then threw her arms around his neck and buried her face in his black and yellow fur. Over dinner, she'd learned that Camo had faced tremendous sorrow as a working military dog, but he'd found a happy ending with Kyle and Arden.

She'd also heard happy stories about the time Arden had

gone to the cabin with Ellen, and the stories Ellen had told Arden about other times she'd gone with her family. It made her sad to think someone would just buy the place and tear it down, or let it fall further into ruin, sight unseen. That was, if she could even find a buyer. And if she did sell the place, she knew that somehow, her family would take it all from her. She'd never see the money, never have a chance to be free. She'd be stuck taking care of all of them like she had since Mama died, with nothing but abuse given back to her.

"I have to do something, Camo," she whispered into the dog's fur.

She couldn't go back. She just couldn't. So that left going forward.

As much as she trusted Arden—and Kyle now that he knew who she was—it didn't feel right to mooch off them. Who knew how long she'd be here under their roof? And she didn't want her family to find out where she was and target them. Not that Kyle couldn't handle that. His entire company as far as she could tell existed to protect, and Kyle wanted to protect his own more than anyone else.

But she didn't want to pretend she was part of that inner circle. At best, she was just passing through. And she had a feeling that if they knew where and what she'd come from, they'd want her to keep on moving, thank you very much.

Too much trouble, that's what she was. Kyle was probably right to mistrust her from the drop. Too much trouble.

But, she was about to change that.

She kissed the top of Camo's head. Maybe, once she got herself resettled, she'd reach out and explain. But not until then. She had a lot of work ahead of her and she didn't want anyone to talk her out of it.

Ellie stood up and put her finger to her lips—as if Camo could understand the gesture. But then again, maybe he could. He sat down and watched her silently as she repacked the few belongings she'd taken out of her backpack and put her jacket on. He stayed quiet as he followed her down the hall to the kitchen where she wrote a quick note. She paused, thinking about how kind Jon Behr had been to her throughout the day. He made her feel like she had a protector all her own. But, that was probably an illusion, too. He was just a quiet and thoughtful man being his decent self, and she wasn't used to that so it felt like more. Besides, he'd said during dinner that he was only passing through Colorado. *A vagrant like me*, she thought. They'd probably never cross paths again.

That didn't stop her from adding one more line to her note, just for him. It was the least she could do, acknowledge his kindness. But just writing the word *Bear* put butterflies in her stomach and they felt too good to be true, especially for a foolish optimist like her.

Even if he had beautiful eyes that seemed to warm every time he looked at her.

She folded the paper in half and left it on the counter. Camo tilted his head when she hoisted her backpack and sleeping bag onto her back. The gun was tucked back in there too. Kyle had returned it to her after she got back from the cabin. She hoped no one had seen her point it at that pimp, but she'd had no choice. Ellie hated carrying it, but needed it for protection.

Arnold would probably shoot me with it himself if he found me.

Ellie shook off the thought. She opened the jar of dog treats on the counter and gave Camo one.

"This is to keep you quiet, buddy."

He snarfed it down, then looked guilty and sheepish as he followed her to the front door.

Along the way, she caught the silhouette of a woman out

of the corner of her eye and her heart skipped a beat. She thought Arden had heard her and was about to stop her, but when she turned her head, no one was there. Arden had joked earlier that the house was haunted by her several-greats grandmother, Nancy.

Just my imagination.

When she got to the front door, Ellie knelt and hugged Camo one last time. He made the faintest, high-pitched whine and tears sprang to her eyes, almost stopping her from leaving. But no. She'd made up her mind and she had no choice. She couldn't let anyone talk her out of her decision and she knew they'd try.

Her bike was still where she'd left it on the porch. Ellie quickly took it out of its bag and unfolded it, then walked it down the steps. She was probably on at least one camera, but she'd have to worry about that later. She'd make sure to go the wrong way once she got past the gates to throw them off. That had worked with evading her family—so far. Ellie shivered in the autumnal night air. Oh, well—she'd warm up quickly enough as she pedaled away.

B y the time she got up to the clearing before the cabin, it was midmorning, sunny, and warm. She'd shed her jacket an hour before and still sweat trickled down her spine. Even though she'd stopped a few times to catch her breath and drink some water, she felt better today than the day before—not a trace of a headache, no stomach ache, and she had leftover biscuits from dinner along with some apples growing wild on a tree beside the road. It was a start.

With the sun out, the aspens looked like trees full of golden coins that spilled out onto the path winding between them. She hopped off her bike and walked it through the grove to the cabin. In the light of a new morning, it looked completely different to her. Yes, the cabin was dilapidated, but it was easy to see that it'd been a happy place once. The outside walls had been white, with trim the color of a blue-gray stormcloud. A wooden bench on the porch was a faded brick red, which would have stood out nicely against the white. The boards that made up the overhang were still good, protected from the sun and rain. They were a light sky-blue and welcoming.

Ellie went inside to really examine the rooms. Sunlight poured in through the windows despite the dirt and dust. Well, she was no stranger to cleaning a house. That was doable, even the windows. She grinned. She could bring the cabin back to life and make this place her home. It would be a lot of work and take a lot of time, but she could do it.

The alternative was unthinkable.

Ellie spent the rest of the day exploring her new property. And what she found encouraged her. The remnants of raised garden beds filled not just with weeds but volunteer onions, herbs, and strawberry plants. A shed behind the cottage held some tools, row covers, building materials and tarps, as if her Uncle Walter had planned on doing some renovations but couldn't get to it. The tarps would help her immediately. She set them up in the cabin areas that needed to be protected the most and laid her sleeping bag down in the driest, most protected part of the cabin—the main room by the fireplace.

She broke for lunch and sat out by the lake. The day had turned so warm, she was down to shorts and a tank top. A trout jumped in the water—a big one—and she grinned. Fresh trout was tasty, and she knew how to cast the rods she'd found in the shed along with an old but well-preserved tackle box as well.

So, she did just that as the sun set, the sky turned violet and the air cooled down. Ellie waded out into the lake, which was quite shallow and warm along the edges, and caught herself a fish. She cooked it over a fire she made in the outdoor pit she'd cleared of grass and weeds. It was the most satisfying meal she'd ever eaten.

The stars came out one by one, and they were *her* stars.

When Ellie curled up into a warm little ball in her sleeping bag she fell right to sleep.

W hen she woke the next morning she was freezing. How could Colorado go from one extreme to another so quickly? She didn't remember that from her childhood whenever Mama got tired of getting hit—or seeing her children hit—and would bring them all out to visit her brother. It was usually summer or winter though, times when her father was the most stressed. Maybe those seasonal temperature changes weren't as extreme as fall and spring.

Ellie didn't want to uncurl from what little warmth she'd generated in her sleeping bag, but who knew if the day would warm up or not? She saw clouds through the newly cleaned windows. Would they stay all day, cooling everything down from the day before?

Well, this was the perfect opportunity to test out the fireplace. There was even a stack of wood beside it to get her started. It would be dry enough to burn easily. Ellie got up and used the sleeping bag as a blanket around her shoulders as she grabbed the box of long matches she'd found in one of the cupboards and wadded up some yellowed newspaper from a rough old box next to the pile of wood. Ellie looked up the chimney and saw sky above, which meant the chimney was open and not blocked. She stacked some split wood over the paper like a teepee and lit the match. The paper caught and the fire spread to the wood. She'd soon have the place nice and warm. *Success!*

Until the cabin started filling with smoke.

SIX

Bear knew his instincts were right when he saw the thin plume of smoke as he drove closer to the cabin. At least she'd gotten a fire going to keep herself warm. He found himself grinning at Ellie's determination and her plain old stubborn grit. He only hoped she'd listen to him. He parked his truck in the clearing and grabbed the bag he'd brought along, then set out through the aspens.

Something wasn't right, his instincts told him again. He smelled smoke, but it was too strong and there was something about it—

Bear broke into a run when he saw the smoky cloud up ahead. He didn't see any flames, but smoke billowed out the open door and windows. There was no sign of Ellie.

He put on speed as he roared her name. Bear ripped the hat off his head and covered his nose and mouth. He pounded up the porch steps and into the cabin—

And ran smack into Ellie, sending her backwards into the kitchen counter.

"Ellie! I gotta get you...out..."

Huh.

Inside, the smoke wasn't that bad. He looked around and where he'd expected to see flames consuming the cabin, he only saw a smoldering fire in the fireplace.

It didn't stop him from picking Ellie up and carrying her out the door.

"Hey!" Ellie said. "I have everything under control. Put me down."

"No, you don't. Cabin's still full of smoke, Ellie. You can't be staying in there."

She stared at him. "It's not that bad and I have the fire half out."

"You stay here. I'll take care of the rest of it."

Before she could protest, Bear turned and walked back up the steps. Now that he was back inside, yes, he had to admit she did have the situation under control. The smoke wasn't that bad, especially with the door and the windows open. There was actually more smoke outside than there was inside the cabin at this point. So what was he supposed to do? Go back outside, pick her up and carry her back inside? And what possessed him to do that in the first place?

I have completely lost my mind.

It looked like Ellie had actually used old ash to cover the fire rather than put it out with water. Really a smart move on her part. Pouring water onto it would have created more steam and made the problem worse. Bear looked closer. Nope, not ash. Sand. There was a small metal trashcan half-full of it on the hearth. When Walter had been well enough to come up to the cabin it looked like he'd kept a pail full of sand beside the fire, just in case. And Ellie had been smart enough to know what it was and how to use it.

The only thing she hadn't done was take a poker and separate the logs first to scatter the embers. That was her only misstep. And not a bad one for sure. Just to make himself feel useful, he did that, then dumped what was left of the sand over the last of the embers. Then he went outside.

Ellie stood in front of the cabin with her hands on her hips.

"Satisfied that I'm not up here accidentally killing myself now?" she asked.

"They're worried about you," Bear said.

"*They* are? Or you are?"

Bear rolled his eyes. "Fine. We all are. Ellie, why'd you leave?"

Even as the question left his lips, he felt stupid for asking. He knew her. Even if they'd only just met again as adults, Bear *knew* her. Knew her stubbornness and independence. Her unwillingness to let anyone make a fuss over her. She didn't want to be a burden. He'd watched her try and take up as little space as possible at Arden and Kyle's place. She'd sat on the edge of her chair. She'd kept her arms tucked in close to her body. She took the smallest share of food and drink. People acted like that, they came from a life where the people around them took and took and took.

Now Ellie was standing in front of him on her own land, elbows way out to the sides, feet spread shoulder-width apart. Literally standing her ground against him.

His heart swelled at that good sight.

"I didn't want..." she started. "I'm..."

He watched her deflate and hated himself for causing it. "Don't worry about it. Not judging you." He turned and started back up the steps, listening to her catch up behind him.

"Wait, what are you doing?"

"Gonna help you clean up. Then we'll have breakfast."

"Bossy," she murmured under her breath.

Bear just grinned.

After Bear had swept the last of the sand and ashes into the fireplace while Ellie fanned the remaining smoke out of the cabin, he took a paper bag full of breakfast burritos out of his backpack and set it down on a wooden table that had seen better days. The cabin was cold, but the sun was coming up over the ridge and the day would be a warm one. Ellie kept looking at the fireplace with a puzzled look.

"It's the chimney cap," he told her.

Ellie looked at him with startled eyes. "How do you know?"

"Noticed it was gone yesterday. That can cause a backdraft."

"I meant, how did you know I was thinking about the fire? I didn't want you to think that I'd left the flue closed, or something dumb like that."

"Didn't think you had."

He offered her one of the foil-wrapped burritos and took out a thermos full of hot coffee and two mugs. She watched him pour the coffee and then wrapped her hands around the mug and held it just below her chin, savoring the heat. If he could, he'd try and talk her into the truck where he could turn on the heat. But there she was, sitting on the edge of her chair just like the other night, only this time like she was ready to bolt at any second. He didn't want to startle her further, make her think he was taking her back. Bear didn't want to risk her disappearing again—this time for real.

She sipped the coffee and closed her eyes. "You think the chimney cap's still around here somewhere?"

"Could be. If not, a new one'll set you back two, three hundred dollars."

Her eyes flew open. "That much?" she whispered.

He nodded and studied her. "And the whole chimney needs repointing. Probably a good sweep, too."

She looked at the old propane-powered stove in the kitchen.

"That looks to be in good shape, but I think the propane tank's empty," Bear said. "Maybe not, though."

"Propane's expensive?"

"Yup. Price's gone up past couple of years. So's labor and delivery."

She gripped the coffee mug again and stared down into its black depths.

"Where you staying, Ellie?" Bear asked quietly.

Her gaze snapped back to his. "Close by. Biking distance."

"Yeah?"

She nodded.

"Why you got your backpack and sleeping bag here then?"

She bit her lip and looked back down into her coffee. "I like to have my things with me. Never know what can happen otherwise." She braved a look up through her lashes at him.

"Ellie." Bear leaned forward and she scooted back. "You're not outright lying, but I think you're in danger of falling off the edge of the truth."

Ellie took a deep breath. "I can't go back." Bear didn't know if she meant the ranch or Illinois. Or if there was even a difference in her mind. "I'm...ashamed."

"Hey." He reached across the little table and lifted her chin. "You got nothing to be ashamed about. You don't have to tell me what it is, but there's a reason why you don't want to go back to Illinois. Arden and Kyle, they care about what happens to you, and you'll never find a more understanding, caring person than Arden."

"What about you, Bear? You seem pretty understanding. And caring."

Bear inhaled sharply. How did this woman know how to shoot straight for his soul?

His thumb stroked her soft cheek. "And you seem pretty damned brave for trying to make this work."

She shook her chin out of his hand, like a bird taking flight. "Or foolish, huh?"

"Nights are only gonna get colder. Gonna freeze to death if you stay here."

She looked back at the fireplace. "If I can find the chimney cap somewhere and put it back on, get it all fixed up, I'll be fine."

Bear wondered what in the hell she was running from.

Hiding from.

"I'll help you. But you're coming back with me to the ranch."

Ellie shook her head. "After I...lied?"

"Told you, they'll understand."

Instead of answering, she unwrapped her burrito and took a small bite. Her eyebrows rose and she took a much bigger one. She devoured the breakfast burrito in record time.

"Good, huh?" Bear asked.

Ellie nodded. "Never had one."

"Santiago's is local."

"No, never had any breakfast burrito."

Bear tried to hide his surprise. He reached for the bag and pulled out another one. "This one's got chorizo. Kinda spicy. You game?"

Ellie grinned. "Give it over."

Bear liked a woman with an appetite. Maybe he could lure Ellie down off the mountain by leaving a trail of breakfast burritos like breadcrumbs.

"What are you grinning at?" she asked between bites.

He just shook his head and drank his coffee. When she shrugged off the sleeping bag, he knew the chorizo was warming her up.

Doing the job *he* wanted.

B ear and Ellie worked on the cabin all day. It turned out the propane tank was not empty, but had been topped off at some point, so Ellie went to work on the stove, making sure it was functional. Bear hunted for the chimney cap and found it in a shed packed with tools and building supplies. It was damaged, but he could make it work for now. No choice because he knew, trail of burritos or not, he wasn't going to convince Ellie to come with him back to the ranch.

At least not today.

While she was inside, he texted Kyle and Arden to let them know he'd found Ellie and she was safe, but that was all he could tell them for now. Then, he turned his phone off and went back to work. Today was for Ellie.

The chimney was in worse shape than he thought. Swearing, he climbed back down the ladder. No damn way she could spend one more night without heat.

When Bear came in, she turned and beamed at him.

"Stove's working just fine. I can catch us a fish and you can stay for dinner."

"That what you ate last night?"

"I did. That lake's full of the biggest trout I've ever seen. Tasty, too."

Big trout, beautiful land with a flowing water source. Bear was positive they'd get the well going again too. She was sitting on a gold mine if she wanted to sell it all.

Something told him she didn't care about gold if it meant selling the view and the peacefulness.

"So will you stay for supper?" she asked, her eyes round and hopeful.

Bear nodded. "I'll stay for supper."

True to her word, Ellie caught a trout, cleaned it—not her favorite task, she admitted—and had it frying in a pan for dinner in no time. Also true—the fish was big. If she caught that from the shore, he couldn't imagine the monsters lurking out in the middle of the lake where the water was deep and they had a place to hide. Bear loved to fish. If he wasn't careful, he'd end up buying a boat just to see what he could catch.

"You're impressed, I can tell," Ellie said as he watched her cook.

"I'm impressed." The fish was the least of it. The cabin looked brand new inside after Ellie had spent the day cleaning it. But that was an illusion. Shadows from the kerosine lamps hid the places where the wind blew right in and made itself at home.

She wrapped the cast iron handle in a towel and carried the pan to the table. She divided up the fish between two plates.

"Where'd the onions come from?"

"The garden beds. There are some volunteers in there already. Once I set up a hoop garden and a rocket stove, I can pretty much grow vegetables year-round."

"You do that back in Illinois?"

She nodded and took a bite of fish. Bear tucked into his and it was delicious. He didn't realize he'd closed his eyes until he'd opened them again to find her staring at him and grinning.

"My turn to watch you."

He smiled back. "That's fair."

When they finished dinner, she left the dishes in the sink. Bear grabbed a gallon of drinking water he'd brought up. Then, she led him outside to the firepit where Bear had laid out wood earlier. Once he got the fire going, he sat down beside her and looked at the stars.

"There aren't half as many in Illinois," she said. "The air's too thick and hazy in the summer, and it's cloudy most of the winter."

"They look the same at the ranch as they do here," Bear coaxed.

Ellie was quiet so long he wasn't sure she'd answer.

Finally, she said, "But here, they're mine."

SEVEN

Bear almost—almost—convinced Ellie to return with him.

But in the end, she walked him back to his truck under a blanket of stars and he insisted on coming back first thing the next morning to check on her. As his red taillights shrank to the size of the most distant stars and then disappeared, she regretted her decision.

When they'd gotten to Bear's truck Ellie was hoping for a hug before he left. So she was thrilled when he cleared his throat self-consciously before wrapping his arms around her and pulling her in close to his warmth. She heard a rumble in his chest and looked up. The stars were so bright, she could see the wondering look on his face as he gazed down into hers. Then his hand was cupping the back of her head and she went up on her tiptoes. Her eyes closed in anticipation. Would his beard feel good scratching against her chin? Were his lips soft or rough? Would he part her lips with his tongue...

And just like that, he let her go. She opened her eyes as soon as his hand dropped from her hair. Bear took off his coat and draped it around her shoulders without a word then turned away to open the driver side door. Harsh light spilled out of the cab and she put her hand up to shield her eyes.

"See you tomorrow," Bear said right before he closed the door and started the engine. Ellie blinked while her eyes readjusted to the darkness, then she watched his truck grow smaller.

"Just wishful thinking," she said to herself. Of course Bear wasn't going to kiss someone like her. *Probably thinks I'm crazy.*

As she headed back to the cabin, pulling Bear's coat tighter around her body against the cold, she thought he might be right.

By morning, she didn't think he was right—she knew it.

Ellie had started out warm enough, but the night grew colder and the residual heat from the oven seeped through the walls pretty quickly. The fireplace still smoked so she'd only kept a small fire going. While she fell into a deep sleep, clouds rolled in with a brief but heavy rain that went straight down the chimney. The hot embers died without her knowing it.

Ellie woke to someone gently shaking her shoulder. Terrified that her brother had come into her room, she jumped up and took a swing only to find she wasn't at the farm and the man shaking her wasn't her brother.

"Hey, hey," Bear said as he stood up and backed away slowly. "Easy now. Not going to hurt you, Ellie. It's Bear."

Breathing fast, she looked around. Yup, the cabin was real, Illinois was the dream. She was safe. Bear was here, not Arnold.

"Bear," she said between breaths, her hand pressed against her chest.

"Yeah, Ellie. It's just me." He took a step closer. "Shouldn't have touched you. That was my mistake and a stupid one."

"It's okay." She swallowed and caught her breath.

I'm safe. I'm safe.

Then why was she suddenly teary?

"Ellie? Come on, Honey. Let's get you warmed up. I got coffee. Promise I won't hurt you."

She looked up at Bear's huge silhouette against the gray light coming in behind him and all her fear dropped away. She reached out and he found her hand.

"I'm taking you to my truck now."

She nodded and let him lead her out the cabin door.

His truck was blissfully warm. Ellie thought he must have had the heat cranked all the way up while he drove to the cabin. For her, maybe? She watched Bear out of the corner of her eye while she sipped her coffee and waited for him to say *I told you so.* It was something Arnold would have said. *You're stupid and I told you so.* Anything to make her feel small and weak and dumb. But Bear only drank his coffee right along with her.

"You warming up?" he asked.

Ellie nodded as she wiggled her thawed-out toes in her sneakers. "Thank you. You make really good coffee."

Bear grinned and she heard an amused rumble in his chest. That sound was becoming common and familiar. She wanted to hear it all the time.

"Good coffee's important," he said.

"Understatement."

"You hungry?"

Ellie hesitated. "No, I'm fine."

"Well, I am. We're heading down for breakfast."

"Bear, I don't wanna—"

He held up his hand, stopping her. "Drive-thru. Not Arden and Kyle's. Not a restaurant. Unless you want that. I'm good with wherever you want to go, but I want food."

"Drive-thru?" she asked.

"That what you want?"

Ellie nodded.

Bear opened his thermos and topped off her travel mug. Then he shifted the truck into drive and headed for civilization. The storm wasn't done with the mountain and they drove in and out of patchy rain. She curled into a tight ball and wondered how she'd make it through the winter.

Any way I can.

Bear turned the heat up even further. She noticed a light glaze of sweat on his temples and turned the heat back down. He frowned.

"I'm good. Nice and warm," she said.

"Sure about that? You look cold, all curled up."

"I'm sure. It's just..." She looked at the rain hitting the windshield and trickling down the side window and felt her heart freeze up with anxiety.

"You're cold inside."

Ellie turned her head to look at him.

"Thinking you can't do this," he added.

"Yes. Exactly." She brushed her eyes before her tears fell. "But I *have* to."

Then her hand was in his oversized paw. His thumb brushed over the backs of her fingers, sending tingles up her arm and down her spine. She waited for Bear to tell her that she was exactly right, she couldn't do it. That she was crazy and stupid to think she could turn the cabin into something habitable.

Instead, he just drove—one hand on the wheel, the other holding hers.

When they got to the fast-food place, Bear asked her what she wanted, then ordered double the amount. They got their food and he parked in a spot facing the red cliffs over Lyons.

"You're trying to fatten me up," she joked.

"Maybe." He pointed at the bag. "Now eat."

"Bossy, bossy." She never would have felt safe saying that to any other human being, but for some crazy reason, Bear put her at ease, even at her most worried moments.

And there went that amused rumble in his chest that made her smile.

Ellie devoured the first sausage biscuit and hash brown, then dove back into the bag for a second one. "Okay, so fattening me up is probably a good idea."

Bear laughed outright. "That'd take a while." She watched his cheeks turn red around his beard. "Sorry, don't mean to say...I mean, you look fine like you are. Good."

It was Ellie's turn to laugh. "No, you're right. I've dropped a few pounds, I think." Her jeans hung lower on her hips than they had when she left Illinois. The bag held two more sausage biscuits, which she figured would feed her over the next day. Maybe the day would stay cold enough that she could keep them fresh until the generator was fixed.

Ugh. One more job for Bear. No way could she ever pay him back for anything he'd done, including breakfast.

Stop thinking like that. You'll figure it out and get on your feet.

Ellie folded the top of the bag over and set it between them.

"Done?"

She nodded. "Thank you. It was good."

"So. Pay me back?"

Ellie's eyes widened. But why should she be surprised?

"My wallet is still up at...what?" Bear started shaking his head the moment she said wallet.

"Not with money. With time."

"Time?"

He nodded slowly. "About an hour should do it. Give Arden a chance to talk to you about coming back down to the ranch."

Ellie turned away and grabbed the door handle.

"Ellie. Stop."

"Nope. I'll find my way back up, thanks. And I'll send you the money for breakfast via Arden's ranch." She opened the door but Bear was already out of his seat and ambling around the front of the truck by the time her feet hit the pavement.

"You're not going anywhere in this weather. You'll catch pneumonia." He didn't look angry. If anything, worry filled his eyes. "Just get back in the truck. Please."

"Can't exactly get around you, can I?" She put her hands on her hips.

Bear grinned. "Nope."

"All right." Ellie turned and climbed back in while Bear circled the truck again.

"If you won't go because you're embarrassed, don't be. They get it."

"So you told them where I was?"

"Had to, Ellie. They were worried. Kyle was ready to send out his team to find you."

That shocked her. "Why? I'm a nobody. And a liar." She looked down into her lap. *A thief* she thought to herself.

"Look at me, Ellie."

She tore her gaze from her hands and looked into Bear's beautiful eyes, trying not to get lost in what she saw there.

"You're right, you are a liar," Bear stated.

She flinched.

"Every time you open your mouth and say something ridiculous like you're a nobody, that's a lie. You're repeating a lie that someone told you."

Her jaw dropped.

"That's gonna stop today, Ellie. You're real important to a bunch of people here, okay? Colorado's your home now and you have family here who care about you."

Ellie frowned and shook her head. "Ellen lives in Arizona and she was all the family I had in Colorado."

"Come on, Ellie. You know better," Bear said softly, and her heart sped up. "The minute Arden saw you, you were part of her family. And I'm not talking about a couple days ago."

Ellie blew out a breath. *Right. Arden.* Yeah, she knew what he meant. She just didn't know if it was really true. So many years had passed. They'd been little girls.

"I see you doubting. Just let me drive you to their house. Don't mean you have to stay. But just hear 'em out." Bear held her gaze until she finally nodded yes.

"All right then." He backed out of the parking space and headed for the ranch.

After a few minutes, Ellie said, "I'm not usually like this."

"Like what?"

"I'm not someone who... Who lies." She nibbled on her bottom lip. *In for a penny...* "Or steals. I'm not a thief, even though I stole the bike from my brother to get out here."

"Honey. I don't know your story. Way I see it though, you did what you needed to do to get away from a bad situation. That don't make you a thief. That makes you a survivor."

The way he said it made her feel like he knew a thing or two about surviving. But of course he would. He told her he'd been a Ranger.

"The bike was already stolen," she continued, cringing at her every word. "That's what he does. He steals things." She shuddered at something—more a feeling than a memory—from her childhood.

Then her hand was enveloped in his big, meaty paw.

"He steals things and sells them."

An unexpected tear slid down her cheek as she drew too close to remembering. Ellie hunkered down in Bear's big coat as if it were a fortress. It smelled like him—fresh air, pine forest, coffee, and something that was a little spicy and a little musky. Bear's skin, maybe. She turned her head and breathed against the collar. Her eyes drifted closed as she suddenly felt safe. Bear squeezed her hand and didn't say another word until after they'd passed through the gate and pulled up in front of the ranch a few minutes after that.

"You afraid?"

Her mouth went dry. Bear couldn't know that Arnold would always ask her the same thing—*Are you afraid?*—right before hurting her.

She opened her eyes to find Bear staring intently at her. She didn't think anyone had ever looked at her with such compassion. Her chest expanded before she realized how shallow her breaths had been.

"They'll understand," was all he said. "Ellie?"

"I'm not afraid," she whispered. And to her shock, she wasn't.

He smiled. "That's right. You're not afraid of anything."

At least not for today she thought. *Not so long as I have you with me.*

The front door opened and Arden appeared, looking worried before she spotted Ellie. She smiled and waved as if they were just stopping by for tea. Bear let go of her hand and was out of the truck and getting her door before she'd had a chance to reconsider.

"Ellie!" Arden said. "Come on in. It's too cold out here today."

Camo trotted out and picked up speed when he saw her. She reached down and buried her hands in his fur and he groaned, making them all laugh.

Inside the house, Kyle was nowhere in sight, which made her feel better. Arden poured coffee and brought the mugs to the big farmhouse table where Ellie and Bear sat.

"Am I keeping you from work?" Ellie asked.

Arden shook her head. "From clients, no. No one's scheduled to come up today. But you know that the work never ends on a farm or ranch."

Ellie smiled and nodded. That was the absolute truth. Even though Arden's ranch no longer had cattle, the horses, alpacas, and goats who lived in the barn took a lot of work. Borders and therapeutic animals for Arden's clients, they were pampered and well cared for.

Arden turned serious. "If there was anything Kyle or I did that made you feel unwelcome here, we apologize."

"No, no," Ellie protested. "You were wonderful. I'm the big jerk who ran and hid."

"You're not a jerk, Ellie." Arden's voice had gone soft and low, comforting her. "And when someone hides, there's always a good reason. I'm not going to pry, but from what I remember about your dad, and about how your brothers acted when they were here, I can't blame you."

Embarrassed, Ellie felt herself blush.

"It's also not your fault. Ellie, if you're in danger—"

She started to stand but Bear laid a steadying hand on her shoulder.

"Are you worried I'm gonna cause trouble?"

"No, that's not what I mean." Arden chuckled. "We can handle trouble—and we have—believe me." She pointed back toward the front door. "I don't know if you noticed, but I keep a shotgun next to the door. Her name's Nancy."

"Like your great-great-great grandma."

"Exactly. Nancy knew how to handle trouble, and so do we. So, if you need a place to stay and a job while you sort things out, there's no better place than here with us." Arden leaned forward. "No one's going to bother you here. No one's even going to know where you are and it's going to stay that way." Her gaze slid to Bear, who nodded.

Arden continued. "I know the cabin must feel safe because it's so isolated, but it scares me to think of you alone up there. This is safer, here with us. I promise."

Bear grunted.

"You don't think I'm dangerous?" Ellie asked, and there went that amused rumble in Bear's chest before Arden could even answer.

With an uncharacteristically wicked look in her eyes and a smile on her face, Arden answered, "Some people think we're the dangerous ones. And that's all right by me."

B y that afternoon, Ellie was the ranch's newest employee. She still had misgivings. Not about the job—she loved working with animals, and ranch work already came naturally to her. And it wasn't about Arden and Kyle, even though she couldn't get past feeling like she was imposing despite Arden's reassurances that she loved having the company and needed the help. She couldn't quite place her misgivings until Bear reappeared with her bike and backpack. He'd taken off earlier, and she assumed that he'd gone to the safehouse to work, until he walked into the barn and told her that he'd left her bike on the porch and her backpack just inside the front door.

"Oh, thank you. You didn't need to do that. I could have gone and gotten them."

"That's a long walk," Bear said as walked over to the alpaca enclosure and scratched the nose of a curious alpaca who decided to come forward and check out the new human.

"Figured you'd want your stuff and I had the truck and the time." He shrugged.

"Well, thank you." She watched his hand scratching the alpaca instead of meeting his eyes. Her cheeks burned. "Really, I didn't want to impose."

"No imposition. How you doing with the rest of this? You're looking a little..." Bear tilted his head. He didn't have to say another word because those gorgeous eyes saw the truth right as it dawned on her.

"Uncomfortable. Yeah. It's just that I don't want to feel helpless. Or...or trapped."

His lips pursed within that thick, dark beard. "You have a driver's license."

She grinned. "You know it. Farmer's daughter. I've been driving all sorts of vehicles since I was fourteen."

He reached into his pocket and pulled something out. "Catch." He tossed it in the air.

She caught it. Confused, she said, "This is the key to your truck."

"Nope. That's *your* key to my truck."

"Bear, I can't." She tried to hand him back the key but he wouldn't take it.

"You can. If I'm working down here on Walter's place and you need to be somewhere, you got two choices now. Bike or truck. Don't mean you have to take the truck, but it's an option. You're not helpless. Unless you *decide* to be."

Dang it. He was right. She pocketed the key.

"Thank you. I promise I'll pay you back somehow."

His eyes darkened, but he smiled anyway. "Not what that's about."

She put her hands on her hips. "You don't feel responsible for me, do you?"

Bear chuckled and waved her off like she'd just said the

most ridiculous thing ever. "Nobody likes to feel helpless. Or trapped." He turned away and walked toward the open barn door.

Did that mean he didn't want to feel trapped by her? Some of the warmth in her chest evaporated. Ellie patted her pocket. She'd just never use the key, that was all.

But it sure felt good there in her pocket.

EIGHT

Bear wasn't sure what to say over dinner at Arden and Kyle's so he let everyone else do the talking. All he wanted was to sit quietly in Ellie's presence. He couldn't stop studying every little move she made like he was watching something wild peeking out from the edge of a forest. He was afraid that if he made the wrong move she'd bolt.

That's what kept him from kissing her the night before when she felt so good wrapped in his arms. Looking down into her pretty face in the starlight made him forget that they'd really only just met, even if they knew each other as kids. She felt familiar to him already and it was only natural for him to bend close and brush his lips against hers—the least of what he wanted to do to her. What he really wanted was to take her back to the safehouse, carry her into the bedroom, and...

Stop he'd told himself right before he almost kissed Ellie. *She doesn't feel like a stranger to you, but that don't mean you aren't still a stranger to her.*

He was used to people giving him a wide berth. Bear was

big and intimidating. Ellie was such a tiny thing. He didn't want her to think he expected her to pay for his help with her body. The thought sickened him. So he'd let her go and left before he changed his mind and did something stupid. It killed him to leave her there—not just because he wanted a taste of the woman who smelled like fresh, sweet berries, but because he worried about her there alone. A million things could happen.

But you didn't force wild things, especially when they were scared. You followed their lead, gave them space, and hoped they'd grow used to you until they approached on their terms.

Then why aren't you practicing what you preach? he'd asked himself a few hours later as he drove most of the way back up to her cabin. Ellie had what she needed—food, a fire, plenty of wood to keep the coals going. What she didn't need was an overprotective Bear stomping in to check on her in the middle of the night and scaring her to death.

So he just parked his truck in the field and got out to make sure no one had come up to bother her. *Good*, no tracks except the ones from his truck. A wisp of smoke rose from her chimney. No doubt Ellie was sound asleep. She was just fine without him, thank you very much.

Bear had gotten back in his truck, feeling like a fool. He glanced at the big thermos filled with hot coffee he'd made right before he left. What he should have done was turn around and driven back to the house, then come up in the morning with breakfast like any old decent human being would do. He even got so far as to turn the ignition.

Then he sat there.

Nothing but more dreams waiting for him back at the house—exactly what woke him up in the first place, with a raging hard on that only took him a few strokes to resolve.

He'd dreamed of Ellie's smile, her laugh, the softness of her hair slipping through his fingers. He'd held her again but this time he did kiss her all over and she tasted like berries and honey and everything good that he never thought could be his to keep.

Still not mine to keep.

Bear was headed to Texas in a few days. A month at most. Shouldn't have stayed this long as it was. Old roots he'd pulled up long ago were threatening to anchor him again if he didn't start thinking about moving on. Sure, he felt peaceful now, but it wouldn't last. It never did. Soon enough, he'd get restless, agitated. Someone would pick up on it in a bar, decide to start a fight with him just to scratch an itch or impress a woman. Bear didn't look for trouble, but trouble found him, always. The note on the door a few days ago was proof.

That's why I need to go. She's already got enough trouble without me.

Instead, Bear got out of bed and paced until he gave up, got dressed, and started the coffeemaker. Now he sat there in his truck, heat on, radio playing low, mind replaying the day he'd spent with Ellie. Peaceful and easy.

He woke to a gray morning, raindrops scattered across his windshield. No smoke coming from the cabin's chimney.

Shit.

Bad enough he'd fallen dead asleep, but he'd missed the rainfall and it looked like her fire had gone out. Bear turned off the idling truck and got out. Damn if the rain hadn't dropped the temperature down almost to freezing.

Ellie was alone and cold.

Bear lumbered through the aspen grove. Sure enough, there was no smoke from the chimney, no sign that Ellie was up and moving. He knocked on her door and when she didn't answer, his fear got the best of him and Bear went inside.

There she was, curled up in a ball in her sleeping bag in a drafty cabin that was almost as cold inside as it was outside. All the way from the door, he could see her shivering in her sleep. He needed to get her warm and fed. She was going to make herself sick if she kept this up. Her stubbornness was gonna get her killed.

He knelt beside her and felt his heart throb when he saw her face. She looked so peaceful. He gently shook her shoulder through the bag and her eyes flew open. He was pretty sure she was still mostly asleep when she shouted and took a wild swing then backed away from him. The way she clutched the sleeping bag around her like it was armor broke his heart. He'd scared her half to death. Stupid of him, doing more harm than good. Story of his life. He should just walk away.

Then Ellie reached out her hand to him. Trusting. Not afraid. And he took it and knew he wouldn't walk away, not until he was sure she was safe. Bear was determined that Ellie would stay with Arden and Kyle.

Wish she'd stay with me.

Stop being selfish. This ain't about you.

He held her hand at every opportunity. *To comfort her* he lied to himself. *Just and only to comfort* her, *not me.*

He was so sure she'd try and bolt again when they pulled up at the ranch. All this talk of her being too much trouble when she was nothing of the sort. Just an excuse to cover her fear.

"I'm not afraid," she'd whispered and he doubted her.

But when he looked into her eyes, he didn't see fear. Maybe she wasn't afraid. What had changed?

"That's right. You're not afraid of anything."

Funny how, sitting here at dinner, Bear was the one who

felt uneasy. What if she disappeared again and didn't go to the cabin this time? How would he find her?

When it came time to leave, Ellie walked him out to the truck. Bear clenched his jaw, so full of all sorts of emotions. He wanted to pull her into another hug. Wanted to kiss her this time. Wanted to extract a promise that she'd still be there in the morning, safe and sound. And all that would damn near guarantee she'd bolt, and what that thought did to him...

Now Bear was the scared one.

"Ellie—"

"Bear—"

They both smiled when they said each other's names at the same time.

"You first," Ellie said.

"No. Ladies first."

She grinned and her eyes sparkled. "Bossy."

Bear laughed.

She slipped her hand into his and his chest went molten. "I just want to say thank you. For everything."

Was that a goodbye?

"Ellie, if you feel like you need to run, you come down and grab my truck, all right? You take a nice long drive, then you turn around and come right back here. You do that a hundred times if you need to."

"No, I couldn't—"

Bear clutched her upper arm. "I mean it, Ellie. You get to feeling caged and you need room to breathe, you take my truck but you come back. Just don't... Don't run away again." He realized he was holding tight to her arm and let go like it was on fire. Here he was, scaring her for sure. She'd probably turn around and bolt right back into the house, grab Nancy the shotgun for good measure and he couldn't blame her. Big, dumb, scary oaf that he was.

Ellie didn't turn around and run. She wrapped her arms around him and went up on her toes until she was an inch from his face. So close, he could smell her skin, the pure sweetness of it, feel her breath passing over his lips, the warmth of her body against his.

"I'm not gonna run, Bear. Not from the good things."

Then she tilted her head, leaned in the rest of the way and—

Kissed his cheek, right above the edge of his beard.

"Bossy, bossy Bear," she giggled beside his ear as his whole body turned to flames. "Goodnight."

And just like that, she was out of his arms and back inside the ranch house, leaving him to smolder as he brushed his fingers over the place where her lips touched his skin, and wonder about her.

Stop. Friends kiss cheeks. If she wanted more, she woulda kissed your mouth.

This time when Bear got back to Walter's old house, there was another piece of paper *and* a photo taped to the door. One look at the photo made him growl.

Not playing fair, assholes.

He stared into the boy's big brown eyes where the hurt lived. The kid's smile wasn't fooling anyone who cared enough to pay attention. He looked about ten, maybe eleven years old, all dressed up for the school picture. Now it was Bear's brain that wasn't playing fair. He kept wondering what put the hurt in the kid's eyes. Or more likely, who.

And if they'd been punished for it.

No. If the photo was taped on Bear's door, it meant someone had hurt this boy and gotten away with it.

And Bear's friends were asking for his help with making that person pay.

He unfolded the piece of paper and read the name, address, and the date—two weeks from today. No asking him to reconsider this time. They knew the photo would do the job for them.

Those eyes.

Not fair.

NINE

I should have kissed him for real.

But Ellie didn't and now she was tossing and turning in bed thinking about Bear. His rough beard and the surprising softness of his cheek above it. The heat coming off his body, pushing away the cold night. The way his beautiful eyes pleaded with her not to run away.

No, she did the right thing by not kissing him. He'd told her he was leaving. Bear had been so quiet at dinner while she, Arden, and Kyle talked. When they thanked him for the work he'd done already and wished he wasn't moving on to Texas for the winter, he just grunted in that inscrutable Bear way. He didn't say he was staying.

He didn't say he was leaving, either.

Ellie turned over. She couldn't afford to read anything more into his kindness. Men like him were heartbreakers. Big, fit, good-looking, they didn't have time for a little mouse like her. He'd drift on down to Texas and find some Southern Belle in a bikini who was ready to play. Why should Ellie hurt herself even more with the memory of his lips on hers while she imagined him sipping Piña Coladas with a beautiful woman. She pictured Bear with his shaggy beard flowing over a Hawaiian shirt, wearing flip-flops and sipping a frothy drink with a paper umbrella in it.

Okay, maybe not a Piña Colada for him. She had to stifle a laugh.

Still, why would he stay in Colorado for her? She was trouble, she'd told him that already. Trouble and a lot of work. Look at everything he'd already done for her—the money he'd spent feeding her, the time away from his handyman job to help her at the cabin. Checking on her and making sure she didn't freeze her dumb ass off when the fire went out. She couldn't believe the look on his face when she'd finally realized where she was and that she was in no danger from him. He looked mortified. Almost...afraid. *As if anything could scare a big man like that.*

Bear was so careful when she was in his arms, treating her like she was made of spun glass. He'd gripped her arm hard tonight but then let go quickly when he realized what he'd done. He looked almost scared after, like he'd hurt her, but he'd never lost control. That's when she'd hugged him, to reassure Bear that she wasn't hurt or afraid of him, not at all.

Yeah, Ellie, keep telling yourself that the hug was only for him and not because his arms feel so good when they wrap around you.

He'd given her a key to his truck. His only mode of transportation, which he pretty much lived in if he traveled as much as he said he did. He'd given her that key even after she'd told him she'd stolen the bike from Arnold.

Don't run away again.

She was reading too much into it. Maybe Bear was only remembering the little girl she'd been and felt sorry for her. He sure remembered her brothers and so did Arden.

Ellie's brothers hadn't always been so bad. When they

were really little, her oldest brother Arnold had even taken a few hits for her and Harlan when Daddy was drunk and swinging his fists. But those days were long gone. As they got older, the boys turned mean, until Ellie was dodging their fists as much as her father's. After their mother died, it was like they'd just given up on being decent human beings. Arnold and Harlan supplemented the farm's income—less and less every year—with stealing and fencing whatever they could get their hands on. Things got really bad when Ellie was fifteen and Arnold made friends with a gang that made and sold meth.

Not going to think about that.

She shuddered as she tossed again and a small sound escaped her. Ellie hoped Kyle and Arden weren't light sleepers. She listened for a moment and heard Camo's dog tag ringing as he must have stood and shook himself off. Then his clicking steps came down the hall and he scratched at her door. Ellie got up to let him in.

"Hey, boy," she whispered as she closed the door, but not enough that he couldn't nose it open if he wanted back out. She went back to bed and he followed her. Camo jumped onto the bed, circled once at the foot of it and flopped down, his head facing the pillows so he could watch her.

Ellie grinned. "You're about as protective as Bear," she whispered as she scratched Camo's head. She got back in under the covers and leaned forward until she could bury her face in the dog's ruff. Then she grabbed the second pillow and laid back down with it beside her. She held it tightly, imagining that it was Bear lying in her arms, keeping watch. Keeping her safe from her own nightmares.

Ellie drifted off with a tiny smile on her face.

It was the first morning that Ellie woke up knowing exactly where she was. She was at Arden and Kyle's ranch in Colorado and she was safe. Not just safe, but warm and comfortable. The guest bedroom that she'd been told to call hers was incredibly cozy. Part of the older house, it had an amazing view of the Rockies rising in the distance behind the pine forest that edged the field where the horses, alpacas, and goats roamed. Right outside Ellie's window was the back yard. And framed perfectly in the window was the single evergreen Arden called the Christmas Tree. Her family had decorated it every year. Ellie smiled to herself, wondering if she would still be here to help Arden and Kyle decorate it, or if she would have her own tree in her own snug little cabin. Because even as she worked at the ranch, she planned to spend every spare minute fixing up the cabin.

Ellie stretched in bed, not quite ready yet to get up. The morning was still dark and chilly, but she knew the day would warm up once the sun rose. Colorado had decided to put off autumn and keep summer going just a little while longer. The two cold nights that she had spent in the cabin didn't seem real to her at this point. she couldn't believe how desperate she'd been not to go back to Illinois and how little she had trusted everyone around her. Everyone except Bear.

Camo stretched and shook himself, then jumped off the bed and trotted to the door. He turned to wait for her.

"All right, buddy. Let's see who else is up." Ellie got out of bed and put on a robe and slippers she'd borrowed from Arden. She was determined to spend her first paycheck on necessities so that she didn't have to borrow anything. She wasn't used to the flowery print on the robe or any girly clothes. Mostly what she wore were hand-me-downs from her brothers, except for the clothes she'd managed to grab from her mother's closet before her father took everything out and either sold it or threw it away. She had to stash Mama's dresses because the first time she'd worn one, her brothers laughed at her and Daddy got real mad and told her if she didn't take it off he'd tear it off her right there. He never wanted to see anything of her mother's again.

Just keep moving forward. Don't need to think about old things that don't matter anymore.

Ellie was the first one up so she fed Camo, let him out, and started making biscuits in the hope that Bear would amble by for breakfast before he started work. She wouldn't have many more chances to cook for him, she figured. He wouldn't be staying much longer in Colorado, and if he left before she got her first paycheck, she had no idea how to get ahold of him to pay him back. The least she could do was fatten him up for the winter. Isn't that what bears liked?

She laughed lightly to herself.

"Good morning." Arden's voice came from the hall as she walked into the great room and toward the kitchen on the far side of it. "What can possibly be so funny before coffee?"

"Good morning." Ellie smiled brightly, genuinely glad to see Arden. "I was just making biscuits and thinking I could fatten up Bear before his winter hibernation if he comes for breakfast."

Arden laughed. "Oh, he'll be around, I'm positive." She poured herself a fresh cup of coffee and topped off Ellie's mug. "Thanks for getting breakfast started."

Ellie wondered at Arden's teasing tone. "Because he comes every morning?"

Arden just raised her eyebrows. "If he didn't before, he will now."

Ellie felt her cheeks grow warm. No, she had to be misunderstanding Arden. It wasn't her bringing Bear around, it was the biscuits of course. But it was nice to think it *was* her.

"How many eggs will Kyle want?" Ellie asked.

"Kyle's already up and at the office," Arden said as she pulled bacon out of the fridge. Something in her voice gave Ellie pause.

"Everything okay?" she asked nervously, afraid that she'd somehow messed things up already and wasn't as welcome as she'd thought.

Arden smiled and draped her arm around Ellie's shoulders for a quick hug. "It's not you if that's what you're worried about, I promise. We're still a little gun-shy around here after a rough summer. Kyle's had trouble sleeping and doesn't want to keep me awake tossing and turning so he gets up and starts work early. Now that you're here, he feels safer leaving me in the mornings. Before, he had Bear checking on me if he went in early."

Ah. So, it was just Bear's nature to be protective. Ellie wasn't a special case after all. She couldn't help but feel her heart squeeze.

"What happened this summer?" she asked to cover her disappointment.

Arden looked down. "I can't talk about it much because it's an ongoing situation." She immediately looked back up, worried. "Though I don't want you to think you aren't safe here. You are. We took care of a big part of the problem."

Now it was Ellie's turn to look away. She pretended to check on the biscuits. She didn't want to jeopardize Arden and Kyle's safety if Arnold found out where she was. Maybe this wasn't going to work after all.

"Ellie?" Arden set her coffee mug down. "I think we need to talk, don't we?"

Ellie covered the frying pan so the bacon wouldn't splatter

everywhere. "Yeah. Look, um, really, if you don't want me here—"

"What?" Arden covered her heart. "Of course we do." Realization dawned on her face. "Do you still think you're going to bring trouble that we can't handle?"

"I..." Tears welled in her eyes. Before she could get another word out, Arden wrapped her up tightly in her arms. Then Ellie's words flowed quickly. "They don't know I'm here. I can't let them find out. They'll take it from me. They take *everything* from me, and they can't have this."

A voice came from behind them. "Who's *they*?"

Ellie looked up as Bear stepped into the kitchen. Behind him stood Kyle. Arden led her to the big farmhouse table and she and Bear sat on either side of Ellie while Kyle sat across from her, a worried look on his face.

"Is it your brothers?" Bear asked, and Ellie nodded. He exchanged a look with Kyle.

"Arnold...I stole his bike," Ellie said, embarrassed to be telling Arden and Kyle the truth. "Well, not *his* bike, techni- cally. He stole it first. That's what he and his crew do, they steal things. But I had to take it when I got the letter from Mr. Cole. I didn't have enough money for the bus fare all the way here and I didn't want to leave from my hometown anyway just in case they figured out where I was going. So I took the bike...and the gun," she added, looking at Kyle, who only looked back with sympathy in his eyes. "I went south instead of directly west in case anyone saw me. I rode for three days until I was sure they didn't know where I was and they weren't following me. When I got to a bus station in Kansas, I took the bus to Colorado from there."

Bear's arm went around her. "You were alone for three days? Just a bike and a gun."

She nodded. "I was okay. Nothing even happened until I got to Denver."

"What happened in Denver?" Kyle asked.

"Some guy tried to talk me into 'working' for him, if you know what I mean."

Both Kyle and Bear growled. Kyle reached across the table and grabbed Ellie's hand. "Ellie, look at me. I want you to know that you are safe here. We aren't going to let your brothers know where you are. The minute you walked onto the property, you became family, I just didn't know it then and I apologize again for scaring you." His gaze shifted to Arden. "The boys you remember have grown into dangerous men." He looked at Ellie again. "I was in the office reading a report on them from a friend of ours who works in the home office. Elissa. She couldn't find a home number or any cell phone attached to Arnold or Harlan."

"They don't have them," Ellie said. "We don't have a land-line on the farm anymore and they only use throwaway phones." Shame heated her cheeks. "I don't have a phone at all."

Kyle nodded. "Figured as much when we tried to find you when you left."

Ellie started to apologize when Kyle held up his hand. "No need, little sister. I get it why you ran. The gang your brothers are connected to, they're bad news. You did the smart thing by getting away and going into hiding, and I didn't help matters when you showed up. But we're past that, right?"

Ellie nodded, grateful tears blurring her vision again.

Kyle's voice softened. "Hey now." He let go of her hand and came around the table. Ellie stood up and Kyle hugged her. "I mean it when I called you little sister. That's who you are to Arden, no matter how much time has passed, and that's who you are to me now, understand?" She nodded and he tipped her face up. "And here, we take care of family."

"I don't want to bring trouble down on you," Ellie said.

"Negative," Kyle said. "Nothing we can't handle easily if they come around."

Ellie heard Bear get to his feet behind her. Kyle let her go as she felt Bear's hand on her back.

"It's true, Ellie," Bear said softly. "We've got you, Honey."

But for how long? Ellie wondered. "I've got to check on breakfast," she said, jogging back into the kitchen so they couldn't see that more tears raced down her cheeks. Why was it that she'd learned to stop crying long ago whenever she took a beating, but now in the face of such kindness, the tears just flowed?

Arden joined her and mercifully she didn't say anything, just helped her plate up and bring the food to the table. Bear smiled big and his eyes twinkled as she set the plate down in front of him.

"I'm feeling spoiled," he said when she sat down beside him. "Thank you."

"The least I can do." The words sounded squeaky.

Bear's leg brushed against hers then stayed there. She didn't move her leg, enjoying the warmth and silent support.

Ellie settled into ranch life much faster than she thought was possible. It helped that Arden and Kyle were so kind. She wasn't used to getting up in the morning to a friendly, *Hello, how are you?* Instead, she'd been used to, *Is breakfast done yet? God, you're lazy.*

Over the next two weeks, she quickly fell into a comfortable routine with Arden and Kyle. Every morning, Ellie got up to help Arden with breakfast. After that, they made the rounds and checked on all of the animals. Arden usually went back inside to get a head start on the paperwork she needed to do for her clients who came to the ranch to ride the horses, pet the alpacas, feed the chickens, and with Arden's help, work on their PTSD.

Meanwhile, Ellie enjoyed quiet time in the barn, taking care of the animals and watching for all the stray cats who called the barn home. They were even starting to get used to her and would come out as soon as she put a bowl of food down for them instead of waiting for her to leave. That is, unless Camo was outside with her. The Labrador struck big fear into their hearts when really all he wanted to do was play.

Bear was always there for meals. He'd gotten quieter—if that were possible—but made sure to thank her and Arden for the food. The way he smiled at her behind that beard when she spoke while they ate gave her the courage to share a few stories. One morning, he brought wildflowers he'd picked on his walk to the ranch house. Ellie thought they were prettier than any roses she'd even seen. Even though she knew they were for both her and Arden, she pretended that Bear had brought them just for her. The first flowers she'd ever been given.

And every passing day Bear gave her more reasons to trust him.

Even though she had sworn never to use his truck, she found herself needing to go into Boulder to pick up a few things along with a surprise thank-you gift for Arden so she wanted to sneak away rather than borrow Arden's car. So, Ellie biked the short distance to her Uncle Walter's old house and knocked on the door.

When Bear opened it, he didn't say a word, just smiled at her through that big beard of his. The day was already warm and he'd taken off his usual plaid flannel shirt. The t-shirt he wore stretched nicely across his broad chest, and she swore she could hear the fabric squeak from the effort of encasing his biceps.

Bear didn't greet Ellie, just took up the entire doorway and stared at her. Ellie didn't say a word right away. She was suddenly empty of words.

"Hi," she finally forced out. "I, um." What was she here for again? It wasn't to stand slack-jawed staring at him.

Bear frowned and quickly stepped back. He grabbed something beside the door. It turned out to be his flannel, which he put on without meeting her gaze again.

"Can I help you?" He sounded all formal suddenly, as if he were a cashier and she'd just walked into his store looking for a pack of chewing gum.

"No." Ellie turned on her heel without thinking, suddenly wanting to be out of there.

"Wait."

She stopped at the edge of the porch like his voice had lassoed her.

"You here for the truck?"

Ellie turned. "It's okay that you changed your mind about loaning me your truck."

"Wait, wait, wait. Who told you I changed my mind?"

Your formal voice is what she wanted to say. "Nobody."

"You sure?" He tilted his head and squinted. "Because I haven't. I made that offer and it stands, Ellie. I wouldn't go back on my word like that." Then his expression softened. "You aren't used to that, are you?"

She shook her head. In Ellie's world, promises were at best maybes and often broken without a second thought.

"Ellie." The soft way he said her name sent delicious

chills down her spine in contrast to the hot sun overhead. "Get used to it, Honey."

"I won't keep it long, I promise," she stuttered. "I just need to go to Boulder to pick up a few things for the ranch."

A strange look passed over his face as if he were thinking about something he didn't like. "Keep it as long as you need, Ellie. You want to keep it overnight, you can."

She thought that was a strange thing for him to say.

"I'm not going up to the cabin today if that's what you're thinking. I'm saving that for Saturday." Kyle had offered to take her up there himself and look around just to make sure it was safe.

Bear nodded. "I know. I'll go ahead and take you up there."

"You don't need to."

"There is need and there is want. Ellie. I *want* to take you up there."

Oh. My. She smiled, not trusting her voice to stay even.

"And if you need me to come with you today, I will."

"No. No, Bear, you have enough to do here, and you've already lost work time helping me out. I'll be fine."

His face fell behind his beard.

"I mean, unless you want to make sure I'm a good driver," she added.

He laughed and shook his head. "That what you think?"

"I wouldn't blame you."

"You're killing me, Ellie. Just flat-out killing me." He stepped back into the house. "I trust you." Then he closed the door, leaving her alone to wonder what she'd said.

TEN

Bear's stomach knotted as he listened to the sound of Ellie returning his truck in the late afternoon. He'd hoped that she'd go ahead and keep it overnight, but of course that was silly—why would she? And even if she had, he could just walk up to the ranch and take it.

So he had his truck back. There went one lame excuse not to go to the address from the note on his door. Not to get involved in some bad business tonight.

He clenched his fists, remembering the pain in the boy's eyes. If he didn't do this he might as well tape that photo to his truck's visor to remind himself that he'd walked away from a situation he could fix.

No, not fix. He didn't have the skills to fix the boy. That was more along Arden's line. He had other skills.

Bear didn't fix people—he broke them. And he wanted to break this man.

He listened to Ellie's steps coming up the walk to the front door. No doubt she wanted to let him know she was back and to thank him. He stood beside the door aching to open it, to pull her inside and slam it shut behind her, shut out the world and make it just the two of them.

She stepped onto the porch and knocked on the door. He reached to open it, saw the tremble in his hand, and pulled back. What would she see in his face if he let her in?

A monster, that's what.

Ellie knocked again, this time a little louder.

Go away, Ellie. Just go away now.

She knocked one more time.

Let her in. Don't let her in.

He heard her sigh, followed by some rustling. A minute later, the screen door opened and shut and then her footsteps receded. Bear waited to open the door until he was sure she was gone. He opened the door to see she'd taken her bike and left a note for him tucked into the screen door.

I knocked but you must be napping. Thank you again for the truck. For <u>everything</u>. I'll see you at dinner? I'm making biscuits!

Ellie

"Ellie." He breathed out her name as he gripped the note. If she knew what he was capable of she wouldn't make anything but tracks—away from him.

Bear parked the truck at the edge of the soccer field. He'd done his homework in the meantime and researched the name so that he had a face to go with it. It didn't take long to find the man. His name was all over the local news, but not for the right reasons. He was a hero at the moment, with only a passing paragraph about allegations brought against him at the very end of the story. An afterthought that should have been the lede.

Soccer practice was over, and the last few boys on the school team were headed for a minivan parked three spots away from Bear. The coach was busy on the field packing up equipment but still had time to wave at the smiling mom and shout something friendly. What a great guy.

If you ignored the truth.

The little boy with the big brown eyes wasn't one of the kids piling into the van. He was off the team, bullied out of playing not by his teammates, but by other parents who didn't want any trouble.

It takes a village to hurt a kid sometimes. The thought made Bear growl.

Three more trucks pulled into the parking lot as the minivan disappeared into the setting sun. Six doors opened and slammed shut. Six men converged and walked in a line toward the coach.

Jon Behr. Shane Foti. Gabe O'Neil. Elias Hunt. Waylon Ramson. Benjamin Massey.

"Knew we could count on you," Shane told Bear.

"Not here for you. I'm here for the kid. Then I'm out."

No one answered.

Catching sight of the men, the coach dropped the net full of soccer balls and took three steps back. Too late, the men surrounded him in a loose circle. The coach reached for his cell phone and one of the men knocked it from his hand then stomped it.

"*Coach* William Schultz," Benjamin said. The word *coach* came out as sarcastically as Bear had ever heard. "You are accused of abusing young boys who were placed in your care. The first accusation went public eight months ago, at which time you were arrested and held for seventy-eight hours until your million-dollar bond was paid by a member of the school for which you *coach*."

"I have nothing to say about that." Schultz turned in circles to face each accuser.

Benjamin ignored him. "One by one, the three children who came forward with descriptions of your abuse rescinded their testimonies. One boy is now in a children's mental hospital in Denver. The other two have moved out of state, thanks to massive bullying. Two more children who did not testify have left the team. What else did you do, besides start a smear campaign, to intimidate them into silence?"

"I don't have to answer your questions."

"How many children have you abused?" Gabe asked.

"That's...they cleared me. Dropped the charges. So no one." Schultz scratched briskly at his face. The man was a liar.

Benjamin stared him down. "One more chance. What did you do to silence the first boy who accused you?"

Now Schultz was rubbing hard at his chin. "I was cleared of all—"

Bam. Benjamin's fist connected with Schultz's nose and his eyes immediately watered as he staggered backward into Bear. Bear turned him around and sent his fist into Schultz's soft gut, connecting with his diaphragm.

"What did you do to hurt them?" Bear growled as Schultz doubled over, wheezing.

"Noth...ing." Schultz clutched his gut. He made a headlong run for it but Bear caught him and gripped him hard.

"Cameras," Schultz wheezed. "You all are fucked." He pointed toward the parking lot where the lights had not come on.

"Funny. Cameras and lights sometimes don't work," Shane said.

"Cowards," Schultz said, struggling in Bear's grip.

"No. We're not the cowards. We're the ones who clean up the shit when the system fails." Shane's fist connected with

Schultz's jaw. His head snapped to the side followed by his body. Bear held him so he couldn't fall.

Waylon grabbed Schultz's chin and lifted it. His eyes streamed, his jaw swelled, and he wheezed.

"You hurt children and you lie about it. People cover for you, all because you win games, and because no one wants to look at the truth head-on. You are a cockroach. No, even cockroaches serve some fucked-up purpose, I'm sure. But you don't. You are toxic shit. You can't even admit to your crimes. And if you disappeared, no one would care. You'd be replaced and forgotten. Maybe then people would come forward and spit on your empty grave with their equally empty excuses for why they didn't do anything while you were alive."

Schultz cringed, and Waylon went on.

"How does it feel to be helpless and scared? Do you even care that you made children feel this way? No, you don't."

Bear braced Schultz as another punch landed in his gut, this time lower.

"What did you do to intimidate him?" Bear asked.

Schultz spit bloody drool on the ground. "He was asking for it."

Bear's hackles rose. "You meant to tell me a kid was asking to be abused? An innocent little kid?" Rage flowed through him like a river of fire, making his skin tingle and his chest burn. He was ready to pop this guy's head off and kick it across the field. His fingers dug into Schultz's arms until the man cried out in pain.

"I...I...I told him I'd hurt his mom," Schultz sputtered.

Bear grinned. "Truth's coming out." He nodded to the others. "Full confession time now. What did you do and who did you hurt?"

Schultz spilled his guts, sickening Bear along with the circle of men hemming Schultz in. And like the rat he was,

Schultz told them about his partner in crime—part of the school administration and the person behind the bail money. The more he talked, the more Bear could smell the flop sweat pouring off him, sour and disgusting. His voice grew more and more strained, his eyes bulged and Bear vaguely wondered why.

"Hey." Gabe touched Bear's shoulder and then jumped back. "Enough."

That's when Bear realized one of his hands had strayed to Schultz's throat. He let go. Part of him still wanted to snap Schultz's neck and leave him there for the vultures and the coyotes, a quick death he didn't deserve. Then he wanted to go after the other piece of filth Schultz ratted out. His fingers flexed open and shut, open and shut, wanting to squeeze something until it broke.

The other part of him recoiled at not realizing he'd almost killed a man. He thought of Ellie. How he was so afraid of ever hurting her. Old shame threw cold water on his rage.

Schultz lay crumpled in the middle of the circle breathing heavily, snot running down his face. Bear looked to his brothers, expecting to see condemnation for what he'd just done. Instead, he saw flickers of understanding. Bear had gone and done what every man there wanted to do.

"You have a couple choices now," Benjamin said. "You can go home and end yourself. Or, you can immediately resign your position in shame, pack all your belongings and leave the state, but you will be watched for the rest of your life. If you ever come near another school, a playground, anything even remotely involving children, you'll wish you'd taken the first option. You are not free, understand? You have built yourself a lifelong prison made of fear and pain and we are your jailers. We are everywhere."

With that, Bear and the others left him lying in the field.

L ater, they all reconvened at Riversong. Here, the men went from cold vigilantes to Bear's old friends, the guys he grew up with, who one by one threw an arm around him and slapped him on the back. It helped take away the chill he'd felt when he realized his hand was around a man's throat. Even if that man was the scum of the earth. Bear wondered if his friends felt the same way every time they did this.

"Good to see you, Bear," Gabe said. "Been a long time."

"First round's on me," Shane said. He went to the counter while the other men pulled a couple of tables together in the back and grabbed chairs. Sonny was working the counter like he'd been the day Bear got to town but he wasn't alone. A woman who looked like she could be related to Sonny was working too. She had a little smile for Shane like he came in here often, but she swallowed it up quick the second he looked at her and replaced it with a scowl when he started stuffing money into the tip jar. She disappeared through a doorway behind the counter.

Bear got the feeling all the men were regulars. Gabe took a seat next to him. Bear noticed the thin, clear wire stemming from Gabe's ear canal. A hearing aid. The rumors were true— Gabe was suffering permanent hearing damage from his final mission with the Rangers. Bear felt bad about that, but Gabe looked like it hadn't slowed him down none.

Shane came back with a tray full of coffee mugs and handed them around. Bear wrapped his hands around the hot white mug and stared down into the black coffee. The shop was empty except for their group and Sonny looked like he was minding his own business up front, giving them plenty of privacy.

"How did you know who he was and what he did, besides

a mention at the end of an article?" Bear asked Benjamin, who'd taken the seat across from him. Ben had always been their leader, even as kids. He was as big as Bear and never liked to talk much in school, earning him the nickname of Moose and a reputation for being dumb. But Ben was anything but dumb, as anyone smart enough to want to be his friend quickly found out.

"Cutting right to the chase, huh, Bear?" Ben asked.

Bear shrugged. "Don't see why I shouldn't, considering I was ready to end him. Figure the source had to be a good one, not just rumors." It wasn't how they worked, not even back in high school. They had always made sure they weren't hurting someone innocent.

"Can't tell you the source," Ben said. "Unless you're ready to join us."

Bear shifted his weight in the wooden chair. He wasn't sure how to answer that. The adrenaline was still running through his body, clouding his thoughts. He'd learned never to make decisions in that state. But what took up the front of his brain right now was a sense of purpose, if only for tonight. He'd chased down a cowardly predator and that felt good. Dangerously good. He hadn't felt this sort of purpose in a long time.

"How long do I have to think about it?" he asked.

"Well, now that's up to you, isn't it? Depends on whether or not you're staying here. I know you had plans to go on down to Texas."

Bear nodded. "I always head south for the winter."

The other men exchanged looks. Shane spoke for them all. "I hear some hesitation in your voice, though," he said from Bear's other side.

Is it that obvious? Even throughout tonight's adventure, a little thought at the back of his mind nagged at him—the thought of Ellie facing a winter in Colorado by herself.

Of course she won't be by herself. That was a stupid thing to think. She had Arden and Kyle now. She even had Ellen in Arizona. But nobody had been up to the cabin to help her. No one except him. Not that they'd known to look for her there that first night. But now that they knew she was absolutely determined to fix it up, they'd help her out.

She didn't need him, did she? Not really.

But that didn't mean he didn't want to help her. And what about her family? Her brothers were obviously no good. And it sounded like Arnold pushed her around like she was a servant. She was afraid of him, afraid of all of them, maybe. The fear on her face the morning he woke her told Bear she thought Arnold had found her. He hated seeing Ellie afraid.

Yeah, Bear thought he might stick around just a little longer this fall. The weather was supposed to turn nice here in the next few days anyway. Forecast said this autumn was going to ripen up into a nice Indian summer for a change. What would it hurt to stay just for a little while longer?

But did he officially want to join his friends? Bear still wasn't sure.

"Yeah, let me think on it," he said and took a swing of his coffee. "But I don't like going into things I don't know. You all understand that. So tell me how you knew about the coach or I ain't doing this for sure."

Again, the men exchanged looks. Ben finally said, "This whole thing's bigger than us, Bear. We're the Mountain Division. There are groups like ours all over the country. Men and women fed up with people not meeting justice. Women and kids getting hurt every day because no one will believe them, or because someone doesn't give a shit about a restraining order and keeps on coming back to dole out more abuse while the cops are either too busy or have their hands tied and can't go after them."

Ben sipped his coffee, his eyes never leaving Bear. "We don't learn about them through the regular channels. So the truth is, we can't tell you how we knew about the coach because the source has to stay anonymous. We just know that we got the message and that the message was clear."

Bear huffed out a breath that was half-growl. "So, you ever been wrong before?"

"Never," Ben said, firm conviction in his voice. "We don't immediately go after someone, just like we're not going to immediately go out after this administrator tonight. Just because that rat gave us his name doesn't mean we're immediately out the door and ready to beat him up. We're not thugs. We'll do our due diligence to make sure he gave us the right guy and we'll pass his name along the chain of command to confirm. But as soon as we know for sure, and if he doesn't do the right thing and resign, you better believe we're going after him, and anyone else who hurt that little boy."

Ben leaned forward, his stare holding Bear's as sure as a snare. "Question is, will you be there with us?"

Each man stared at him, waiting.

Dammit. Bear nodded. "If he checks out, yeah. Yeah, I gotta see this through. But no promises after that. And I ain't waiting around forever."

"Understood, Bear." Gabe clapped his hand on the big man's shoulder. Thanks for your help." One by one, Bear's friends shook his hand.

"Now," Shane said. "We have some catching up to do."

"Feels like the coffee shop's about to close," Bear said.

"Sonny will let us stay after hours," Shane said. He looked up at the counter, but Bear realized he was actually scanning a doorway behind it where the woman disappeared..

"You a little interested in that woman, Elk?" Bear teased his old friend.

"Yeah, you could say that," Gabe laughed. "He's got a thing for Sonny's daughter, April."

Bear glanced up toward the counter to see if Sonny had caught his name or his daughter's. But either the man was deaf or busy ignoring them.

"What's Sonny think of that?" Bear asked.

"Well," Ben said, raising his mug. "Seeing as his niece is engaged to another friend of ours, our coffee's free, but Shane's always sticking a couple extra twenties in the tip jar." He glanced at Shane who had just sat up straighter.

"Don't know what you're talking about," Shane muttered. Bear couldn't help but notice red creeping up the man's neck. He chuckled.

"Yeah, laugh it up, Bear," Shane said, then looked at the other guys. "This asshole here rolls into town and in less than a month, he's already found a woman."

"Whoa!" Waylon said. He elbowed Elias. "Our little cub's all grown up."

Bear smiled as he raised his middle finger.

"What?" Elias set his mug down. You didn't date in middle school or high school. Was wondering when you'd stop bein' a wallflower."

Out of the corner of his eye, Bear noticed the way Gabe studied each man as he spoke and wondered how much lip-reading he was doing. His reactions were just a moment behind everyone else's. But he must have caught the drift because now he clapped Bear on the shoulder.

"What's her name?" he asked.

"Not a girlfriend," he mumbled.

"Didn't catch that, Bear," Gabe said.

Shit. He didn't mean to leave Gabe out. The beard probably didn't help.

"He said she's not his girlfriend," Shane said, leaning around Bear so Gabe could see him. "I beg to differ."

"Shane," Bear warned. But once Elk locked horns, he couldn't ever let a thing go.

"She's staying up at the ranch," Shane said as he picked his coffee mug up. "And all of us already know her."

"Whoa!" "What?" "Who?" The questions rounded the table.

"You all know Mr. Sanders and his daughter, right?" Shane asked, despite Bear's warning glare.

"Yeah," Elias said. "God rest his soul."

"Remember how his nephews used to come to town?"

"Shit, yeah," Waylon said. "They turned into little pricks by the time they were teenagers."

"Remember their little sister? Hung around with Arden?"

The men got quiet for a second then Bear watched each one remember.

"Yeah. A little thing, wasn't she?" Gabe asked. Shane nodded. Bear felt his chest tighten.

"She's back in town and staying with Arden. Something about an inheritance?" They all looked at Bear for an answer.

Dammit. Why couldn't Shane keep his mouth shut? But why should Bear be upset? His friends were the biggest gossips he knew.

"Mr. Sanders left an old fishing cabin to Ell—Elinor," Bear stumbled over her name and tried not to wince.

"Cool," Waylon said. "So why's she staying with Arden and Kyle when she's got a place already?"

"It needs work." Bear squeezed his coffee mug. He hated how he felt like he was somehow ratting Ellie out. "We're fixing it up."

"Told you he had a woman." Shane smirked and drank his coffee.

"And I told you it ain't like that. Ellie is...she's..."

Too good for me.

"Guys," Ben said with plenty of warning in his tone. "Does she need any help, Bear? Anything we can do?"

A wave of possessiveness threatened to drown Bear. His instinct was to tell them to back off, he had everything under control. But the truth was, Ellie was going to need all the help she could get.

Maybe not just quite yet. Bear wanted to see how much he could get done on his own. And besides, he didn't want to scare her off. If they were to all pull up to the cabin, she might think she owed them—or him.

"I'll let you know," he grumbled. He swigged his coffee.

The conversation switched the old days when they were kids messing around in the woods, and Bear felt himself relaxing at last. Yeah, maybe he'd let them help Ellie after all.

Just...not yet.

ELEVEN

Ellie woke up feeling excited before she remembered exactly why. Then it came to her—it was the weekend and she would spend it up at the cabin with Bear. Her heart pounded faster just thinking about having him to herself. They'd crossed paths over the past couple days since she'd borrowed his truck and eaten dinner together, but someone else was always around. Ellie wanted to ask him where he'd been when she returned his truck. He'd seemed a little quieter since then, and she was worried that it might be something she'd done. And yet, when they were together, she could see a little sparkle in his eye, one she hoped she wasn't misreading.

She stood on the front porch waiting for Bear to pick her up. Just when Ellie was afraid that Bear wouldn't show, she heard the truck making its way up the long driveway. She tried to hide her smile but gave up pretty quickly. Besides, she was already bouncing on her toes—nothing subtle about her. Bear parked the truck and got out while Ellie picked up a basket she borrowed from Arden and bounded down the porch steps. The air was chilly but not as bad as it had been the nights she'd spent at the cabin. The day was supposed to warm up even more as they headed into a couple weeks of extended summer weather.

"Whatcha got there?" Bear asked as he looked at the wicker basket.

"Can't expect you to work on an empty stomach, so I made us breakfast and lunch. I figure we can catch dinner from the lake. If you still like fish?"

Bear chuckled as he took the basket from her. "Bears always like fish." He opened the lid and sniffed until his grin grew wider. "And we love biscuits and honey. Yours are the best."

Ellie felt her heart fill with exploding stars. "Grab one while it's still warm."

They ate biscuits and honey on the way up to the cabin. Neither talked, but the quiet wasn't uncomfortable. Nothing about being with Bear was uncomfortable as far as Ellie was concerned. She dribbled honey onto a third biscuit and handed it to Bear and he growled a thank you. Arden had told her that he seemed like a different person. Bear was always grumpy but ever since Ellie arrived, he smiled more and even cracked a few jokes. Ellie had joked that it was her cooking, but Arden only lifted an eyebrow that morning as Ellie took the biscuits out of the oven.

Then Arden had changed the subject to something Ellie absolutely didn't want to talk about.

"Have you talked to a real estate agent yet?" she'd asked Ellie.

Ellie's stomach clenched. "I made a list of some and I'll call them next week."

"Good. If I were you, I'd keep any repairs to a minimum. Chances are, if someone buys the property they either won't care about the cabin and just own the land as a tax write off, or they'll scrape it off to build a new house."

"Mmm-hmm." Ellie packed a jar of honey into the basket with jam and an insulated lunchbox full of sandwich fixings she'd pulled from the fridge.

"You will want to make sure the well is either dug deeper or find a new one. That will be important."

"Yup."

Arden stopped and looked at Ellie. "I don't mean to tell you what to do, but I do think it's best that you sell it. You can stay here as long as you like. Then when the sale goes through, you can go anywhere and do anything. That land will go for a lot, I guarantee."

As Ellie sat beside Bear in the truck she absentmindedly nodded like she had to Arden.

"What's that sigh for?" Bear asked.

"Did I sigh?"

He nodded without taking his eyes off the narrow switch-back up the mountain.

"Just thinking, that's all." She waited for Bear to demand what she was thinking. Back home—no, back in Illinois because this was home now—she wasn't allowed a private thought. But Bear stayed quiet, letting her have her space.

He parked the truck in the meadow just before the aspen grove and came around to let her out. She'd learned to wait for him, ever since she'd jumped out on her own once and he'd grumbled about not being allowed to be a gentleman. She'd called him bossy and as usual, got a quiet grin back. Holding the picnic basket, he opened the truck door and offered his other hand to help her down.

What if I didn't let go of his hand this time? she thought, and her stomach did a backflip. But as soon as she jumped to the ground, Bear turned her hand loose and cleared his throat.

"If we're gonna be bringing bigger things up here, we're gonna have to widen the path through these aspens," he said, looking away from her. "Can't be carrying a pellet stove from here to the cabin."

"A pellet stove?"

"I think it would work better than the open fireplace. And you could have a second one upstairs in the bedroom, keep you nice and toasty through the winter."

Ellie bit her lower lip and pushed down her excitement. The thought of having the cabin fixed up and all hers by winter gave her hope. But Arden was probably right. She was crazy to think she could keep this beautiful place. She needed to sell it and move on, maybe someplace her family would never expect to find her. She was only kidding herself that they wouldn't look for her here, where they had family, even if they'd been out of touch since they were little kids.

"Ellie?" Bear said softly. He brushed her arm gently, raising goosebumps under her shirt.

But if she was going to sell, there was no reason for them to be up here now. She was wasting Bear's time, his weekend, even. He had better things to do. Friends to spend time with before he took off for Texas.

"I..." She looked up into Bear's face, which was full of concern and unease. "Don't you have someplace better to be today?"

She couldn't believe the hurt look on his face. He opened his mouth, then closed it and stalked toward the aspen grove. Ellie felt her face grow hotter. She wasn't sure how he'd taken what she'd said, but it wasn't good. Did he resent her asking because he did want to do something else and she had called him on it? Or was it something else?

Now, this felt familiar—being in trouble and not knowing

what it was or how to fix it. Bear had been too good to be true, she knew it.

"Bear, wait." She followed in his wake, jogging to catch up to him. He stopped and turned, still looking upset. But as soon as he looked at her his expression softened and his shoulders relaxed.

"We're not gonna to do this," he rumbled.

"I understand. The cabin's way too much work. If you could just drop me back off at Arden and Kyle's, you can go—"

"Wait, wait, no." Bear shook his shaggy head. "I don't mean I ain't gonna help you with the cabin. What I mean is, we're not gonna second-guess and misunderstand each other. I *want* to be here, all right? Ellie, I'd tear this cabin down with my bare hands and rebuild it board by board if that's what you wanted."

"You would?"

"Yeah, Honey, I would." His voice had gone softer and deeper, sending shivers up and down her spine. "Problem is, see, I don't think you know what you want. I thought just now that you didn't want me here. But it's the cabin, isn't it?" Bear's cheeks flushed red. "It's not me, it's the cabin." His beautiful eyes turned uneasy. "Right?"

Ellie grabbed his big hand in hers. "It's not you at all, I promise. You've been so good to me. I...I like you." Now Ellie's cheeks felt warm. "It is the cabin. Arden keeps asking if I have a real estate agent yet, and I know she's looking out for me. But..." Ellie looked around at the aspens, the mountains in the distance, the little creek running past the cabin. "I'd never be able to afford a beautiful place like this again, so if I can make this cabin work, I want to live here. No one understands that."

Bear gently squeezed her hand. "I understand it. It's beautiful here. All this land, and the ridge. So quiet. Peaceful. Like stepping back into a simpler time."

Ellie nodded. Bear got it. "And no one's around. I feel hidden. Safe." She wrapped her arms around her torso, suddenly afraid of everything vanishing before she even had a chance to enjoy it. A chance to finally *live*.

Without a word, Bear pulled her into his arms and held her. She felt his lips brush the top of her head, feather-light and impossibly gentle for such a big man.

"You're safe with me, Ellie. I'm not gonna let anything get near you. And if this cabin is what you need to finally feel protected, then we're gonna make it happen."

Ellie tucked her face into Bear's chest and breathed deep. Flannel, pine, cedar, Bear. He could hold her forever like this and she'd be content.

But they didn't have forever. They had until Bear headed south.

Ellie pulled away and looked Bear in the eyes. "Thank you. I think you're the best friend I've ever had."

He studied her face, his expression unreadable. Then he let her go.

"Let's get started. Got a lot to do."

The day passed quickly—too quickly. The hours Ellie spent with Bear always seemed to go that way. Not enough time. She couldn't believe they'd gotten to know each other again over less than a month. To Ellie, it felt like they'd been friends ever since they were kids and not lost touch, that's how comfortable they were with each other. They didn't need to speak to know what the other one needed—a hammer, a saw, a broom. They both got hungry at the same time and stopped for lunch. Over sandwiches, Bear told her he'd found a surprise in the shed—an inflatable raft that looked like it was still in good shape.

Ellie beamed at him. "We could take it out on the lake."

"Exactly what I was thinking. Maybe after supper, huh?" He looked in the picnic basket. "I think we still got enough food here we don't have to fish. We can just relax tonight out on the water."

"Sounds like heaven."

Did Bear just shiver? The day was warm—hot even. She must be imagining things.

He got quiet after that, and as soon as they'd finished eating, went right back to work. He'd brought roofing materials up in his truck and was determined to patch up the roof so they could get to work replacing some of the walls and flooring inside. Ellie was determined to learn everything she could so that once she was alone she could manage repairs on her own. Bear turned out to be a good teacher—patient, calm, clear with his explanations.

Which contradicted everything Ellie was feeling inside. It was like her chest had filled with fizzy soda and the bubbles were rising and popping in her brain. Part of it was anxiety over how she'd ever be able to afford everything that the cabin needed. But the other part came from being this close to Bear, watching him move with such confidence and skill, listening to his voice as he explained things, the occasional brush of hands or bump of shoulders when she leaned in close to watch what he was doing.

Sweet torture, that's what it was. And she wanted more.

Bear had long since taken off his flannel and folded it neatly on a chair on the porch. His dark green tee pulled tightly across his broad back and chest. The sun was intense overhead, as hot as summer. When it finally slid toward the tops of the mountains to the west, they both breathed a sigh of relief.

"That's enough for today," Bear announced. He covered what was left of the work—surprisingly little—with a tarp and started down the ladder first so that if Ellie slipped, he'd be there to catch her. Halfway down, Ellie looked over her shoulder at him waiting for her at the bottom. He seemed so *there*, like he was made of the mountain, and she wasn't afraid at all to climb down, despite her slight fear of heights. Fear hadn't bothered her on the roof, either, not with Bear.

"We've got enough light to inflate the raft and take it out on the lake if you still wanna," Bear said. He was right—pine tree shadows were creeping around the cabin, but the meadow with the big lake was still bathed in sunlight and would be for a while.

"Let's do it," Ellie said with a grin.

TWELVE

Bear kicked off his boots at the edge of the lake and watched Ellie do the same. He offered his arm to steady her and she took it. Every touch sent electricity through him and flipped his heart right over.

I'd never be able to afford a view like this again, so if I can make this cabin work, I want to live here. No one understands that...I feel hidden. Safe.

After saying that, Ellie had wrapped her arms around her body in a way that broke Bear's heart. He wanted to pick her up and carry her away from the rest of the world and promise her she would always be safe so long as he was around.

And at that moment, he knew.

He knew he wouldn't be leaving once the job at Watchdog was done. No. He'd stay and help her as much as she'd allow. Then and only then would he be on his way.

Unless she wants me to stay here.

Bear shook the thought from his mind and the hope from his heart. *Friends.* They were friends and that was all. Which made his attempts to touch her at every opportunity seem wrong, but he couldn't resist. She was so pretty, and funny, and she smelled like summer berries. Irresistible. He couldn't take advantage of her or she'd think he was expecting something in return for his help.

Which was another problem—He'd bought the excess roofing materials off Kyle and Ellie tried to write him an IOU. She was letting her pride dictate how much she'd let him help and he knew it wouldn't be enough. She was strong and determined, no doubt about it. She'd work herself to the bone to make this place her sanctuary. But she was small and inexperienced and had no money resources. With a Rocky Mountain winter bearing down in another couple months, she had little chance of succeeding if she tried going it alone.

So, he'd just have to be quiet about it. Maybe not let her know just how much help he'd give her. Bear knew more than just how to fix things. He had resources he hadn't tapped yet, just sitting and growing over time. He didn't know what to do with it until he'd met Ellie. Now, he knew exactly what he wanted to accomplish with what he'd been given. It was good and right that he did this. For her.

He just needed to figure out how to do it in a sneaky way, so she'd accept it without fighting him.

Bear didn't want to lie or deceive Ellie. After the cabin was finished, after she had her cozy little home and it was too late to turn him down, then he'd tell her how much he'd helped her.

Maybe.

That was tomorrow's problem though. Today, he needed to think about how to get his resources into her hands and close her fingers around them, thinking they were hers all along.

He also decided he was being stubborn. He'd wanted to have Ellie all to himself, to enjoy the quiet and the soul-deep peace he found when he was with her. She didn't need that, she needed a team at her back, working on the cabin before winter came.

And what better team than his friends? If they wanted his help with the administrator, he'd ask for their help in return. Not that he wouldn't go after the son of a bitch just to see the man suffer for the pain he'd caused. But Ellie needed the manpower.

"Whatcha thinking?" Ellie broke into his thoughts, making him think he must have been scowling. One look at her worried face told him yup, he'd been frowning. He quickly smiled at Ellie.

"Nothin' much. Like I always do." He winked.

She laughed. "You don't fool me." She tapped his forehead. "Lots goes on up there."

"Just planning for tomorrow."

Ellie brightened. "You don't mind working tomorrow? Don't you need a break?"

"This *is* my break, Ellie," he said softly. "Getting away from civilization."

Spending time alone with you.

Ellie nodded to herself. Bear steadied the raft in the knee-deep water and Ellie got in. There were signs of an old pier that had fallen into the lake. Bear would get on that, too. He stepped into the raft and they paddled out onto the lake. The water was taking on the color of the sky—sunset peach and orange and light blue. When they got toward the center, they set the paddles aside.

Ellie trailed her hand in the water. "This water's warmer than I thought. Wish I had a swimsuit."

Bear suppressed a shiver at the thought of seeing Ellie in a swimsuit. *Or skinny dipping.*

Shut it down, Bear.

He plunged his hand into the water, wishing he could

dive into it and escape his feelings. He looked up into the sky, then at the cliff, the meadow, and the cabin back under the trees. "So beautiful here," he growled out instead of telling her what he was feeling.

"It is. But...am I crazy for keeping it? The cabin needs so much work, and if Arden's right, I could sell this place and set up somewhere else."

Bear chuckled. "No crazier than a woman my grandpa met once."

Ellie tilted her head. "I sense a good story."

Bear shrugged. "He was just a kid, my grandpa, when he and his dad were driving down into Leadville." He paused. "That's way south of here, and west. We used to have property in the mountains there." Bear kept it at that. "About a mile from town, my grandpa's daddy sees someone walking along the side of the road and he pulls over. At first, my grandpa thought it was a small man, maybe a prospector, the way he was dressed in baggy pants and a flannel, but he saw it was an old woman when she got into the car. She turned and smiled at him and asked him his name. He told her, then she went back to talking to his daddy. They let her off at a general store in Leadville and he told her he'd be happy to take her back home but she declined. When my grandpa asked who she was, his daddy said he'd just met a very famous lady. Baby Doe Tabor." Bear paused again. "You know who that is?"

"I don't," Ellie admitted.

"She was notorious in her day for marrying a silver baron named Horace Tabor. He was twice her age and left his wife for her. They lived high on the hog before they lost everything in the silver crash of 1893. He died a few years later and on his deathbed, he told Baby Doe not to give up the Matchless Mine, that it would come back to life one day. So Baby Doe went to live in a cabin there for thirty years."

"Wow. And your grandpa met her?"

"Yup."

"Did he ever see her again?"

"Nope."

"What happened to her?"

Whoops. That's when Bear realized his mistake. *God, I'm stupid.*

"Bear?" Ellie urged.

"She, um, well, she was old."

Ellie drew her eyebrows down and mock-frowned. "What aren't you telling me?"

"Nothing. Dumb story."

Ellie shook her head. "Oh, no. That's the most I've ever heard you say at one time." She crossed her arms. "Continue."

"It's not..." He looked away, angry at himself.

"Bear."

"Look, the point of the story is, she believed in her land. She loved it, and she lived there to the end of her days."

"They found her dead in the cabin, didn't they?" Ellie said flatly.

Bear blew out a breath. "Yeah. After a cold winter." God, could he fuck this up any worse? He was going to chase her off for sure. "But like I said, that's not the point of the story, Ellie."

To his surprise and delight, Ellie laughed. She covered her mouth and tried not to, but the laughter bubbled out around her fingers. "I'm sorry. I'm not laughing at her. That's tragic."

"Then what *are* you laughing at?"

"Maybe a little bit at you?"

That took him aback. "You should probably jump out of this boat and paddle back to shore away from me after I tell you a story like that."

"Why? Bear," she reached across the boat and grabbed his hand. "I love that you shared a story with me. It's...special."

"I'm not gonna let you freeze like Baby Doe did, I promise. We're gonna have your place fixed up and warm and you can keep it forever and be safe and happy here." The words rushed out of him.

Her confident smile was all he needed. But when she said "I know" it sent him over the moon. She trusted him. Believed in him. Completely.

"Promise, Ellie," he whispered, squeezing her hand.

"I know." She looked into his eyes and he was lost. "So." She let go of his hand and leaned back. "That was your grandpa. Now, tell me more about you."

"Me? Nothin' much to say."

"Oh, come on." She pretended to splash him. "You were a Ranger, right?"

Bear nodded. And found his tongue was stuck to the roof of his mouth. He didn't want to talk about it. Couldn't. He looked up into the sky which was indigo blue now. Venus was shining bright, and the first star twinkled far away.

Ellie followed his gaze. "So beautiful. I'd never seen so many stars before coming here. I tried to count them as they came out one night and I couldn't."

That tickled him—the image of Ellie trying to count the infinite. "Maybe start with the constellations instead." Bear pointed at the first star. "That's Vega. It's in the constellation Lyra. It's between Hercules and Cygnus, which is supposed to be a swan but always looks like a cross to me."

"Oh." Ellie's voice was filled with wonder. "I didn't know you knew so much about stars."

Bear nodded. "Have to. If you don't have a compass or a phone or something like that, you need another way to figure out where you are."

"You did that as a Ranger?"

"Sometimes, yeah. My unit learned it. Came in handy when our GPS crapped out." Bear hoped Ellie wouldn't make him dig into that. "I had a head start cuz I used to do it as a kid. We all did, all my friends."

Ellie's smile lit up the twilight. "Oh, I remember now. You all took Arden and me out looking for bats one night in the woods. We had to find a clearing so we could see them and you all started naming off the stars. Remember?"

"Huh. Yeah, I do now. I'd forgotten." The memory was coming back to him. He and Sean and Ben and the rest decided to show off for the girls, but he wasn't about to admit that. And there was something else about that night, something that didn't want to be remembered so he left it buried.

"Will you teach me about the stars, Bear?" Ellie asked. "I don't ever want to be lost up here."

"I'll teach you anything you want," Bear said around the lump in his throat.

Ellie grinned—the one that made her nose crinkle and her freckles dance. "I only know one constellation. The Big Dipper."

"You know what it's also called?"

"What?"

"Ursa Major."

"Ursa?"

"Yeah. Ursa means bear."

"Ha! Big Bear."

"Yup. And you can use Ursa Major to find the North Star, and once you find the North Star, you can navigate home."

"Home," she whispered. She looked up again and pointed. "Oh, there's a new one out. What's that star called?"

Bear spent the next hour naming the stars and constellations for Ellie. The lake was so clear and still it reflected the stars perfectly.

"It looks like we're right in the middle of them," Ellie said. "Like we're in a spaceship instead of a boat."

"Good thing I'm teaching you to navigate then. Don't wanna get lost in the stars."

"Oh, I wouldn't mind that right now," she said, looking at Bear through her lashes. Bear was glad it was too dark for her to see the red creeping into his face.

"You think God can hear us better from up here?" she asked.

Bear grinned. He wasn't much of a believer after all the bad he'd seen in the world, but he could see her point. "If there's a God and if God listens, I think maybe, yeah. Air's thin, place is beautiful." *You're here* he thought silently. "So, why not?"

Ellie tilted her head. "You don't think there's a God?"

"I don't know. The question's bigger than I am."

She nodded. "If God's a loving God, then I don't think He minds our doubts about Him. But, I think God does mind us doubting ourselves."

"You'd better never doubt yourself, Ellie."

"Neither should you, Bear."

The wind kicked up, chilling the air and they rowed back to shore. Bear quizzed Ellie on directions and she passed with flying colors.

"Follow the stars and you'll always find your way home," Bear said.

THIRTEEN

Bear picked Ellie up bright and early the following Saturday.

She'd crossed paths with him all week, but he'd been scarce, saying he needed to finish up Walter's house and get started on another one. He was his usual quiet self at meals, though they'd been joined by one of the other Watchdog bodyguards, Brock 'Badger' Jones and his fiancée Brianna one night. Brianna worked at Riversong with her family but really, she was a musician. Ellie couldn't believe how talented she was when she pulled her fiddle out after dinner and played for them. Sitting beside Bear, Ellie imagined having Brianna and her friends up to the cabin the next summer to play, maybe on the Fourth of July. Would Bear come back? Maybe if she invited him.

One thing he did do was take her out back and give her another lesson in navigating by the stars every night right before heading back to Walter's.

Ellie had dreamed of Bear each night and now all she wanted to do was curl up against him while he drove.

"I have a surprise for you," he said when they got into his truck. Her stomach quivered. "What surprise?"

"You'll see." He chuckled.

"Something at the cabin?" He couldn't have gone up there and left something already, could he?

"Just gonna have to wait, Honey."

"Bossy."

That got her a full-on laugh. But no hints or answers.

When they pulled into the field, another truck she didn't recognize was already waiting for them. Ellie's heart sped up with fear. Had her family found her and sent someone to bring her back? No—Bear was at ease, grinning even.

"Is this my surprise?" Ellie asked, uncertain. The driver's door opened and a Bear-sized man stepped out and waved.

"Don't recognize him?" Bear asked in a teasing voice as he parked beside the truck and killed the engine.

"Should I?"

Bear just got out, went around the truck, and let Ellie out. The other man followed him.

"Ellie?" he said. "It's Ben Massey."

"Oh!" Of course—this was one of Bear's old friends. "I sort of remember you, from when I was a kid."

Ben just nodded, then he looked at Bear. "What are we starting on first?"

"Wait," Ellie said, looking back and forth between the two men. "You're helping today?"

"That's right."

Ellie's heart clenched. She didn't have the money to pay Ben. "Um, I...I can't..."

Another truck drove up just then, followed by two more. Each had a tarp-covered load in their beds. Ellie recognized Shane from Watchdog but the other three men were strangers...until they got closer. Wait, yes, she did recognize each man, but she hadn't seen any of them since she was a girl and they were young teens.

"Hey, Ellie," Shane said. "Heard you could use some help, so here we are."

"Surprise," Bear said, dropping his arm around Ellie's shoulders.

"But..." She looked at the six men towering over her. "I can't afford... I don't have the money—"

"You do," Bear said. "Called your lawyer. There's money in that trust fund along with the cabin."

Ellie's jaw hit the ground. "I...have money?"

Bear nodded. "For repairs and whatever the cabin needs." His smile went from ear to ear. "Surprise for real. That is, if you still want to keep the cabin. If not, I can always take everything back—"

"No way!" Ellie said, laughing. "Not a single nail. This place is my dream come true."

"Congratulations, Ellie," one of the men said. "I'm Gabe O'Neil, by the way."

Bear scratched his beard and looked at the trucks. "Went ahead and ordered some things, hope you don't mind. Nothin' you can't afford, I promise. I—"

But anything else he was about to say whooshed out in a breath as Ellie threw her arms around Bear and squeezed him tightly.

"Thank you." She pressed her face into his shirt to stifle a sob. How could this be? Mr. Cole had never mentioned any money in the trust Uncle Walter left her. Or, maybe she'd misunderstood him the only time they'd spoken. She'd put off talking to him again, not wanting to discuss selling the cabin.

I've been an idiot. All this time, and I could have been paying Bear back.

"You okay, Ellie?" Bear asked. He'd hugged her back and

was stroking her hair. The other men were laughing and chatting, and one was actually clapping.

"I'm stunned, that's all." She reluctantly pulled away from him and looked up to see his eyes beaming back down at her. He looked as happy as she felt, if that were possible. "But now I can actually pay you."

Bear shook his head hard, his longish hair swinging back and forth. "I ain't taking a dime. And neither are they."

A chorus of nopes and no-ways filled the meadow.

"But—"

"They owe me, Ellie, at the least."

"And we just want to help," Shane said.

Ben stepped forward. "We, uh, remember your brothers, Ellie," he said in a strong, quiet voice. "And we want to do whatever it takes to make you feel safe."

Ellie closed her eyes. She felt a little unreal, as if she were still dreaming. She was also filled with gratitude.

"Thank you. Thank you so much. I don't know what else to say."

"Tell you what else you can say," the second man who drove up said. "You can tell us where you want to start. We've got all day, the weather's holding good, and I think we can have this place habitable by tonight if we get started now. I'm Elias Hunt. I was and still am the handsomest one out of this bunch."

"Ha! No way," the last guy said. "That would be me. You remember me, Ellie? I'm Waylon Ramson."

Ellie laughed even as she wiped tears from her eyes. "I remember all of you. And you're all gorgeous, inside and out, every single one of you."

They just laughed—all except for Bear who grinned down at his feet, his ears turning bright red. Waylon and Elias tagged him on the arm as they all walked past Bear to check out the cabin.

"Very cool," Shane said. "You could have some awesome barbeques here."

"Check out the lake." Elias pointed toward the water in the distance. "Bear said it was full of fish."

"Big ones," Ellie confirmed. "And you're welcome to come up any time to fish, all of you."

"Ha! Careful what you promise this group of miscreants," Ben said. "They'll fish you out of house and home, some of them. Bear especially." He winked at his friend.

"I'm counting on it," Ellie said as she grabbed Bear's hand and squeezed. His ears turned even redder, which delighted Ellie. This big guy was fun to tease. How could he ever think Ellie was afraid of him when all he ever did was watch out for her and treat her so gently?

If only we could have more.

Bear squeezed her hand back before letting go and walking away. "Lemme show you guys where to start. Got our work cut out for us."

———

Bear and his friends worked all day, stopping only for lunch, which Shane pulled out of his truck—a big cooler packed with food, compliments of Arden.

"She was in on this?" Ellie asked, amazed. Her friend had never said a word or given anything away all week.

"She was," Shane confirmed.

Ellie pulled out her new phone. "I need to thank her."

"You can thank her in person later." Shane handed Ellie a sandwich. "She and them are coming up here tonight for dinner." Shane looked at Bear. "Or was that supposed to be another surprise?"

"Well, it ain't one now," Bear grumbled.

"Ooops."

"Who all's coming?" Ellie asked. She suddenly felt a little embarrassed. It was amazing what the guys had accomplished already today. The roof was patched good as new though Bear said he'd like to re-do the entire roof eventually. They'd replaced the broken window and storm-proofed the rest of them and shored up the sagging porch overhang. Best of all, they installed two pellet stoves with heat exchangers in the fireplaces. Bear knew about plumbing and was already starting on turning the little bedroom downstairs into a bathroom and replacing the pipes in the kitchen. The well probably needed to be dug deeper with a new pump installed but Bear had already arranged to have that checked out and it was scheduled to happen in two weeks.

And that's what embarrassed her along with the peeling paint—no indoor plumbing. It was fine for the guys—more often than not, they went off into the woods to pee anyway. But what would Arden think, let alone any other women she might bring with her up to the cabin? Ellie had been bullied by other girls growing up—teased for living out on a farm and wearing boys' hand-me-downs to school. She knew Arden was too kind to say anything, but that shame still clung to Ellie as an adult. What if other women came up and judged her?

"You all right, Ellie?" Bear asked.

She put on a bright smile. "Yeah, I'm great. Just a little tired is all."

Mistake. Bear immediately went into action. He practically dove for the cooler.

"Lemme get you some water, you haven't been drinking enough. You got a headache? I have aspirin." He thrust a water bottle into her hands as his other hand went to her fore-head. "I'll turn on the air in the truck and you go lay down in there."

"Bear, I'm fine, I promise. It isn't altitude sickness." Before she thought about it, her hand went to his face and she stroked his cheek. He went statue-still at her touch and closed his eyes. Her fingers trembled.

"Thank you," she whispered. "Thank you for taking such good care of me. You're wonderful."

His stare was heavy when he looked at her again. He opened his mouth and she hoped...for what? For him to say that he wanted to stay in Colorado? That he cared about her beyond sympathy or pity? No, men like him weren't attracted to mice like her, she told herself for the thousandth time. It was just some misplaced sense of obligation, like she was a stray dog he'd found. That wasn't far from the truth.

Bear closed his mouth again without saying a word. He gave her a small smile and grabbed a bag of potato chips for her.

"Just in case," he finally said, then went to sit over by Elias.

The best part about having Bear's friends around—beyond the obvious—was that they told stories about Bear during lunch. Mostly about when they were all growing up together, but some were about Bear's time as a Ranger. Gabe had served with him in the same unit so he had the most to say. It became pretty clear to Ellie that Gabe looked up to his friend and that Bear didn't even realize it.

"He saved my life, Ellie," Gabe said.

But instead of looking pleased, Bear actually looked

ashamed. "Had I been faster, you wouldn't have been injured at all," he murmured.

Gabe tilted his head and turned to Ben. "Did he say what I thought he said?"

"He said he wasn't fast enough and that you still got injured." Ben had raised his voice and suddenly Ellie realized Gabe was hard of hearing.

"We've been over this, dude." Gabe frowned as he looked at Bear. "You. Saved. My. Life." Ellie's suspicions about Gabe's hearing were confirmed when Gabe signed each word as he said it. Then he added, "You're my brother, always."

Bear waved him off and walked into the cabin as he mumbled again, something about needing to get back to work. Ellie's heart fell. These men so obviously cared for Bear and he wouldn't let himself feel it.

Gabe shook his head. "Stubborn fool." He got up and went in the opposite direction toward the trucks.

"Bossy, too," Ellie added.

Ben chuckled. "Truth, Ellie."

"Is *that* why he won't stay here?" she asked quietly. "He feels guilty?"

Ben shrugged. "Hard to say. That man plays his cards close to the vest."

"Too close," Waylon added, giving Ellie a sweet smile. "And one day, he's going to regret it if he isn't careful."

L ate afternoon, Ellie felt her stomach knot up. Not one but two Watchdog SUVs parked in the meadow. How many people had come up? Ellie wiped her sweaty palms on her work shirt and tugged at the hair tie holding her ponytail, which had become a complete mess throughout the day. She imagined her face was streaked with dirt and sawdust and God knew what else.

Nothing to do about it now she thought. She swallowed hard and tried to smile but felt the corners of her mouth quivering. She'd been less nervous in the Denver bus depot when that asshole had tried to 'recruit' her. He didn't matter. These women did. And she was about to make a terrible impression.

Of course you are her brother's voice echoed in her head. *You're small and ugly and I can't understand why Tibbs sees anything in you.*

"No," she whispered as she closed her eyes at the bad memory of Tibbs. Her fingers curled into fists.

Two big hands grasped her upper arms and she felt a strong, solid body standing just inches behind her. She smelled Bear's good scent, even after he'd been working all day, and she relaxed instantly.

"It's okay, Ellie. It's just friends." His voice rumbled in his chest. "You're safe."

"I'm not used to friends," Ellie whispered even as she took a step backward until her spine pressed against his chest.

"That's gonna change right now, Honey," Bear murmured just inches above her hair. He turned her in his arms and smiled down at her.

Ellie smiled back to please him but he saw right through it.

"They'll like you just as you are, Ellie. Because there's a lot to like." He turned her back around and took her hand. "Let's go see who all came up."

As the sun turned the meadow golden, several women got out of the SUVs. They carried baskets full of food and wine and flowers and a big red-and-white checkered tablecloth for the long plank table the guys had set up beside the cabin with a perfect view of the lake. Three of the women Ellie didn't recognize but she knew the others—Arden, Charlie, Jodie from Watchdog's kennels, Brianna, and the biggest surprise of all—Ellie's cousin.

"Ellen!" she shouted as she ran to her cousin. They hugged each other tightly before Ellen held her at arms' length.

"Let me look at you! I can't believe you're here."

"Me neither. Thank you again."

"For?"

Ellie shrugged then swung her arms around. "Everything."

"That was Dad's doing," Ellen said.

"He was too generous," Ellie said as her cheeks flooded with heat. She couldn't imagine how much Walter had left her in the trust fund. All the materials Bear and the other men brought up—and Bear said there was still plenty more coming —told her it was a lot.

"Nonsense. Dad had it to give. Now, let's go see what you've done to the place." The skin around Ellen's eyes crinkled and she looked mischievous. "We brought up a few housewarming gifts. Things men don't think of." She chuckled as she put her arm around her cousin and started walking her back to the cabin. "But we'll get to that later after dinner."

Time seemed to slow down and turn to butterscotch—sweet and warm as Arden introduced Ellie to her friend Harper and Harper's fiancé, Flint who worked at Watchdog, and to Brianna's sisters April and Hannah. They skipped the formalities and just hugged Ellie.

"We're going to be friends anyway," April explained. "Why not start from the jump?"

By dinner time, the table was covered with the big red-and-white cloth, the plates were set, and the wine glasses sparkled from the battery-powered fairy lights strung in the pines overhead. The whole place had turned magical in the span of an hour. They insisted on Ellie sitting at the head of the table. She made sure Ellen sat on one side and Bear on the other.

"Before we eat," Ellie said as she raised her glass, "I just want to thank all of you for welcoming me." Her voice almost broke. "Visiting Colorado as a girl were the best days of my life. But I think even better days are coming. All of you are invited up her any time you need to get away from the rest of the world." She couldn't help but glance at Bear. "Besides, it's all of you who are making this a home."

Cheers ringed the table and they dug into the food. Ellie felt Bear's leg press against hers and she smiled at him. He raised his beer and gave her a little toast and a wink and set her heart flying.

The evening cooled around them when the sun set, but the cabin was toasty warm with the new stove going. The women wasted no time and got to work making the cabin even cozier. Ellie had cleaned the place top to bottom earlier in the day and now they added all the accents that made it a home. Rugs, throws, pillows, new dishes, and best of all—Ellen brought a patchwork quilt Ellie's mom had pieced and sewn together over one especially long summer visit.

"I thought I'd dreamed she made this," Ellie said as she rubbed her cheek against the soft cotton. "We didn't have it at the house."

"She left it with us," Ellen said with just a touch of sadness and Ellie knew why—it was a nice thing her father might have ruined just because he could.

"Thank you for keeping it for me," she said gratefully.

"Let's get it on the bed upstairs."

"What bed?" But just as the words were coming out of her mouth, Bear, Kyle, and Shane were carrying a bedframe through the doorway.

"Hope it's okay." Bear cleared his throat. "I picked it out."

"It's perfection," Ellie gushed. And it was. It was like Bear could see right into her heart and made real all the dreams she hid there.

The quilt fit perfectly over the feather mattress.

FOURTEEN

Ellie's guests left around ten o'clock until Bear and Ellie were the last ones standing on the porch. Ellie looked to Bear like she was in a dream. He couldn't have been happier. His scheming had worked.

There was no money in the trust fund for Ellie. At least not in the one from Walter.

Bear had spent the week setting another one up for Ellie out of his own funds. His money had been sitting there for years collecting interest. The seed money had come from decades of his family's land and estate sales, mineral and water rights, and good investments. You'd never know it looking at Bear, but he was worth money.

A *lot* of money.

And he'd had absolutely no use for it until now.

So, he'd set up a blind trust for Ellie through Walter's lawyer.

"This will backfire, Mr. Behr," Cole had told him. "The amount you're putting in—"

"She won't know the amount," Bear had told him.

"She'll have an idea based on how much you're spending on fixing up that wreck of a cabin."

Bear had growled at that.

"Hey, I've been up there," Cole said defensively. "I know what it is and what it isn't and when it's all said and done it would probably cost less to buy a nice place in town—"

"She don't want that. I'm giving her what she wants."

In the end, Cole had shaken his head and done the paperwork. Bear went ahead and bought what Ellie needed before the trust was even funded—he only needed it to look like the money was coming from Walter.

By the time she'd find out the truth, if ever, Bear would be gone.

He didn't belong here. He kept telling himself that over and over despite what he wanted and what he felt for Ellie. His friend Gabe was a living reminder of how Bear had failed him. And the other night when he'd roughed up the coach and almost lost it, almost killed the man...

No, Ellie didn't need a violent man in her life. She was running away from violent men and making a fresh start.

"I can't believe everything that got done today." Ellie looked around as if it all might disappear.

"Still not all done though," Bear said. "Generator's going good now, but you'll want to hook up to the power grid sooner rather than later. Or maybe go solar. Then there's the well and plumbing, and the chimney still needs—"

"Bear." Ellie laughed. "I know it's not perfect, but it's habitable now. I just never thought..." She shook her head and wiped at her eyes.

"You up for some stargazing?" Bear asked. Ellie was acting like she wanted to stay up at the cabin for the night and he didn't want to leave her just yet. Truth was, he didn't ever want the night to end.

"I'd like that." Ellie grabbed Bear's hand and led him out to the little plywood bridge that crossed the stream to the ridge on the other side. They sat on the ridge and looked up at the stars. The Milky Way spilled across the sky, the air was so clear. It looked like its name—cold milk spilled across a dark table, with diamonds scattered all around, twinkling.

Bear noticed Ellie shiver. "You were right; even after a hot day, it gets cold up here once the sun goes down," she said.

He took off his heavy flannel and draped it around her shoulders. She slid her arms into the comically long sleeves and he couldn't help but smile.

"Thank you."

"It's pre-warmed. You should stop shivering here soon."

She scooted closer to him until she was right up against his side. "You're warm too." She smiled up at him. "A big warm bear."

His heart filled with wonder at this beautiful woman. She might look plain to others, but her smile brought such beauty to her face, and his heart heated up whenever she gave it to him. Like now.

It took a surprising amount of courage because he didn't want to ruin this perfect moment, but he put his arm around her and stroked her shoulder with his thumb.

And she responded by snuggling even closer. He felt her arm go around his waist and he took her opposite hand in his.

"Cold," he said as he rubbed his fingers over hers, trying to generate heat.

"They'll warm up," she said. "You'll make it so."

The certainty in her voice went right to his core. Her complete trust killed him. She had no reason to trust him— they barely knew each other and she'd had her trust betrayed so many times. Plus, he tended to scare off women. 'Big bear' was right—gruff, grumpy, tending toward solitude. He knew how to please a woman in bed, but he didn't know how to make one stay after a night or two with him. One woman had called him cold after he'd gotten up to leave her house. He didn't mean to be that way, but he didn't talk much and he tended to end up with women who asked him endless questions he didn't feel like answering.

That's why he liked Ellie. She was quiet too, but in a thoughtful way. Her bright eyes took in everything, soaked up every little detail. He liked that about her. And right now, he really liked the way her body felt against his as they sat and admired the stars.

"Let me know if you get too cold," he said, worried that she might not speak up.

"I will. But this is comfortable right now. Won't you be cold though, without your shirt?"

"No. You're keeping me warm, too."

She looked from the stars to his face again. "I'm not used to feeling like this. Comfortable with someone. Safe."

He swallowed. She felt safe with him? He could crush her if he wasn't careful—not that he wouldn't be. He'd treat her like she was made of crystal, something precious and rare. Especially if he ever had the amazing luck of finding himself in bed with her. That stirred him. The idea of holding her close all night long. Kissing her long and slow and sweetly. Discovering her body inch by inch. Her wild-berry smell was so good. Her hair was soft and he wanted to know how it would feel brushing his chest as she rode him. She'd have to be on top because he'd be too afraid of crushing her otherwise. But he could see her up there riding, bringing them closer and closer to ecstasy...

He needed to stop. Why dream about something that would never happen? He knew she wanted solitude as much as he did, maybe more while she healed from whatever she'd left behind. Tonight, sitting with her body against his was probably as good as it got. Tomorrow, they'd go back to being friends. He'd eventually finish work on the cabin, she'd move in, he'd move on. That was how it should be. That was how he'd keep from hurting her. How he'd keep from hurting himself with unfulfilled expectations.

But he couldn't keep his thoughts from drifting to how good he knew she'd feel. How delicious her berry-scented skin would taste. How warm and sweet and tight she'd be. His eyelids dropped to half-mast and the stars blurred even as his heart pounded harder with every thought.

"Do you want to kiss me?"

Her voice drifted up through the dark as if conjured out of his fantasies. He had to shake his head to determine if he'd imagined her voice, or if she'd really spoken. He felt flushed as he looked down into her face, turned up to his like the full moon.

"I'm asking because I want to kiss you, and I know how quiet you get," she continued. "But the way you're rubbing my hand and my shoulder, the way you suddenly feel a lot warmer and your heart is pounding, I thought maybe—"

He let go of her hand and cupped her face as he dropped his big shaggy head down to hers. When he found her lips they were even sweeter than he'd imagined. She kissed him eagerly as her fingers tangled in his hair. Without breaking from her sweet mouth, he picked her up until she was straddling his lap. He cradled her in his arms as they kissed. The cold night was a distant memory as heat grew between them.

"I want more. I want to make love with you," he dared to breathe against her lips before he could stop himself out of fear. He knew better. It would kill him to be rejected, but he couldn't ask for less. Not now that he'd tasted her, and that he knew she'd wanted to kiss him.

"I want that too, Bear. Let's go back to the cabin."

He pulled away from her and cupped her face. "I won't leave you tomorrow."

"Okay." She sounded uncertain.

"I mean, I've...I've made love to other women, but I've always left the next morning. Sometimes, in the middle of the night, I've left. But I don't want to do that with you. I want to stay. I want to be there in the morning. With you. I want to see your hair mussed and your eyes half-open in the morning light. I want to smell your bed-warmed skin and I want to be with you. Understand?"

She nodded mutely and he hoped he hadn't frightened her. His voice had gotten loud.

"Is that okay?" he asked, quieter.

"That's okay, Bear. That's more than okay with me because I want that too."

He hugged her tightly to him. She wrapped her legs around his waist and he stood, still holding her. He carried her in a dream through the piney air, under the sharp white stars, out of the frigid night and into the warm cabin. Fresh-cut cedar wood scented the air. The fire he'd banked in the stove before they went outside heated the cabin beautifully. She wouldn't be cold tonight. He wouldn't be, either. No cold, lonely bed for either of them.

He carried her up to the bedroom, to the bed with the feather mattress and the patchwork quilt. He set her down and turned on the little lamp on the bedside table. It gave off a honey-colored light he liked. Her bare skin would look good in that light. He wanted to see her as he made love to her.

She pulled back the quilt to reveal the white sheets under it. Ellie took a deep breath and slipped his flannel shirt off her shoulders. She laid it down carefully and smoothed her hand over it as if it were a fancy suit she didn't want to rumple.

He chuckled. "It's just my old shirt."

"I know."

Those two words were filled with such gravity his heart stuttered. He ran his hand over her hair. He'd never been treated like he was something special, something someone wanted to keep. He didn't know what else to say, so he whispered her name reverently.

Then he took his time undressing her until she stood completely naked before him.

He was right—her skin looked gorgeous in the honey-colored light. The lamplight picked out golden highlights in her fox-brown hair, like a tiger eye stone. Her nipples were small and pert and rosy. Berries. He bent to lick them one at a time and she shivered and gripped his shoulders each time.

She tried to undress him several times but he wouldn't let her. Not yet. He didn't want to disappoint her with his hairy chest. Women wanted smooth men, didn't they? Manscaped, or some damned thing. Normally, he didn't care. He figured if a woman had let him into her bedroom, she wanted to have sex with him. But Ellie was different. She said she wasn't scared of him, that she wanted to be with him, but would she change her mind once he was naked?

So he set her on the edge of the bed and distracted her with kisses and touches, grabbing her hands and kissing her fingers each time they reached for the hem of his shirt. He kissed up her arms to her throat where he lingered in her scent—blackberries, raspberries, something wild and hidden in the deep dark forest, a sweet treat to be found and claimed. He kissed her breasts, swirling his tongue around her nipples, pulling them into his mouth and sucking on them. He restrained himself until she begged him to suck harder. He didn't want to hurt her but he also wanted to give her everything she wanted.

"Let me undress you," she pleaded. "I want to play with you too."

"In a minute," he said before dipping back in for another taste of her mouth.

She bent away from him. "Are you shy?"

That made his chest rumble with laughter. "Do I seem shy to you?"

"With this, yes." Her eyes had gone serious. "You don't want me to see you naked?"

"It's not that." It was totally that.

"I like what I've felt so far." She ran her hands over the front of his shirt. "And I'm pretty sure I'll like everything I haven't felt yet." A blush rose up her chest into her face, prompting him to laugh again.

"Well, they don't just call me Bear for my last name."

Now she laughed. "Come on. A little hair doesn't scare me." She slowly reached for the hem of his shirt again and this time he let her take it and pull it up until she couldn't reach any higher. He helped her from there until his shirt was off.

"See?" Warmth flooded his cheeks as she looked at his chest. He'd never felt this self-conscious. Then again, he'd never cared this much.

"Not as much hair as you were making it out to be. And I like it," she whispered. "Can I touch you now?" She looked up at him through her lashes.

He nodded.

"Good." Then she attacked him.

She ran her hands over his chest and down his abs. She circled his belly button with one finger—not feather-light, but pressing hard—until he groaned. She ran her hands around to his back and kneaded his muscles. This brought her close enough to kiss his chest so she did until his cock ached and threatened to push right through his pants. In the meantime, he explored her bare skin. She was soft where he was rough, curvy where he was muscular, small where he was big.

Finally, he'd taken as much as he could.

"Want you," he said as he nuzzled into her hair.

"Want you, too." She grinned up at him after covering his chest with kisses.

"It's okay if I take my pants off?"

"Yes." She chuckled, surprising him with her eagerness. He'd expected her to be hesitant at best and afraid at the worst, after what she must have been through. He didn't even know all the details, but he sensed enough that he wanted to go slow and careful with her this first time, let her lead so that he didn't overstep and make her uncomfortable.

But tell that to his weeping cock. All it wanted was her warmth and softness in a place he was sure would be snug and tight and feel so damned good.

He let her undo his pants, and as quickly as she went, it still wasn't fast enough. He was breathing heavy now, running his hands up and down her arms. She pulled both his pants and underwear down at the same time and he bent to get his boots off. He grabbed his wallet from his pants' pocket, remembering to pull out a condom at the last second. He ripped open the foil and quickly sheathed himself. When he stood straight up again he brought her up to standing with him and pulled her in close. His cock pressed hard against her belly, seeking her softness. Her face was chest-level and she covered it in kisses as he held her, trying to maintain control. She felt amazing and he wasn't even inside her yet. The thought sent a shudder through him.

She turned her face up to his. She slowly went to her tiptoes, her belly pressing and sliding against his hardness—pure, sweet torture—until the head of his cock nestled against her pussy. He slid his hands down to her ass and picked her up. She was so light in his arms and yet so strong. He buried his face in her neck again and breathed in her sweet scent like it was pure oxygen.

"I want you inside me, Bear," she begged. "I've wanted it for a long time now."

"Honey," he growled. "I want to kiss you all over first."

"No. Later." She squirmed in his arms and he laughed when he realized that she was trying to impale herself on his cock.

"What? You're laughing at me." She had the funniest pretend pout on her face.

Bear just laughed harder. Then he captured her mouth as he lowered her body the tiniest bit until the head of his cock pressed against her hard little clit. She ground against him. Her wetness felt incredible as they slid against each other. He lifted her up again.

"Hang on to me, Honey."

She gripped his upper arms and tightened her legs around him as he grabbed his shaft and lined himself up. Then he slowly lowered her onto his cock. The look on her face was a beautiful mingling of pleasure and relief. Her half-masted eyes looked into his and he groaned. He never wanted to look away. So much beauty there, all for him. He couldn't believe it.

As she clung to him, Bear gripped her legs and thrust himself deeper into her. She was just as warm and tight and perfect as he'd imagined she'd be. And when she squeezed around him he nearly lost control. He turned and sat down on the edge of the bed. Once he was down, she lifted herself up and bent her knees until her weight was on her shins on the bed and she had more control over her movements. She pulled herself up, gliding slowly along his shaft until he nearly slipped out, then back down again, squeezing along the way.

Up and down as he clenched her ass and divided his kisses between her breasts and her throat.

"God, so good." His voice rumbled against her skin. "Can't believe how good you feel." He leaned back with her on top of him until he was lying down. Then she brought his fantasies to life. Ellie rode him hard as he watched her. He stroked her back first, then brought his hands around to play with her taut nipples, rolling them and pinching when she begged him to.

"Pinch harder, Bear. It feels so good."

"I'm not hurting you?"

"No. Yes. Yes, please...feels *good*."

He squeezed harder and she closed her eyes and moaned.

"Promise me I'm not hurting you," he whispered. "Never want to hurt you."

She shook her head wildly, her hair flying, and moved faster. He moved his hands down to her hips and encouraged her as he felt his orgasm mount.

"That's my girl. Ride me." He brushed her clit with his thumb and she cried out. He rubbed harder until she came for him. At her clenching, he pumped into her, his orgasm the best he'd ever had.

Ellie laid her body down on his and he wrapped his arms around her. Her heart pounded against his chest in tune with his own. Her soft hair brushed his skin with every breath. He never wanted to let her go. He wanted to hold her like this forever.

"I love you, Ellie." The words came out on their own and they should have surprised him. Instead, he felt their truth down to his soul. "I love you so much."

"I love you too, Bear." She lifted her head and looked into his eyes. "I wanted to say it first, but you beat me to it." She brushed his cheek and gave his beard a little tug as she smiled.

"So instead, I'll tell you it's the first time I've ever said it to anyone."

"Anyone?"

She nodded. "Never had anyone I could say it to."

Ellie spoke so matter-of-factly and so casually that he felt his eyes prickle. This sweet, warm, incredible woman had no one in her life she'd felt safe enough to love and that was a damn crime. So here he was, the luckiest bastard in the world—

"But now I have you," she added, also matter-of-factly.

Bear blinked quickly as his chest tightened. He inhaled as best he could through the squeeze. Then he cupped the back of her head and kissed her. She laid her head down again, snuggled into him, and that's when he felt safe enough to let the first tear fall. Never in his life did he think he'd find a woman like her, one who made him brave enough to open his heart up like this. No way would he ever—*ever*—want to leave her.

Another tear slid down his cheek. He couldn't even explain what emotion he was feeling except that it was deep, stronger than anything he'd ever felt before. It hurt and it felt good all at the same time, like jumping into the coldest, clearest mountain lake on a hot day. Without meaning to let it, his chest hitched. Ellie held him tighter. She didn't say a word and he was glad for that. She just held him, and he clutched her to his chest until they both relaxed and let sleep take them.

FIFTEEN

Ellie woke the next morning wrapped up in Bear's arms. It was the first time she'd ever awakened next to a man, let alone beside one who she loved, and who loved her so well in return. She never wanted to wake up any other way again. As the sun rose and her attic bedroom caught the light, she studied Bear's face in sleep.

Why do you have to leave?

She knew right then that as much as she loved her cabin, she'd sell it all if he asked her to go with him.

But he wouldn't. What man helps a woman fix her place up—no, build a *home*—then asks her to give it up for him? A selfish man, and that wasn't Bear. She pushed a stray curl off his forehead.

Please stay.

Was Ellie being selfish if she asked him to stay? Bear was obviously running away from Gabe and some weird sense of failure for not saving his friend in time to spare his hearing. She hated that for him, especially since Gabe didn't hold any grudge and was actually thankful.

She decided she'd have a talk with Bear after she sussed

out the situation between the men a little more. She had half a dozen people she could ask, especially after last night. Ellie smiled as she remembered the magical dinner outside under the fairy lights with all their friends gathered there. Yesterday was definitely the best day of her life. She wanted so many more of them in her cabin.

Her home.

She needed to contact Mr. Cole and ask about the trust fund. She didn't want to burn through it and not be able to pay Bear back. She could even pay Arden and Kyle back rent for letting her stay. She knew they'd fight her on it, but it just didn't feel right to mooch off of them. Once she saved up for a car she could move in here full-time but for now she didn't mind staying at the ranch. She wanted to keep her job too—it was fun, it was something she could do, and it would keep her from getting lonely once Bear left.

Don't leave.

Stop being selfish, Ellie. Don't cling.

But Bear had said he loved her last night. More than once. Why couldn't she trust that?

Because no one could ever love you Arnold's voice insisted in her head. *You're fucking lucky Tibbs wants your sorry, ugly ass.*

Ellie squeezed her eyes shut against her thoughts. They were all back in Illinois with no idea where she was.

Yet.

I'm here. I'm safe. All that matters is that today, I'm safe.

Bear stirred in her arms and opened his mouth to yawn before he opened his eyes. When he did, he blinked at her sleepily then smiled. And that smile was everything. All her doubts vanished. There was nothing but love and care in Bear's beautiful eyes.

"Morning, honey," he said as he pulled her close and kissed her forehead.

"Good morning."

"Lookin' serious," Bear said as he stroked her cheek.

"Just thinking. I need to contact Mr. Cole and find out how much is in that trust fund so that I don't overspend. And if there's enough, maybe I could buy a used car so that I can stay here."

Bear frowned. "There's enough. Guy who left it to you made sure of it." He kissed her again, long and slow. "I can take you car shopping if you want." His smile was back. "We can do whatever you want today."

So they did. They started with Ellie making breakfast while Bear checked on the roof and made some phone calls about the chimney and the well. Ellie was happy—blissed-out even—but under it lay an anxiety she couldn't name.

It's just that you aren't used to being safe, that's all. Not used to someone taking care of you, and it feels weird.

She called out the door when breakfast was ready and Bear came in a few minutes later. He was covering his forearm with his opposite hand.

"Let me wash up first," he said as he headed for the water cooler set up over the sink in the kitchen. He turned on the spigot and ran his arm under the water.

"You cut yourself," Ellie said. She set the plate she was carrying down and picked up a clean dishrag. "Let me take a look."

"It's fine," Bear said.

"Let me take a look," Ellie insisted. "Lord knows how dirty it is. I have iodine and antibacterial ointment." She grabbed the small first aid kit she'd stashed in a cupboard over the sink.

"I got it." Bear grabbed a different towel she'd been using and Ellie placed her hand on his arm.

"Not that one, it's dirty. Please let me help you."

Something about her voice stopped him. He studied her face then nodded.

"Let's go over to the chairs by the window. I need light."

Ellie studied the cut—a little deep but not jagged at least. Bear had done a good job rinsing it out.

"I have a butterfly bandage for it." Ellie took out the bandage and the iodine from the first aid kit. "What happened?"

"Just me being clumsy up on the roof."

Ellie cringed. "I'm sorry. This wouldn't have happened if I didn't need—"

"Nope," Bear said. "Not another word. I like helping you, Ellie. This is nothing."

Ellie applied the bandage and studied her work. She thought it would heal up nicely. "Who takes care of you, Bear?"

"What do you mean?"

"You're taking such good care of me, but who takes care of you?"

The shrug was all she needed.

"Can I?" She cradled his arm.

"Can you what?"

"Can I be the one to take care of you?"

Those big, thoughtful eyes closed for a moment, then opened slowly. Bear's lips twitched and his jaw clenched for a moment before he said. "Yeah. Yeah, I'll let you do that."

She smiled, relieved. "Good. I have some ideas about how to do that." She lowered her chin and stared into his eyes as sternly as she could. "But you have to let me. I'm only telling you that because you're really a lot bigger than I am, and you're bossy, and I can't force you to do a darned thing. So, I have to tell you to let me. You gonna let me?"

Bear's mouth twitched again and then he was chuckling. "Yeah, I'm gonna let you."

"Okay, good. Glad that's settled."

"Ellie?"

"Yeah?"

"The truth is, you can always get me to do anything you want."

Ellie shivered. He was serious.

"You're not afraid of me, are you?"

"Never, Bear." She hugged him tightly, wishing he'd believe her. "You take the fear out of everything."

He squeezed her back, his chest rumbling.

"I mean it, Bear." She pulled back so she could gaze into his eyes and make sure he understood her. "You've asked me before and I'm telling you, I've spent my life being afraid— right up until you handed me a bag of potato chips because you knew I wasn't feeling good. I'd never be afraid of someone who does that." She shook her head. "A man who cares about you like that, well, he's someone you love without fear. And that's how love is supposed to be."

Bear said nothing back. He simply wrapped her up again and held her.

"What's *that* for?" she asked him, teasing.

"For loving me without fear." And then he added a few short words that spoke a library of meaning. "Fear kills happiness, doesn't it?"

"It does," Ellie agreed. "But not this morning. Not for us."

Bear tucked her in under his chin. "We're not afraid of anything, are we, baby?"

"Nope. Not as long as we're together."

B ear drove them to Walter's house so they could take a quick shower before heading down to Denver. Ellie barely recognized the inside of the house with its new furniture, paint, polished floors, and all the other upgrades and repairs Bear had made.

She tried to get Bear to shower with her, but he refused.

"We want to get stuff done today, right?" he asked as he handed her a brand-new, fluffy towel. "You pull me in there with you and I'm liable to just keep you here all day."

So Ellie reluctantly showered alone. The warm water streaming down her body only made her want Bear more as she remembered the previous night. She quickly washed her hair and body, then toweled off and got dressed. Bear had used the other bathroom and was already dressed when she came out.

Darn it.

Much to Ellie's surprise, car dealerships were by law closed on Sundays, which meant they could still go on the lots and look without being pestered by salespeople. Ellie wanted a truck—nothing fancy or new, but something that could get her reliably up and down the mountain in winter and let her haul stuff. They went south around Denver and Ellie could feel her skin begin to crawl, remembering her encounter with the pimp at the bus stop. She still couldn't believe she'd pointed a gun at him, but she'd do it again in a heartbeat if she needed to defend herself. She'd been lucky so far, and maybe that was the cause of her anxiety. Ellie never stayed lucky or kept nice things for long, and now she had so much and so much to lose. It was only a matter of time.

Bear grabbed her hand and squeezed it. "We can wait on the truck if you want."

"No, it's not that. I need to look at them before...before the weather turns bad again." She could bring herself to say *before you leave*. But the words hung silently between them.

Not afraid of anything? Not true. She was afraid of losing Bear.

The last person Ellie had in her life who loved her was her mother. When she died, all the sunlight went out of Ellie's life. Now that she had it back, she wanted to keep it forever.

They looked at a few dealerships but trucks—even used ones—were *expensive*.

I might as well be buying a second house Ellie thought.

Bear didn't blink at the stickers on the windows. "We'll find you one, Ellie. We can look online too. But I want to go with you if we do that." He already had his arm around her and he pulled her closer. "Don't want nothing happening to you."

"I don't know if I can afford, well, anything," she whispered, feeling ashamed.

"You can, honey. You can."

And there was that anxiety again. Bear was so confident she could afford a truck. Why? And why did it bother her? Ellie decided she'd talk to her cousin and give Mr. Cole a call on Monday.

Just to make sure.

"I'm getting hungry again," Bear said, patting his stomach. "Lemme take you out for lunch and then we'll head back ho... to your cabin."

Ellie didn't miss his slip and neither did her heart, which clenched before speeding up with happiness.

They struck out trying to find a truck, but that didn't mean they'd had a bad day. Bear took Ellie to a great pizza place in Lyons that had the old arcade-style video games in the back. She challenged him to a game of Space Invaders and beat him three times in a row, but he got her back on Donkey Kong right after that.

"I guess you're just better at saving damsels in distress than I am," Ellie joked.

Bear grinned through his shaggy beard. "Guess it's your job to save the whole world from aliens."

She pretended to consider it. "Okay. I'll do it."

He pulled her close for a kiss. "You ready?"

"Yup. Let's head home."

She felt Bear's body go stiff for a second. Then he placed his hand on the small of her back and they walked to the front of the restaurant.

"Got a surprise for you," he whispered in a gruff voice as the tips of his ears turned bright red.

Ellie couldn't wait to see what it was.

When they got back to the cabin, Bear swept Ellie off her feet and carried her upstairs. Instead of laying her down on the bed like she expected, he set her gently on her feet beside it.

"Wait," he whispered as he kissed her. Then he added, "Be naked when I come back."

He turned and went back downstairs. Ellie stripped quickly then trembled with anticipation until she heard his footsteps coming closer on the stairs. He was carrying a dark bundle that looked like a folded-up blanket. He stopped dead in the doorway as his eyes took her in.

"So damn pretty," he said, making Ellie's knees go weak as her chest flushed with heat.

"I've had this for years," Bear said as he came back to himself and cleared his throat. "Never used it for this, though I've thought about it. A lot." Bear crossed the room, stood beside the bed, and shook out the blanket—which turned out to be—

"Is that...mink?" Ellie gasped. The blanket covered the entire bed. Ellie had never seen anything like it. "It can't be real."

"It is," Bear said. "My family had a mink farm for a while. I hope you don't think it's cruel," he added quickly. "I have a deep love for animals, but minks are mean little critters."

She tentatively reached out and ran her hand through the dreamy softness. "Farm girl, remember? I know the difference between pets and livestock."

Bear laughed and before Ellie could stop him—as if she ever would—he'd picked her up and laid her down on the warm fur. It smelled sweet, like it had been stored in a cedar chest.

"I've dreamed of making love on this." Bear's voice was little more than a rumble in his chest as he climbed onto the bed and straddled her. He stretched her arms out over her head and ran his hands down her sides while his eyes devoured her. "I could look at you all night, Ellie. Can't believe you're mine. Something so precious." He bent and kissed her softly. She tugged at his thermal, trying to pull it up.

"Don't you want to feel some softness, too?" she teased, grinning when she saw his eyes go misty with desire. He got off the bed in one surprisingly graceful move and grabbed the back of his shirt between his shoulder blades. With one pull, he was bare-chested and Ellie feasted her eyes. How could he ever be self-conscious of his body? He was a solid wall of muscle that made her core turn molten at the sight of his six-pack. She watched him undo his belt then unbutton his jeans. His erection pressed against his boxer briefs as if it were fighting to get to her. He stepped out of his boots and pulled off his socks, then pulled down his jeans. His gaze never left her.

When he grabbed the waistband of his boxer briefs, Ellie said, "Wait. Let me do it."

Bear groaned and climbed back onto the bed as Ellie sat up.

"Let me take care of you, Bear," she whispered. She tucked her legs under her, loving the way the fur felt against her skin, and wrapped her arms around Bear's chest. They barely made it all the way around. She pressed her body against his, making sure to brush herself against his straining cock, and got the groan she'd been looking for. She did it again.

"Don't tease me like this, honey," Bear warned.

"Told you I'll take care of you, Bear. Just be patient." She kissed him and he ran his hand up into her hair, keeping her steady while he kissed her hard and hungrily. She ran her hands back down to his waistband, loving the shivers they produced. She realized that as big and strong as he was, she had complete power over Bear right now and it excited her.

Ellie pulled Bear's boxer briefs down over his meaty thighs, freeing his cock. It brushed against her breasts as she went down and he raised himself up to straighten his leg so she could slip the briefs off. Once he was naked, she stared at his cock. A bead of wetness formed at the tip under her gaze. She bent to lick it off and Bear's chest rumbled when her tongue licked his tip. She swirled her tongue around the head of his cock while he gripped her upper arms, head thrown back and eyes closed in ecstasy.

"So good and sweet," he said as she ran her tongue up and down his thick shaft. "Can't believe how good that feels."

"It's only going to get better," she murmured against his cock before taking him into her mouth. She twisted her head slowly as she descended along his shaft. Bear dug his fingers into her shoulders before letting up. He was still so aware of his size and strength versus hers, even when he was lost in pleasure.

Ellie felt his balls tighten as she played with them so she wasn't surprised when he pulled his cock out of her mouth.

"Close, honey. Don't want it to end yet." He eased her back until she was lying on the mink again. He spread her legs and buried his face between them. His beard scratched against her legs even as his tongue laved her sweetest spot. Soft and rough, pleasure and the barest edge of pain and Ellie was spinning, her heart pounding against her ribcage, feeling like a bird trying to escape. Bear held her firmly by her hips, keeping her steady and grounded as he drove her wild with his tongue. Ellie gripped the mink blanket while primal sounds escaped her, sounds she couldn't believe she was making as she felt the tide of her orgasm rising.

"That's my wild thing," Bear said between licks. "Let yourself go. I've got you."

He pressed his mouth hard against her and Ellie moaned out her pleasure as she arched against him. She fell back against the fur, feeling like her bones had turned to water. She panted as she tried to catch her breath, still fuzzy headed from her orgasm. Bear kissed his way up her body until he covered her. Somewhere along the way, he'd put on a condom and he was rock-hard. She expected him to plunge straight into her but instead he cradled her face in his hands.

"I love you, Ellie. I really, really love you."

She grinned up at him. "I know, Bear. I love you, too."

"I just... I want you to know it. No matter what."

Ellie kissed him. "I know, Bear. I promise." She pressed up against his cock, not wanting to think about what he meant by *no matter what*. If he was leaving, she didn't want to think about it right now. She only wanted to live in this moment.

Bear lined himself up with her body and slid home. Ellie wrapped her legs around his torso until she couldn't tell where her body ended and his began. He rocked inside her and she felt another orgasm building right along with his.

"Love you, Ellie," he growled in her ear. "Love you so much." He moved faster and Ellie held on as her pleasure grew until she couldn't hold it anymore.

"Bear," she gasped. With one final thrust, Bear threw back his head and groaned as Ellie came with him.

After that, he wrapped them both up in the fur and they slept safe and sound in Ellie's new cabin.

SIXTEEN

Illinois, *a week after Ellie left*

Arnold Jameson paced the length of the farmhouse's front room while his father eyed him from the ratty old recliner he practically lived in. If wishes came true, his fucking bitch of a sister would be dead at his feet, or maybe tied up in Tibbs' shithole of a trailer and at the bastard's complete mercy. Yeah, that would be way better. That way, her suffering wouldn't end for a long, long time.

And she deserved to suffer for what she did.

"Fuckin' dirty little thief," Arnold mumbled under his breath.

"All women are," Dad confirmed.

"Didn't ask you, old man," Arnold snarled.

"Boy, I will beat the shit out of you."

Arnold laughed. "Love to see you do that now that you can barely walk."

He really should kill the old man too, he thought for the millionth time. Except the son of a bitch was still useful. There were the disability payments and social security deposits, and every now and then he still came up with a good idea or two. Arnold hated that. He consoled himself with knowing that as long as Dad was still alive the old man was suffering. That almost made up for having to listen day in and day out to the bastard whining about how much pain he was in, and what shit kids he'd had to raise by himself after their mother died.

Arnold kicked the recliner's raised footrest on one of his turns just to hear the old man swear in pain. "Help me think of where Ellie mighta went."

"How'm I s'posed to know?"

Arnold started pacing again. The old man was worthless. "She took my shit, including my bike."

"Wasn't your bike."

"Shut up. She took my bike, which means she's going somewhere far and don't want us to know instead of going to a friend's place nearby."

"Because she don't have any friends, dumbass," Dad said. "Last time she had friends was back when your shit mama took all you kids out to Colorado whenever she was on the rag."

Arnold stopped pacing. "You think?"

"Do I think what?"

"That's where she went? Colorado?"

"Didn't Tibbs say they tracked her south?" Dad started coughing into his hand, big phlegmy hacks from years of smoking.

"Yeah, and then lost her. Guy they got on state patrol thinks she kept going into Missouri." Arnold rubbed his cheek. "But there'd be no reason. We don't have family down there, but we do in Colorado."

"Haven't heard from Walter or Ellen for years," Dad said, his voice now raw and rougher after his coughing fit. "She might have gone anyway." He examined the palm of his hand before he grabbed a tissue and wiped it off. "Why won't you tell me why you want her back so bad? You want someone keeping this place up, just take one of Tibbs' women. Less hassle than your sister."

Arnold sneered. "That's not the reason. She has my shit and I want it back." He wouldn't tell the old man the real reason, which was that he owed Tibbs money—big money he couldn't pay back—and Tibbs had agreed to take Ellie instead. Yeah, Arnold wasn't about to tell him. Not because the old man cared about his daughter, but because he'd laugh at Arnold for getting in too deep with Tibbs' outlaw MC, when he'd warned Arnold against it a year ago. He hated when the old man was right.

"So get new fuckin' stuff. That's what you do."

Arnold started pacing again. Ellie had taken more than a bike and some camping gear. She'd stolen Arnold's gun, and not just any gun, oh, no sir. She'd taken the one he should have gotten rid of immediately, the one that would send him to prison. He still had stippling on his finger from the night he killed the pawnshop owner who was blackmailing Arnold, threatening to go to the cops with information on his fencing operation.

The metal under his skin itched. What if Ellie knew about the murder and had taken the gun to turn him in? But if she'd done that, why go so far away to do it?

Well, besides the fact that he'd kill her too once he found her. Use the same damn gun, why not?

Could she turn him in from Missouri? Or from Colorado?

Maybe she took a page from the pawnshop guy and planned to blackmail him with it instead.

"I need to look up Uncle Walter," Arnold said as his pacing took him back to his father. "I don't remember where they lived."

"Colorado."

"No shit. Where in fucking Colorado?"

"Fuck you." The old man gave him the middle finger.

"You want your meds or not, fucker?" Arnold replied cooly.

The old man's yellowed eyes narrowed. "Northern Colorado along the Front Range. Hills near Lyons. Don't remember where exactly."

"Good enough." Arnold pulled out his phone to look up Walter Sanders near Lyons, Colorado. "Says here he died earlier this year."

"Then I guess your sister ain't staying with him."

"Might be with Ellen." Arnold did some further digging. "Shit, looks like she sold the house before he died. Holy shit," he added when he saw what the house went for. He looked up at the old man. "Dead end."

"Well, Ellen's not dead. She's gotta be living somewhere."

"Yeah..." Arnold was already back on his phone looking up Ellen Sanders in Colorado but not having much luck. Maybe he'd ask Tibbs to use his connections for that too. It was a long shot, but the best one he had. He looked again at the sell price for Walter's house. "She's living someplace nice, based on what she sold Walter's house for."

"Might be worth lookin' up Ellen just for shits and giggles," the old man said.

"You think she inherited everything?"

"I sure as shit didn't get anything." The old man started coughing again. "Why don't you send Harlan out there?"

Arnold snorted. The idea of his little brother finding his own ass on any given day was comically funny, let alone their sister. He smoked almost as much meth as he cooked.

Arnold looked at the old house listing and the high six-figures next to the word *sold*. Just for the shits and giggles his father was talking about, he checked other listings around the area. Was everyone in Colorado a goddamned millionaire? Some of those places sitting on postage stamps went for more than what he could sell the whole farm for. Not that he would —Tibbs needed an out-of-the-way place to cook meth and store shit and the fact Arnold let him use the farm was about all that was keeping him alive at this point.

Arnold looked up acreage for sale in the mountains. A few of those lots sold for more than the houses in cities. One parcel with water rights was going for north of a million. Another with a state easement, a lodge, and a bunch of outbuildings was...holy shit, five million.

Walter had a shitty little cabin somewhere, too. He'd taken Arnold and his brother up there once, trying to 'straighten them out' using some back-to-nature, feel-good bullshit talk. Arnold remembered a big lake full of fish. He wondered how much land Walter owned and if that had been sold too. He skimmed through the listings to maybe find it but damn if he had any idea where that cabin might be, either.

Still, it stuck in his mind like the slivers of metal in the stippling.

Arnold tapped on his contacts list and fired off a text to Tibbs:

Need your friends to look somewhere else for me.

SEVENTEEN

In Bear's world before Ellie, he was always waiting to be deployed again whenever he was home. He hated that itchy, waiting feeling. He felt like he could never start a project or a real relationship because he'd just get yanked away again. He'd wished he were a real bear that could go into hibernation between deployments. Expecting to be called up at any moment led to Bear pacing his bedroom, sometimes all night, the rising sun bringing him no relief.

His only relief from the endless waiting was when the call finally came. That was when he could finally grab some sleep, whether it was a few hours before wheels up, or for the better part of a day, or sometimes only on the flight to whatever godforsaken place he'd been deployed to.

Bear thought the restlessness would end once he retired. He wouldn't be waiting for the next call and could finally relax. But instead, the restlessness got worse with nothing to end it. So he bought a truck and hit the road with the idea that once he could sleep regularly through the night he'd be ready to come back home and settle down.

Sleeping through the night never came. Didn't matter if

he was somewhere in the sleepy Midwest or beside the calming ocean or lost in the woods up north. Bear couldn't rest. Every little sound made him jump, even when the sound was only in a dream.

Okay, especially when it was in a dream.

Bear dreamed the same things over and over. Dusty places, cold places, unbearable sun overhead, sweating, freezing. He was always in enemy territory, always looking over his shoulder, keeping his ears and eyes open for danger, doing everything he could to keep his brothers-in-arms safe.

In his dreams, like in life, he failed when the IED went off and Gabe was injured.

So when Bear slowly awoke to the gentle sounds of Ellie's steady breathing and realized he was in the same position he'd been in when he fell asleep, he figured he'd gotten two, maybe three solid hours of good sleep and thanked his lucky stars he hadn't woken up thrashing around and scaring his woman to death.

He still hadn't forgiven himself for making her startle away from him when he checked on her that cold morning. Someone had messed with his Ellie growing up and he could guess who. Scared her so often she startled awake, ready to defend herself. Even though she told Bear time and again she wasn't afraid of him, he couldn't shake the memory of how terrified she'd looked. Yup, someone had messed with his Ellie and Bear had been an idiot and set her off.

Stop it he told himself now. *It's all in the past. She's fine. You're fine.* He kissed the top of her head and she murmured in her sleep. God, he adored her. He didn't want to move for fear of waking her. Maybe he could go back to sleep. He carefully lifted his head and nudged his phone on the bedside table to check the time. He couldn't believe his eyes.

Five in the morning. They'd finally gotten to sleep around eleven the night before. Bear had slept all night long.

"Ellie," he whispered. "Honey, time to get up if we want to get you to the ranch for work."

She stirred and stretched, then half-opened her eyes and smiled. "Don't wanna move."

He chuckled. "Me neither. But I don't want to get you in trouble, either."

"What time is it?" she mumbled.

"Five."

Her eyes opened all the way. "No way. I don't think I moved all night."

"Me neither."

She snuggled down into the fur and tucked herself closer to Bear. "Best sleep I've ever gotten."

"Me too, honey." He nuzzled in her hair, loving her wild berry scent. He couldn't get enough of her.

"And you want to know what the good news is?"

"Sure."

"Last night, Arden told me to sleep in today. She has the morning chores covered. We can go down for dinner if we want, which I do, so that I can see Ellen again. She's only staying a few days. And then after dinner I'll help Arden button up the ranch for the night. Sound good?"

"Anything you want, honey."

Ellie burrowed in against him. She ran her hand down his body to his morning wood and stroked the tip, eliciting a rumble.

"How about we do something *you* want, Bear?"

They slept again after making love. When they woke again, Ellie sighed and tried to sit up but Bear wasn't about to let her escape the bed without a few kisses first.

"Keep doing that and we won't have breakfast," she giggled as he nuzzled her neck.

"I should keep you here for the rest of the week," he teased.

"But then I'll lose my job."

"Okay, then lose your job," he said against her skin as she laughed. Truth was, she could—thanks to the trust he'd set up. He'd just keep feeding it.

He ignored the voice in his head saying that it was a bad idea and he needed to tell her *right now* what he'd done.

No. Not until the cabin is finished to her liking. Better to ask forgiveness than permission.

"Bear?" Ellie pulled her head away and looked at him. "You okay?"

"Never better." And he meant it.

Over a breakfast of coffee, eggs, bacon, and toast, they talked about the cabin.

"I've been studying a map of the surrounding land. A new development went up in the last couple years over to the west and there's a road servicing it. I'm gonna see about getting a driveway connecting the property to it. Easier than trying to pave the old route. And we've gotta think about getting the septic tank in and the plumbing—"

Bear stopped himself. He'd said 'we' as if he were talking about his own property.

"The tank and plumbing? Something wrong with putting it in?" Ellie cocked her head.

"No. Nothing," he said, covering. "Just gotta figure out the best way to get it done."

"I imagine you could just carry the tank on one shoulder." She playfully reached across the table and squeezed his arm.

Bear grinned. "That's a lotta faith you're putting in me," he joked back.

"Faith in you is a no-brainer."

Bear felt heat creeping up into his cheeks and knew he was probably turning bright red at the compliment.

"And there's that blush," Ellie confirmed.

"Hate it," he said, rubbing his cheek like his blush was a stain he could wipe away. As a smaller, much scrawnier kid, he'd been teased mercilessly about how easily he blushed.

"Really? I love your blush. Shows you aren't an emotionless jerk." She bounced in her chair and nodded, and he felt the little kid inside him smile. He felt seen. Accepted.

Where were you when I was younger?

Silly question. She'd been right here, he just hadn't seen her. Or rather, he had, but it was easier to look away from the little girl who was so quiet and shy. He was too busy trying to fit in himself. This sudden, unexpected acceptance touched him deeply and went a long way to heal some of the old hurts he'd temporarily patched over like a hole in the roof.

This was Ellie taking care of him, even when she didn't realize it.

Then she frowned and slapped her forehead. "God, I'm being selfish. Do you have work to do today for Kyle? Am I keeping you from it?"

"Nope."

The truth was, Bear had planned to drop Ellie off at the ranch then stop at Walter's house to shower and change clothes before he went on to a different safehouse to do some fiddly work with the security system there. Wasn't too much work left for him at Watchdog. Bear was torn between being efficient and slowing the last few jobs down just to stretch them out as an excuse to stay longer. He'd been thrilled this morning at the idea of putting off his work one more day to stay up at the cabin with Ellie.

But why play that game?

Nothing and no one but Bear himself said he couldn't stay on in Colorado after he was done with the repairs and upgrades. That impulse to keep moving was an old one and hard to shake he realized. He had Ellie now and she hadn't batted an eye when he said *we*, like the cabin was his too.

I'm staying.

The thought was solid in his head. He'd start looking for a place nearby, maybe something west of Lyons so he could be closer to Ellie.

What if she asks me to live with her?

He felt his cheeks redden again. He'd never, ever assume or ask for that.

But if she asked him...of course he'd say yes.

Bear tested out that feeling for a minute, letting it settle into his gut. He'd had women ask him to stay before—nothing serious, just one or two asking casually in Corpus when winter came to an end what his plans were. Nothing had ever made him pack his bags faster.

But the thought of Ellie taking his hand, looking up at him, and asking if he'd stay on with her, sank deep into his heart and settled it. His gut felt the same.

Ellie was *home*.

The day was much cooler than it had been the previous week but it was perfect for working outside. Bear was behind the cabin figuring out how best to install the septic system when he heard Ellie's shouts.

"No! No, please! Go away!"

Jesus, no. Arnold found her.

His blood froze as vague and terrible memories from childhood threatened to surface.

I'll kill him this time.

The thought was emotionless, a cold fact. Arnold needed killing and Bear was the one to do it. Simple math. Basic subtraction.

Bear rushed around the corner of the cabin to the raised garden beds where Ellie was working. And stopped short.

Ellie was alone. She was holding a broom out in front of her like a knight with a lance, aiming it at a clump of bushes between her and the creek. And damn, she looked scared.

A rattler? But Bear didn't hear the telltale rattle that was the snake's way of saying *fuck around and find out.* The bushes were too small to hide a full-grown coyote and she wouldn't be afraid of a fox. He got ready to block the way between Ellie and whatever danger lurked in the bushes.

"Ellie, honey. What is it?"

"Skunk!" She waved the broom. "It tried to get under the porch."

Bear chuckled with relief and relaxed. "They make good pets." He started walking toward her slowly, so as not to further startle the critter in the bushes.

She looked at him like he'd baked his brain in the sun. "They make stinky pets."

"Only if you provoke them." Bear wrapped one arm around her and his opposite hand around the wooden broom handle but didn't take it from her. He'd learned over the past month how much she hated it when people took things out of her hands, how it made her feel helpless and stupid. Bear looked at her for permission to take the broom. After a moment, she nodded slightly.

Bear eased the broom out of her hands while he held back his laughter. He wasn't laughing at her, just at the situation. Here she looked like the big bad wolf was going to jump out at her, when all it was, was a little skunk.

And little was right. Bear spotted it under the bushes. It wasn't yet full-grown. And to his surprise it wasn't angry or intimidated. It was lying down and blinking at them with its little black eyes.

"Aw, this one's sweet, honey. You don't have to be afraid."

"I'm not afraid. I just don't want it stinking up our cabin."

Our cabin. That slip of the tongue sent a golden warmth spreading through him.

He set the broom down and she took two steps back. Bear reached into his flannel pocket and took out a peanut. He always kept a few in case he ran across a critter looking for a snack. He crouched down and Ellie took another five steps back until she was behind him.

"Let me remind you we don't have any running water, Bear. When he sprays you, you're on your own."

He laughed. "There's always the creek or the lake. But, we'll just see about that."

Bear stretched his arm out and offered the peanut to the skunk. His little black nose twitched as he craned his head forward. Bear set the peanut on the ground and sat back. The skunk watched him, looking as wary as Ellie did. But she was turning brave. She walked back up behind Bear and put her hand on his shoulder, her eyes never leaving the skunk. She crouched down, using Bear as a shield, which cracked him up.

The skunk got tired of stretching his neck forward and stood up. Ellie jumped a little behind Bear and he put his hand over hers on his shoulder.

The skunk practically tiptoed up to the peanut, his neck jutting forward the whole time. He stopped, lowered his twitching nose, and the peanut disappeared with little chomping noises. Then the skunk looked at Bear as if to say *got any more?*

Bear slowly reached into his pocket, took out several peanuts, and laid them on the ground just a little closer. The skunk didn't hesitate to snarf them up. When they were gone, he sat back on his haunches and waved his front paws in the air, begging for more.

Ellie giggled at the skunk's antics.

"Not so bad, huh?"

She grinned. "I guess not. As long as he doesn't turn around and give us the business end."

"He won't, so long as we don't give him reason to." Bear held out his hand to the skunk. Three peanuts sat in his palm. Nose twitching, the skunk barely hesitated before grabbing Bear's big hand and eating right out of it. Bear felt Ellie shaking behind him as she held in her laughter.

"Telling you, they make great pets," he said.

"You're pulling my leg, Bear."

"No, I'm not. I had one as a kid. You think I'm lying to you?"

"No, I don't. I know you'd never lie to me, Bear."

His heart thumped in his chest at that. He thought of the trust fund and pushed down his guilt.

"So, what did you name your pet skunk?" she asked.

"Skunky."

Ellie laughed.

Bear shrugged. "I was little."

"Skunky. I think that's adorable, actually."

Bear extended his finger and the skunk let him run it over his head and down his back while he chomped on the last peanut. "What do you want to name this one?"

Ellie hesitated, her expression turning serious. "We can't really keep him as a pet, can we?"

We. She was killing Bear by inches.

"Honey, this is your place. Your home. You can do whatever you want," Bear said, trying to reassure her.

The sudden wetness in her eyes and her rapid blinking took him aback. He felt his own eyes sting abruptly.

"I didn't mean to hurt you, baby."

Ellie sniffled and wiped away the tears as she shook her head. "You're not hurting me at all, Bear. These are happy tears. I have nothing but happy tears when I'm with you. That's what you do for me."

Bear's heart swelled with love and happiness at her words. He pressed a gentle kiss to her lips, grateful for the chance to make her happy. "Then we'll figure out a name for this little guy together."

Ellie grinned and threw her arms around Bear's neck. "Thank you," she whispered.

Bear's chest rumbled. There was nothing he wouldn't do to make her happy.

The skunk retreated under the bushes, curled up into a furry little ball, and closed his eyes. Yup, looked like they had a new pet.

They. Now he was doing it.

"How about Spot?" he asked.

"For a name? Wouldn't Stripe be more fitting?"

"Naw, too obvious."

"Says the man who named a skunk Skunky."

Bear's chuckle rumbled through his chest.

"Actually, I kinda like Spot. Let's think about it." Then she kissed his nose as if she'd been doing that for years and stood up.

He watched her in wonder, stunned by the perfect happiness of an ordinary day with the woman he loved.

Simple math again. Addition this time.

Ellie went back to the garden beds and started wrestling with some thick, white sheet plastic. Scattered on the ground around her were long, thin metal poles.

Bear stood. "What are you doing there?"

"I'm building a tunnel garden for the winter crops. If I can trap enough sunlight and heat, use a little rocket stove for the coldest days, we can have some fresh root vegetables for stew. I used to be able to overwinter tomato plants on the farm, but that was in a real greenhouse and might be a stretch up here. I'll have to give it a try though—"

She didn't get anything else out because Bear had wrapped his big arms around her and gathered her up for a long, hard kiss.

"What was that for?" she was finally able to ask as she gasped for breath.

Bear screwed up his courage at last. "You keep saying *we*, Ellie." His voice was barely above a whisper, softer than what he used on the most timid of wild animals.

"Of course I'm saying *we*." Ellie looked like she was screwing up her courage, too. "You have your plans already and it might be selfish asking, but... I want you to stay here, Bear. I can't imagine getting through a long, cold winter without you. Please tell me you'll stay."

Bear swallowed hard as his heart pounded double-time. "I never would have asked to stay."

"I know, Bear. It's not your way." Ellie brushed his shaggy

hair back from his face. "So I'm asking for you. Will you stay here with me in *our* cabin?"

He answered her with another long, hard kiss.

That evening before going to dinner at the ranch, they drifted in their boat on their lake to gaze at their emerging stars.

EIGHTEEN

Ellie was surprised to see the number of vehicles in the long drive leading to Arden and Kyle's ranch house.

"Did they say anything about a party?" she asked Bear.

He shook his head. "Not a party. Arden loves company. Ellen's in town. That's all the excuse she needs to invite a crowd."

"I wish I'd known. I would have had you swing by the store so I could bring something." Ellie felt guilty as it was for taking the day off; now she didn't have a dish or even flowers. "When we have our cabin all done, I'll be able to cook for real there. I'll always have something to bring. And we'll have parties, too."

She glanced at Bear, who had gone even quieter than usual. The big man was beaming, grinning from ear to ear.

"You like parties?" she teased, her heart thumping because she knew the real reason he was smiling.

"I like *our*. I like *we*." He pulled into a gap between vehicles on the driveway and parked the truck. Then he looked at her. "And yeah, I'll like it when *we* can have *our* friends up to the cabin for more parties." He reached across the bench and grabbed her hand. "I love you, Ellie. So much."

How? How could this man have fallen in love with her? Her heart melted as she gazed into Bear's sincere, loving eyes. Maybe the how didn't matter. The truth was right there in his eyes. He loved her.

"I love you too, Bear."

She undid her seatbelt and leaned in for a kiss. He pulled her close and turned their kissing into something warm and passionate that threatened to keep them from going inside. At least they were staying at Walter's for the night and didn't have a long drive back to the cabin ahead of them. She didn't want to wait too long before she could get Bear naked again.

And he'd brought the mink blanket.

From the steamy look Bear gave her, he was thinking the same thing. Then he confirmed it when he chuckled and said, "We should at least eat first. For energy."

"Good plan." She turned her expression serious. "And Bear?"

"Yeah, honey?"

"Ask for seconds."

Ellie imagined everyone inside could hear his roaring laugh.

"Does everyone here know each other?" Arden asked over the talking crowd gathered in the ranch house's great room.

"We're not putting on nametags, Arden," Shane said, laughing.

"I just want to make sure no one's feeling left out," she

answered him as she wove through the crowd with a tray of drinks.

"Let me get that for you," Ellie said, taking the tray from Arden.

"Does it look like we're all strangers?" Shane added as he swept his arm around the room. "Relax, Arden. Everyone's having a good time."

Ellie shook her head, but he was right. She'd known most of the men in the room from when she was little, but just over a month ago they were strangers about to arrest her for trespassing. The women who she hadn't known before—Harper, Brianna, Charlie, Jodie—already felt like old friends. And of course Arden and Ellen were here. Her true family, not the people back in Illinois.

Somehow, Ellie's life had gone from dark and dangerous to full of love and light. All she needed to do was take a risk.

A big risk.

Ellie suppressed a shudder even as she handed Kyle a beer with a smile. In some other world, there was a version of her who was not happy, not surrounded by friends and family, not safe and loved by a good man. That poor Ellie was a slave to Tibbs, sold to him by her own brother.

It didn't happen. You saved yourself.

And Bear would keep her safe. They all would.

What if they come after you? What if they know where you are right now and are just waiting?

"Thanks, Ellie," Waylon said as he grabbed a beer off the tray.

"You're welcome, Ram," she answered, using his old childhood nickname. His eyebrows rose and he smiled, saluting her with the beer before taking a drink.

She remembered all their childhood nicknames. Waylon Ramson was Ram. Shane Foti was Elk. Benjamin Massey was Moose, poor guy. Gabe O'Neil was Timberwolf. Elias Hunt was Lion, befitting his golden hair. And Arden's brother Sean had been Hawk. Bear was Bear of course, which fit him now, but had been ironic at the time. He was a short, skinny kid, she remembered in retrospect, and everyone outside of his friends teased him for his size, Ellie's brothers especially.

I don't want to think about them. Not tonight. Not ever.

So why was she?

I'm safe. I'm not used to that, so my brain is bringing them up.

Maybe.

Ellie returned the empty tray to the kitchen. Her cousin waved her over to the couch and patted the empty spot beside her. She sat down and received a warm, one-armed hug. Ellie clamped down the urge to confirm once again that her cousin was all right with giving her the cabin.

Arden stood with Kyle in front of the fireplace.

"Can I get everyone's attention?" Arden asked. The room quieted down.

"I just want to thank you all from the bottom of my heart for being here. This is the house I grew up in. It's been in my family for a few generations now." Arden looked around the great room. "It was cold and empty for a while after I lost my parents and Sean. And so was I." Then she looked at Kyle with eyes full of love. "Until California here came along and reminded me that it was okay to come back to the land of the living."

Kyle smirked. "Kinda ironic, considering that you were bent on sending me to the Great Beyond the night we met."

Arden waved him off, laughing. "What else was I supposed to do with a man pounding on my door in the middle of the night, demanding that I give him my dog?"

At that, Camo perked up, wagged his tail, and trotted over to the couple as everyone laughed.

"Not gonna let anybody forget how you brought us together, are you, buddy?" Kyle said to the dog as he and Arden both gave him pets.

A man named Alex stood and raised his glass. Ellie had met him and his fiancée at dinner a few nights ago. Alex was the kennel master at Watchdog and he and Kyle went way back. His fiancée, Sylvie was a police officer who used to babysit Arden.

"And from there, you started Watchdog," Alex said. "Creating an even bigger family and community. Here's to Pup and Arden. And Camo most of all. Cheers."

"To Camo, the way it should be," Kyle said as he roughed up the fur on top of Camo's head before taking a drink.

Ellen smiled at Ellie. "How did the repairs go today?" she asked.

"Great," she answered brightly. Maybe too brightly. Yup, Ellen tilted her head ever so slightly.

"I don't know how to ask this delicately, without giving you the wrong impression. I'm glad my dad left you the cabin, so let me start there."

Despite her cousin's reassurances, Ellie's stomach tightened. She blinked and nodded rapidly. "Okay."

"I talked to the lawyer about it today. Since the cabin was in a trust fund with specific instructions, Bruce told me he couldn't reveal the trust to me when my father died. And he still can't reveal all the details." She paused. "You said you were funding the repairs with money from a trust fund my dad left you."

It wasn't a question, but when she paused again, Ellie nodded yes. Her stomach was turning into a pretzel. Almost as a reflex, she glanced around the room until she found Bear, who was talking to his friends. Except now he was looking right at them, and he didn't look happy.

Ellen continued. "And...you have enough money for everything? I mean, I saw how much progress was made yesterday and it was a lot. Not to mention all the new furnishings we bought with the funds. Bear said there was no problem at all when I asked him about it."

Now Ellie was nauseous. She hadn't bothered to call Mr. Cole and ask about the trust fund, relying on Bear instead, who seemed to know exactly what she could spend. She felt stupid. Not that she didn't trust Bear, or that he was trying to swindle her, but it really was *her* responsibility and she wasn't stepping up.

"Anyway, I just want to make sure you aren't over-spending on the wrong things and end up with no plumbing or whatever else needs updating."

Ellie took a deep breath. "I... I mean, I've let Bear be my general contractor, basically. I trust him." Another glance his way showed her that he was reading her distress and getting worried himself.

"I do, too, sweetie," her cousin reassured her. "I've known him all my life. He's trustworthy." She smiled. "And it's more than obvious he's head over heels for you."

Ellie blushed and nodded again.

"It's just that... Well, the numbers don't add up for me. My dad did well financially, don't get me wrong. I knew he'd made some good investment choices, and property around here did nothing but go up over the last decade. Plus, Watchdog completely overpaid for our house. But, that was late in the game and I don't think my dad had the kind of money that you seem to be spending on the cabin when he set up your trust, so I worry that you might be nearing the end of it. Or that you might even be overdrawn. Bruce sounded a little nervous, or off, or...something when I was asking him."

She grabbed Ellie's hand. "I'm not trying to scare you or anything, and again, I'm happy that you have the cabin and the money to cover repairs, but something just isn't adding up and I want to make sure that money is really there." She shook her head. "But Bruce Cole and Bear wouldn't steer you wrong. Maybe I'm worried over nothing and I shouldn't be stirring you up."

Ellie placed her hand over her cousin's. "No, I appreciate it. I really do need to look into it and I haven't. I've put that responsibility on Bear when it's mine. Time for me to grow up."

Ellen's expression turned almost pitying. "Sweetie, I don't know if you were ever allowed to be a child. I think it's wonderful that you have people watching out for you now and that you still have the ability to trust another human being after everything you've been through, and I don't even know the half of it, I'm sure. So, don't be hard on yourself. Actually, I feel bad that my dad and your mom fell out and we lost touch."

"It was a long time ago," Ellie said. "We were both kids. Hard to keep in touch, you know? The internet wasn't quite what it is now."

That wasn't the only reason, but Ellie didn't want to get into it. Her mom had warned her against staying in touch. She'd been so upset at Walter. What it boiled down to was that Walter had told his sister that she and Ellie were welcome at any time—but not Arnold and Harlan. He was afraid for his own daughter's safety during what became their final visit. Ellie wanted to ask what her cousin remembered about that visit, but she'd been too afraid to bring it up.

"Do you..." she started. "Did Arnold or Harlan...did they

hurt you the last time we visited? My mama hinted that the reason we didn't come visit anymore was because Uncle Walter didn't want my brothers around you."

Her cousin squeezed Ellie's hand. "No, they didn't." Her expression darkened. "But, my dad tried to talk to them at one point. It didn't go well. And then he either found something or one of the other boys told him something Arnold did. Something that disturbed him enough to talk to your mom about not brining Arnold and Harlan back. I don't know what it was."

Ellie nodded and shivered. She could only imagine.

"I know my dad always felt bad about cutting *you* off, Ellie. He was worried about his sister of course, but also about you. So, I'm not surprised that he made sure you were okay after he passed."

Ellie tried not to tear up. "I am so thankful." She bit her lip. She couldn't tell her cousin how close she'd been to losing her life. After she'd learned that Arnold was going to turn her over to Tibbs, she would have run no matter what, of course. But she'd be on the street now with nothing if it hadn't been for her Uncle Walter's generosity. "I'll call Bruce Cole first thing tomorrow morning."

Ellen smiled and patted her knee. "Oh," she said, and picked up her purse beside her feet. "I think that's my phone." She pulled her phone out and frowned when she looked at the screen before answering.

"Yes?" Her expression went from puzzled to upset.

"What is it?" Ellie mouthed. She glanced over at Bear, who was already starting across the room.

"I see. Yes. I'm out of town. Okay. Yes. Thank you. I'll...I guess I'll cut my trip short. Thanks, officer." Ellen disconnected the call. By now, Arden and Kyle were at her side, too.

Her cousin looked at Ellie, then Arden. "My burglar alarm went off tonight. I think I was just robbed."

Arden covered her mouth and looked at Kyle, who'd gone from relaxed to high alert. He caught Alex's eye and he and Sylvie stood up and crossed the room.

Kyle leveled his gaze at Alex. "Ellen's house was broken into."

Sylvie's mouth went firm. "Do you think...?" She trailed off but shared meaningful looks with Kyle, Arden, and Alex.

"I'll have my friends look into it on that end," Kyle said.

"What's going on?" Ellie asked. She gripped her cousin's hand.

Ellen shook her head. "Kyle, there have been robberies in the neighborhood. Teenagers breaking into cars and such. I don't think it's..." she glanced around. "I don't think it's any more serious than that. But, I do want to go home."

"I'm sending one of my bodyguards with you," Kyle said.

"What's going on?" Ellie asked. "What could be more serious?"

Ellen shook her head and tried to give her a reassuring smile. "There's a reason your uncle and I sold our house to Watchdog, but I don't think I can talk about it." She looked at Kyle for confirmation and he nodded. "It's all right. I don't think, I mean, after all this time—"

"I'm sending someone just in case," Kyle said. "Please, humor me, Ellen."

Ellen stood up. "All right, just to humor you." She smiled. "Thanks, Kyle."

The not-a-party dispersed not long after Ellen received the phone call. Ellie and Arden helped her pack her things as she arranged for a red eye flight out of Denver and Kyle assigned Charlie to accompany her. Ellie wished she knew what had happened when Ellen and Walter sold their house, but she didn't want to add to the stress. She hugged and kissed her cousin goodbye and she and Bear walked her to the waiting SUV. From there, Bear drove her to Walter's house.

"Do you know what's going on?" she asked him.

"Only a little, honey. I know that Kyle and them tangled with some really nasty folks this summer and that's why they were on such high alert when you showed up."

"What do they have to do with my uncle and cousin? They'd sold the house and moved away before then."

"Don't know, honey. Sorry. It was before my time."

Ellie nodded, knowing that Bear wouldn't hide anything from her. If he didn't know, he didn't know.

"Don't worry." He reached across the seat and grabbed her hand in his big paw. "Kyle's not gonna let anything happen to her."

"I know."

"What is it?"

"I don't like secrets is all."

She felt Bear stiffen.

"What's wrong?" she asked.

He didn't say anything until he'd pulled into Walter's driveway and parked the truck.

"Let's get inside. We need to talk, honey." He looked straight at her and swallowed hard. "Let me start by saying, I'm sorry."

NINETEEN

Stupid, stupid, stupid.

Bear knew it the second he saw Ellie talking to her cousin. The concerned look on Ellen's face and the way that Ellie looked back at him while they talked told him that of course Ellen called Bruce Cole and asked about the trust fund money. Bear had just hoped she wouldn't get suspicious enough to look into it right away, that he'd get everything done with the cabin first. If Ellie decided to reject his money—reject him—she'd never get the job done. She wouldn't have a home, and Bear would have failed her.

But it was wrong to hide the truth from her, too. Maybe that was worse than trying to get her to agree to his generosity. He only did it this way because he didn't want to hurt her pride or risk her saying no. But that was wrong for him to do. Maybe it was his own pride he was trying to protect.

Stupid. You fucked up again. Idiot.

The best thing he could do was to come clean right away. This was his only chance to try and explain why he'd gone and made her a second trust fund. Funny that they were called that, when after tonight, she might not have any trust left in him.

Bear led the way into Walter's house. The mink blanket he'd left draped across the top of the couch mocked him now. He'd never feel his Ellie lying on it while he made love with her again. He'd never again wrap up with her in its soft warmth and hold her all night.

Ellie sat down on the couch and curled her legs under her. She leaned back against the fur and stretched out her hand to Bear. He took it as he sat down. He expected Ellie to look mad or upset, but she looked more concerned about him.

"Now," she said as she squeezed his big hand with her tiny one—a mouse's paw in a big bear paw. "What can you possibly be sorry about, Bear?"

"Ellie," he started. He took a breath, held it, and released it slowly to try and slow his racing heart. "I mighta sorta lied to you."

Her eyes rounded but she wasn't looking angry—at least not yet. "Go on."

"I did it because I love you, Ellie. I've never loved any woman like I love you, so I didn't know what to do about it. And I was stupid. I didn't think you could fall for a man like me. And I didn't want to force you to, and it might have looked like that was what I was trying to do, to force you."

She took his hand in both of hers. "Forced me to do what?" she asked quietly.

He shook his head. "Maybe not forced. Maybe buy you is a better word."

She shivered and it killed him. Just stopped his heart right then and there.

Ellie blinked and took a deep breath. "*You'd* never do that. You wouldn't." She shook her head as she spoke.

"No, I wouldn't and that's why I did what I did. But, you

might see it that way. It's the cabin. Ellie, Walter...he didn't leave you any money, just the deed."

She frowned. "But, you said..." She bit her lower lip. "I mean, all the materials, the furniture. You said there was money for it."

He nodded. "I did say that."

"So there's no money?"

"Oh, there's plenty of money, Ellie. I didn't lie about that."

"Okay, am I in debt now? Wait, are *you* in debt?" She looked devastated. "Bear? Did you take out a big loan? You shouldn't have done that, not for me, not—"

"No, honey." He grabbed her hands with both of his now and squeezed. "No loan, not for you and not for me."

"Bear, I'm really confused right now. Can you please just tell me straight—what did you do?"

Bear took one last look at his beautiful Ellie and closed his eyes. "I told Bruce Cole to set up a trust for you using my money and giving me access to it. You wouldn't know who set it up and I hoped that you'd just keep on thinking that it was from Walter, at least until we got the cabin done."

"So that's why Ellen was confused," Bear heard her say. He kept his eyes closed like a damn coward, afraid to see disgust or anger or even hatred on her face.

"She didn't see how Uncle Walter could have left me that much money," Ellie continued. "But it was *your* money. You set it all up so I wouldn't know it was from you. That's it?"

Bear nodded. "Ellie." He looked down before he opened his eyes. "I wanted to help you and I was afraid you were gonna be all stubborn about it."

"I'm not stubborn. I just don't... I don't want to owe anyone."

Bear felt her shiver again. God, what had he done? He didn't dare lift his gaze.

"It's not about owing me, Ellie. It's about me wanting to take care of a woman who I'm so crazy in love with I want to give her the world. You haven't had much kindness in your life so you don't know how to accept it."

"Bear. Please look at me."

He closed his eyes one last time, then looked up and opened them. There was no hatred in her face. No anger. Only sadness.

"I'm not happy with what you did. I want that clear."

Bear nodded, ready to take her back to the ranch, to tell her goodbye, pack his things and leave, never to show his face in Lyons again.

"You should have talked to me instead of assuming what I'd think and how I'd act."

"I know. It was wrong."

"It was. But I get that you wanted to help me and you thought I'd fight you on it. We'd only just met. I mean, as adults."

"So why did it feel like no time had passed, Ellie?" Bear asked. "I felt like I've always known you, like you've always been in my heart and I was just waiting to find you again."

Ellie's eyes watered and it killed him that he was the one who put the tears there.

"You don't know me," she whispered.

"Honey—"

"Bear, the day we met...I pointed a gun at a man that very morning. Right at his chest. If he'd kept bothering me, I would have shot him. I know I would have. And...I wouldn't have felt bad for him. I would have felt bad for *me*, that I had it in me to kill someone. But not for him. I don't know if that makes me a terrible person but it makes me *feel* terrible. Do you want to be with someone who would kill a man and not feel bad that she'd done it?"

"Honey. I could ask you the same question. You know I was a Ranger. I've killed men. And I still sleep soundly at night over it. I..." He paused and swallowed hard. "I was afraid to tell you this, but since coming here I've beaten up a man. I almost killed him and would have if...if someone hadn't stopped me."

Ellie squeezed Bear's hand. "I'm sure if you beat up a man he had it coming. Why were you afraid to tell me about it?"

"I didn't want to scare you. I know I'm big and scary—"

"Not to me, Bear. Never to me." She shook her head. "You keep asking me if I'm afraid of you. Once and for all, I've never, not for one second, been afraid of you, and I never will be. That man had to be bad for you to almost kill him. I know it. You're gentle by nature. I see it in your eyes every time I look into them. I see it in the way you care for animals, for your friends, for the cabin, for me. You're good, Bear. A *good* man. If you lose your temper it's justified, I know that in my soul. If you told me who that man was and what he did, I'm sure I'd want to kill him, too."

"You might, Ellie, if you knew. You just might."

"Then why do you think I'm afraid of you or think you're bad for trying to rid the world of garbage? Why do you think you failed Gabe when you saved his life? Bear. You're wonderful. I love you. Please. Do I have to set up a blind trust fund full of love to trick you into taking it?"

The ridiculous thought tickled both of them at the same time as they looked each other in the eye. Ellie was the first one to crack with a giggle.

"I love you, Ellie. I don't care if you pointed a gun at a man. He had it coming if he tried to hurt you." He let go of her hand to brush her cheek with his thumb and cup her face. "I *do* know you. I want to be with you. I want to stay here as long as you'll have me. Please tell me I didn't ruin my chance."

Ellie smiled, setting Bear's heart at ease. "No, you didn't. But, you can only stay on one condition."

"What's that?"

"That you understand the cabin is yours, too. It's only right that you live with me there. Because then, you've used your money to build yourself a home, too."

"Ellie, honey. I used my money to fix up a cabin, and that's all well and good. But *you* are my home, no matter where I lay my head at night." He grinned. "Thing is, I want to lay my head next to yours every single night."

Ellie grinned back. "I want that, too. I love you, Bear. You're my home, too. The day I decided I wanted to keep the cabin, it wasn't just because of the view, but because it made me feel safe."

"I remember that. It broke my heart to think it."

"Truth is, it wasn't the cabin that made me feel safe, not entirely. I've come to realize that. Now I feel safe wherever I am, so long as I'm with you. I think for the first time in my life."

"So...you forgive me for lying about the trust fund?"

"I do. So long as you promise to talk things over with me from here on out."

"I promise." Bear scooped her up and set her in his lap. Ellie grabbed the mink and he helped her wrap it around them both.

"Bear? Can I ask another question, one that might sound weird?"

He chuckled. "You can ask me anything."

"Do you really have enough money to pay for all of it? Are you tapped out? I'd feel bad if that's the case."

"Naw, honey. I still got plenty."

"You sure?"

Now he laughed. "When I call or go into my bank, which

ain't often, they remember me and call me sir. I can show you the amount I got tucked away if you want. Be happy to if it makes you feel better about what I've spent on our home."

Ellie looked up into his face. "I think the temperature just rose from your blushing." Then she snuggled into him and he thanked the stars he had a woman full of forgiveness.

The next morning Bear drove Ellie to the ranch to start her day before the sun even came up, then came back to sort out his day. He'd just finished his second cup of coffee and gotten his list of tasks squared away when there was a knock on the door. It was a heavier knock than what he was used to from Ellie and if she'd forgotten something, she would have texted him, so he was immediately on guard.

When he opened the door, Shane and Gabe were standing there grinning like fools and Bear's stomach plummeted. He knew that look.

"Yeah, what?" He growled as he let them in.

Shane laughed immediately. "Wow. So grumpy. Ellie must not be here."

"She's over at the ranch working hard, unlike two guys I know."

Gabe clapped his hand on Bear's shoulder. "Hey, I'm happy for you, man. We should all be so lucky to find a woman like her."

If it had been anyone but Gabe, Bear would have immediately shrugged off the friendly gesture. Gabe still filled him with guilt. Instead, Bear smiled and nodded.

"Yeah, she's...wonderful is not a good enough word for what Ellie is."

Shane was already halfway to the kitchen. "Don't let Gabe fool you. He's got his eye on someone," he shouted.

Bear glanced at Gabe to see if the man had heard Shane. When Gabe didn't immediately react to Shane's ribbing, guilt flooded him.

Gabe narrowed his eyes at Bear. "I see that look, Bear. Did it occur to you that I'm just not rising to our friend's bait?"

Yeah, that may be true, Bear thought. But Shane had also yelled it pretty loud—louder than necessary.

Shane reappeared carrying a mug of coffee.

"Where's mine?" Gabe asked.

"There's half a pot left. Get it yourself." Shane took a seat on the couch. "Or did you get your fill at Riversong earlier?" Shane's cocky expression told Bear he wasn't just talking about coffee.

"Speaking of women at Riversong Coffee, You could take a lesson from April on customer service next time you're attempting to flirt with her." Gabe tagged Shane on the shoulder as he made his way to the kitchen.

"What? I'm not a barista." Shane took a drink. "And who says I'm flirting?" he shouted toward the kitchen.

"Everyone with eyes and a brain, Elk," Gabe said as he returned with two steaming mugs of coffee. "But I'm the better barista." He handed one to Bear and sat down at the opposite end of the couch from Shane.

"And you've got a thing for the woman who sits by the window every morning." Shane pointed at Gabe. "Don't deny it, brother."

"So you two just come here to gossip and drink my coffee or what?" Bear asked. "I got shit to do over at the other house."

"You've got something else first," Shane said. "Couple things, actually. Rest of the pack's on their way over."

The pack. The old nickname for themselves when they were kids. Bear hadn't heard it for a long time. Mountain Division business, must be. They hadn't talked about the coach since that night. Was he still being a problem? Or were they finally going after the administrator who let the asshole get away with hurting kids?

"Kyle's coming over too," Shane added. Bear frowned. Kyle wasn't a part of this, or had they recruited him?

"Bear, just take a seat," Gabe said. "It's about Ellie and her cousin."

"What about them?" Bear's stomach tightened.

"Kyle wants to talk about it."

"Can't be good," Bear growled.

"Nope."

"Ellie say anything to you about her family?" Shane asked.

"She doesn't have to. They're bad news." The time that Bear had tried to bring them up after Ellie first told them about stealing the bike, she had physically shrunk into herself and he stopped asking immediately. It was on the way up to the cabin and he'd been afraid she would open the passenger door and jump out, so he stopped talking and turned up the radio until she relaxed again.

"I remember when Arnold caught that little brown bat in the woods out behind Walter's house here," Gabe said as he stared into his coffee.

Shane shook his head. "That night was messed up."

Finally, the bad memory Bear had been fighting surfaced and he actually fought to keep himself from shaking with growing rage.

"Arnold didn't let it go."

The other two men looked up suddenly. "What?" Shane said.

Bear shook his head at the bad memory. "After we were all running around in the woods with a flashlight trying to see the bats in the trees."

"Trying to impress the girls," Gabe said.

Bear nodded. God help him, now that he was digging that dirty old memory out of his head, he remembered that there were two younger girls tagging along—Arden and Elinor. His Ellie.

Come on, bitches. Keep up!

Arnold's fifteen-year-old voice had echoed through the woods and now again in Bear's mind. He'd hated that Arnold called them that—called his own little sister such an ugly word. But as a twelve-year-old at the time, Bear hadn't yet grown into his body. He'd even lost weight at the beginning of the summer, not realizing he was just starting a growth spurt that wouldn't end until he was big enough to have college coaches coming to his high school football games when he was a defensive lineman, hoping to recruit him.

No. Bear had been small and scrawny back in those night woods when they'd gone bat hunting and Arnold was being a complete dick and his brother was no better and the worst was yet to come.

"Arnold only said he let the little critter go. But he didn't," Bear said. He suppressed a shudder. "I didn't trust him—"

"None of us did," Shane interrupted.

"So I followed after him back into the woods when he said he was gonna let it go." Bear realized he was mumbling when he saw Gabe's brows pulled down in concentration. *Fuck.* "I followed Arnold back into the woods to make sure he was gonna keep his promise," he said louder.

"I remember that now," Gabe said.

They'd just wanted to see the bats, not hurt them. Bats were cool—all animals were cool to Bear. But Arnold had blinded a bat in a tree with his flashlight and thrown a rock at it. The bat fell and Arnold went running after it. He caught the bat to try and scare the girls with it.

I'll let it get all tangled up in your hair he'd threatened. But instead of being scared of the bat, they'd been scared *for* it.

Please let it go, Arnold. Bear remembered Ellie pleading, tears in her eyes. *Don't hurt it.* She couldn't have been older than six, maybe seven, and such a tiny little thing standing up to her bully of a brother even then. He laughed at her and kept laughing when the other girls begged him to let it go. Bear joined the protesting along with Shane, Waylon, Elias, and Sean but it only made Arnold more adamant to keep it. Harlan was no help, standing there watching the whole thing and laughing along with his older brother. The perfect toady.

Ben was the one who finally got Arnold to quit and make the promise to let it go. Ben, who'd always been big for his age, the one who got called Moose at school and not in a good way. He was quiet so people thought he was stupid, but they were the stupid ones. Ben was smart, real smart. He took that nickname and made it his. He started the idea of them all as a pack with animal names and he knew his friends had his back when he stood up to Arnold.

Let it go, Arnold. Ben was two years younger than Arnold but towered over him. Bear wasn't sure if it was Ben's height or the fact that he was speaking for once that made Arnold stop teasing the girls.

Fine, I will, if you're gonna be a pussy about it. Arnold turned and stalked away into the woods. The other kids wanted to leave him there so they turned to go back to Sean and Arden's house.

Bear didn't. He sneaked away after Arnold to make sure the bastard kept his promise.

"What happened, Bear?" Shane asked.

Bear pinched the bridge of his nose as the memories grew clearer. He'd pushed that night down so deep that he'd completely forgotten the quiet voice behind him.

Don't. Please don't go after him. He'll hurt you, too.

Ellie's voice trying to keep Bear from harm.

He should have stopped and comforted the little girl instead of going after Arnold and the bat. But hindsight was everything and twelve-year-old boys from families who loved and cared for them didn't know that there were little girls whose families were nothing but a world of pain and suffering. He didn't stop to think that Ellie knew Arnold would try to hurt Bear because that's what he did to Ellie on the regular.

I'll be all right. You go with the others he'd told Ellie. And he'd left her there.

Standing in Walter's living room, shame coursed through his veins. Shame, and the sense of having lost something good he never even realized could have been his all this time. What if he'd listened to her? What if they'd talked more that night, maybe become pen pals after that? He could have saved her long ago...

"Bear?" Gabe said. "You don't need to relive this, brother, if it's dredging up old shit better left alone."

Bear cleared his throat, a gravelly sound. "No. You gotta know what he is and what he's been for a long fucking time now." He leveled his gaze at his friends—his pack. "He's a sick fucking monster." Bear wouldn't let himself remember those details. He'd seen enough pain and torture in his lifetime and somehow, suffering animals always hit him harder. "I was too late to save the bat. He'd...done things to it. All I'm gonna say."

Gabe nodded. "All you need to say, Bear."

"Son of a bitch," Shane murmured.

"Said if I ratted him out, he'd do the same to me. He liked hurting things. But I couldn't stay quiet. I told Walter the next day. Everything. Walter promised he'd keep it secret, who told him. He went out back and found what was left of that poor little critter himself, so he didn't even need to say anyone'd told him about it. He must have talked to Ellie's mom or showed her or something, because they left that night." Bear rubbed his face. "If I hadn't said anything—"

"Then you'd be as bad as some of the men we go after, "Gabe said, putting his hand on Bear's shoulder. "You would have been protecting a monster."

"But I ended up putting a little girl in more danger."

"Bear, you were just a little kid. Kids shouldn't have to be the protectors. It was the adults who failed to protect her. So, dump that guilt right now. Ellie's here now, She's safe. You're seeing to that. We all are."

An SUV pulled into the driveway and Bear heard several people get out. By his count, there were five—most likely Kyle and the rest of the pack. He went to the door to let them in.

"Mornin' Bear," Kyle said. Camo stood at his feet wagging his tail and watching Bear. "Ellie at the ranch already? I've been at the office."

Bear only nodded then bent to pet Camo. "Good boy." *Nothing like a dog to chase off a bad memory.*

The rest of the men filed in and Bear was right—it was the entire pack plus Badger, which made him curious. Badger had become best friends with Sean as a Swick and had come to Lyons when Kyle offered him a job, but Bear wasn't sure what he was doing here now.

Bear went to the kitchen to empty the rest of the coffee into mugs and start another pot while they made themselves comfortable. While he was in the kitchen, Alex and Sylvie showed up. Sylvie was an officer out of Boulder but was on hiatus, something to do with trouble over the past summer, and he wondered if there was some connection with Badger.

"What's up?" Bear growled a few minutes later as he handed the last mug of coffee to Ben.

Kyle scratched Camo's head while he spoke.

"First, Ellen's home and safe in Arizona. I'm getting updates from Charlie. She says it wasn't much of a burglary." He looked at Alex and Sylvie. "They took a couple little things, a mason jar full of change sitting on her desk. They mostly went through her office. Went right past her bedroom and a jewelry box sitting on her dresser."

Sylvie shook her head. "Even if they got interrupted, they'd hit her bedroom first looking for jewelry and electronics." She paused, looking like she'd taken a bite out of a sour lemon. "You're thinking Capitoline."

"Affirmative, that's what's got me worried. We've always known they might come back. They can't hit us here, so they might be going after her in Arizona."

Capitoline. Bear had heard the name. Like he'd told Ellie, he didn't know all the details, but they were some huge group that Watchdog and his own pack had tangled with. Sylvie and Alex must have been part of that mess.

"Looking for what?" Alex asked. "It's been a while since she was in their sights."

"Don't know. Ellen said they'd gone through her files but nothing was taken. She didn't have anything important, just receipts, bills, the usual. She alerted her credit card companies in case they were going for credit card numbers, but there wasn't any unusual activity. Either the assholes were slow trying to charge shit on it or they weren't after that. I've asked her to send me copies of everything in case I'm missing something. Charlie's staying out there until I'm sure the coast is clear."

"She need backup?" Badger asked.

"Not from us. Home office in Los Angeles sent a man. They got their own troubles with Capitoline and want to keep an eye on this just in case." He looked at every person in the room one by one. "You all helped Watchdog last time and I'm forever grateful."

"That goes double for me," Alex said, putting his arm around Sylvie who was also nodding.

"I wouldn't be here," she added. "God knows what would have happened to me without you all. Thank you."

Badger raised his mug. "Same goes for Brianna and she'd say thank you if she were here."

"It's what we do," Ben said. "What we'll do again if you need us."

Kyle nodded his thanks. "We're here for you all too, brother. I'm telling you to watch your backs, just in case. Anything looks suspicious or goes sideways, let us know." He looked at Sylvie. "I let George know already." Bear knew George was the sergeant for Lyons and Sylvie's adopted father.

Sylvie took a last swig of her coffee and stood up with her eyes on the kitchen. Bear straightened up.

"I'll get you more coffee, Sylvie."

She smiled and shook her head. "Thanks, but I'm out. I'm on leave from the department but there are some things coming up I probably shouldn't hear. Plausible deniability." She went into the kitchen and Bear heard water running in the sink as she washed the mug.

"Telling you," Kyle said when she came back in the room, "you've got a job waiting at Watchdog if you want it."

She grinned at him, then looked at Alex who'd stood. "I'm thinking it over. I would like my new co-workers there," she winked at Alex, "but I think my partner would kill me."

"Kill you?" Alex chuckled. "She'd probably follow you."

"Gentlemen, we'll leave you to it," Sylvie said as Alex opened the front door.

"See you at the kennels," Kyle told Alex. Then he turned his attention back to the rest of the men—Bear, Gabe, Shane, Elias, Waylon, Ben, and Badger.

"Got some more intel on Ellie's brothers," Kyle started, looking at Bear. He nodded back and braced himself. "Looks like they've been engaging in a lot more than farming. They're running a fencing operation that's spread over three states. And they're growing more meth than corn on their land. They're tied up with this son of a bitch." Kyle opened a folder and passed a sheet of paper around with a man's mug shots on it. When Elias handed him the sheet, Bear burned the man's face into his brain. He was big, probably worked out but to build bulk, not cuts. Dirty blond mullet. Bloodshot eyes, but there was some intelligence in them. No soul though—that was obvious.

"Name's Tibbs Hackett," Kyle said. "Family's in law enforcement but old Tibbs here just has to be different. We're looking into his cousins, too. One's a state trooper, one is a sheriff. A couple of complaints lodged against the trooper but that could mean anything. Tibbs and Arnold seem to be working together, but something tells me Tibbs has the upper hand." Kyle grinned. "That something is the difference in their bank accounts. I'd say Arnold is in to Tibbs for at least a hundred grand."

"For what?" Bear asked.

"Well, they ain't farming much these days. Arnold sold off the equipment, but the land's still mortgaged to the gills. I imagine Tibbs loaned Arnold money for leverage and now he's set up shop on the farm. Great spot—it's out in the middle of nowhere. I've got some satellite photos here and we can play a game of Spot the Meth Lab without too much effort."

Bear suppressed a shudder thinking of Ellie living in a place like that.

"Here's Arnold these days." Kyle passed around another page. Bear grabbed it from Elias and looked into the face of the man who loved to torture anything smaller and weaker than him.

The scrawny kid that Bear had been, *that* kid expected to see someone bigger than him looking out from the photo, but that wasn't the case. Arnold wasn't small, but he wasn't as big as Bear was now. He looked old before his time like he'd lived rough, and there was a meanness to his face that had only gotten worse in the passing years.

"And finally, we have Harlan," Kyle said. "He's Tibbs' cooker." Kyle handed that photo around. Harlan was missing half his teeth and his face looked sunken in. His skin was gray and covered in sores. He was skinny, and something about him made Bear think of a spider. It was obvious he got high off his own supply. Bear spared him a second of pity—he'd never had much of a chance living in Arnold's shadow.

Then again, neither did Ellie, but she turned out just fine.

"We'll be keeping an eye out," Kyle said, "just in case they decide to come to town. Bear, Ellie hasn't said anything more about them?"

Bear shook his head. "No. They haven't tried getting in touch. Haven't seen 'em either. When she left, she tried to throw them off her trail. Mighta worked, but I'm not counting on it working forever."

"You got the security system set up in the cabin?"

"Yup. Was hoping I could tie it up to Watchdog's today."

"Affirmative. Anything you both need."

Ben handed Kyle the photos. "We appreciate this."

Kyle stood up and Camo got to his feet. "Anything we can do. Badger, we'd better get back to Watchdog."

Once Kyle and Badger had left, Ben started in. "Well, we have one bit of good news. The school administrator is stepping down."

"So we don't need to pay him a visit?" Shane asked.

"Not this time, according to my contact. She says to give it another couple of days though just to make sure it isn't just talk."

"She?" Elias asked. "You know our contact?"

Ben frowned. "That's all I'm saying. She's risked a lot to help us and I'm not too keen you all know she's a she. I won't tell you anything else about her."

"Fair enough," Waylon said. "But does she know who we are?"

"No. What we're doing isn't exactly above board—"

"But it's righteous," Shane said. "It's justice."

Ben gave him a long look before he nodded. He turned his gaze on to Bear. "So. I take it circumstances are changing for you?"

Bear nodded. "They are."

"What about your plans? Are you sticking around this time?"

Every man in the room stared at Bear.

"I am. For Ellie."

"And if *we* need you?"

"I'm here, brother," he told Ben.

"You one of us?" Shane asked.

Bear looked from one man to the next around the room. His brothers. His pack.

"Always."

TWENTY

Arnold was scrolling through Colorado property listings on his phone—his new hobby—when the call came through from Tibbs.

"Yeah?"

"She's not there," Tibbs said.

So Elinor wasn't staying with their bitch cousin in Arizona. Another dead end, or were they one step closer to finding her?

"They find anything?" Arnold didn't have much faith in the men Tibbs had sent to break into Ellen's house.

"They got interrupted, but yeah, they did."

That surprised him.

Tibbs continued. "They found a printed out copy of a plane ticket. Ellen's back visiting in Colorado for a week."

"Interesting timing," Arnold said as he began to pace his bedroom. Outside the window, he watched his idiot brother walking along the old dirt tractor path that led to the trailer where he cooked all day and into the night for weeks on end.

"I thought so too," Tibbs said. "So, I had my people look at some footage there."

"Footage?" Arnold knew Tibbs had law enforcement connections so it could be anything.

"I'm done talking. Check your email." Tibbs disconnected.

"Shit," Arnold swore as he crossed the room to his laptop. Tibbs hated saying anything over the phone for fear it was being picked up by the ATF or DEA or fucking E.T. The bastard was super paranoid. But then again, like the old saying went—it ain't paranoia if they're really after you.

Arnold opened his browser. He wasn't stupid enough to use one of the main ones—everyone knew those were monitored—and checked his email. Tibbs had sent him an attachment which he quickly downloaded. He opened the video file and watched the footage.

And as he watched, he smiled.

The footage was grainy and the lens was dirty and smeared, but he knew exactly who was sitting on that bench, digging into a bike bag. He watched as a man approached her and started talking. It didn't take a genius to know what the guy wanted. Fuck, if he'd taken Elinor and was pimping her out in some Denver back alley, he could keep her. Tibbs wouldn't even want her then. Damaged goods. Fuck, with Elinor gone, how was Arnold supposed to pay—

His thoughts screeched to a halt when his little sister pulled out the gun and pointed it at the pimp. Arnold actually laughed when the big pussy turned tail and ran. Elinor pointed the gun after him for a second before she put it away again.

"God damn. Didn't know you had it in you, you little bitch."

But her hands shook as she hid the gun, and she moved like a little rat that just wanted to scamper away into a dark corner and hide. Oh yeah, Arnold had seen that behavior before. He recognized when something was weak and scared but defending itself anyway.

In Arnold's experience, those pathetic little animals were always fun to play with and they always lost.

He watched Elinor squirm into his stolen backpack and take off on his stolen bike with his stolen gun until she was out of the frame and the video ended.

Well. At least he knew where she'd been a few weeks ago. Chances were good, old Ellen went out to meet with her. But why?

Arnold closed the video. He noticed that Tibbs had also attached a PDF file. Arnold opened it and smiled again.

Police were looking for any information about a mysterious woman who pulled a gun on a man at the Denver Greyhound bus station.

Arnold could give them plenty of information if it came down to that.

If Elinor refused to turn over whatever she'd inherited. Because Arnold was positive now that she must have gotten something out of old Uncle Walter. And he had a good idea of what it was.

Arnold went back to his phone and the listings. Uncle Walter's land wasn't for sale and he was tired of waiting to see if it would go up. He knew which parcel it was now from looking up old public records. So if his cousin Ellen wasn't selling the property, then maybe she was doing something else with it. Maybe he just needed to expand his net.

Yeah, this might require him going out there and taking a look around himself.

But not alone.

Arnold made his plans.

TWENTY-ONE

"Repeat after me, honey. I'm not afraid of anything."

"I'm not afraid of anything."

"Now, hold your breath. Aim. And pull."

Bam. The glass bottle exploded on the old tree stump.

Ellie beamed as she lowered the rifle. "I hit it!"

You sure did, honey."

Ellie felt giddy as Bear put his arm around her and pulled her close. This was their third shooting lesson in a week. Just because Ellie had a gun didn't mean she knew how to use it. No one had ever taught her to shoot—about the only smart decision Arnold had ever made, Ellie thought. She shivered. No, she didn't have it in her to shoot anyone, despite what she'd told Bear about the pimp at the bus station. In the end, she couldn't have shot him.

She still didn't tell him that, even though he was teaching her how to handle both long guns and handguns. He wanted her to be able to defend herself when he wasn't around. He used the excuse that there were real bears in the mountains, and moose and lions too. If she wanted to walk her land, she needed to be able to defend herself if she was alone.

Not that he'd given her a moment to herself since Ellen left. He'd finished up the odd jobs on Watchdog's safehouses, installed the last security system, and now he spent his days at the ranch, helping her with her job and getting underfoot.

She didn't mind that. She loved having him near. What she did mind, was that he was sticking close because—despite what *he* said—he was afraid. Afraid that Arnold would show up any minute. No one said it out loud, but Ellie knew.

"Let's switch to the handgun now," Bear said as she handed him the rifle. He set the rifle on a foldout table they'd set up close to the lake—Ellie wanted their shooting lessons far enough away from the cabin that the shots wouldn't scare away Spot, who'd made himself at home under the deck with her blessing—and handed her the revolver.

"Make sure the safety's on first," Bear told her.

Ellie frowned at his perfectly straight face until he cracked a smile.

"Just because I asked *one time* about the safety on a revolver doesn't mean I haven't learned my lesson," she told him.

"I know, honey. It's just cute to see you screw your face up at me like that."

Ellie rolled her eyes.

"And I'm trying to get you to laugh and relax," he added. "You're doing great. Now, show me how you check the chambers."

Despite Bear trying to set her at ease, Ellie still wasn't entirely comfortable with the gun. She pressed the cylinder release—the button she'd thought was a safety the first time Bear showed her the gun—and it swung out to the side. It was fully loaded. She pushed it back into place and cocked the hammer. She started to aim at one of the beer bottles on a closer stump when Bear stopped her.

"Guns still scare you."

She set the revolver on the table, remembering how she'd pointed Arnold's gun at that man, hoping that there were no repercussions.

"Yeah, they do." She sighed. "Are you disappointed in me?"

"Never, honey. Come here." He opened his arms and she happily hugged him, pressing her cheek against his chest.

"Arnold held a gun to my head once." The words popped out of her mouth without her realizing they were right there, waiting to be heard. "I was in bed one night, sound asleep and he came into my bedroom. I woke feeling the tip of the barrel against my forehead. He told me he was the one who decided if I lived or died and to never forget that. Then he walked out and didn't say a word about it the next morning. We never talked about it, but we didn't have to. He'd made himself clear."

While she spoke, Bear's body stiffened. She looked up at him. "It's not that I'm afraid of guns themselves. Just..." She stopped, not sure what she was trying to say.

Bear brushed her cheek, his beautiful eyes full of love and understanding despite her inability to explain herself.

"Thank you for telling me that, honey. That was brave."

She shrugged. "It's easy to be brave with you right here, Bear."

His chest rumbled as he closed his eyes. Then he opened them again as his lips curved into a gentle smile.

"I want for you to be brave all the time, Ellie. No—I take that back. Being brave means you're scared and doing the right thing anyway, which means you've already been brave all your life. I want you fearless. That's why I'm teaching you self-defense. I love that you feel safe with me, honey, I do. That means the world to me. But I want you to feel safe because you know you can defend yourself."

"It's not about wild animals, is it? You think he's coming for me, don't you?" Ellie whispered.

Bear's eyes turned sad. "Honey, I think it's only a matter of time." He stroked her face. "I want to know you'll be safe even if I'm not here, but more than that—I don't want you living in fear."

"I can't shoot my brother." There. She said it. All his teaching was for nothing. Her heart raced.

"Don't expect you to. That's not what defending yourself is about. I want you brave up here." He tapped her forehead. "So that when you do face him, you know that you hold your own life in your hands now."

Her heart settled at Bear's reassuring words. She nodded. "We're not afraid of anything."

"No, babe. We're not."

Ellie's phone started buzzing. She picked it up off the table and looked at it. "That's the alarm. We've got to pack up and get going if we want to go out with the others." She smiled up at him only to find he looked nervous.

No, that couldn't be right.

"What's wrong?"

"Nothing." He turned to gather up the guns and put them in their cases. Ellie helped him put everything away and carry the guns back to the cabin, then they headed for Bear's truck and Walter's house. Bear had started on the plumbing but it would take a few more weeks to finish it—something Bear wanted to do before winter set in. In the meantime, they showered at the safehouse and spent the night there if Ellie had to work early.

Speaking of winter Ellie thought as she watched out the

window. Both the days and nights had turned cold and snow was predicted for the next week. She worried about how she was going to get to and from Arden's ranch for work if she got snowed in this winter. Even a truck would be challenging to drive over logging roads if the weather got bad. And she and Bear couldn't expect to stay at Walter's house anytime they wanted once it became a safehouse.

"Whatcha thinking?" Bear asked her.

"Oh, just looking ahead to winter. Things might get complicated." She told him her worries. "I might need to find work closer to the cabin, or figure out how I can work from home."

Bear grinned. "I've got some ideas myself about that."

"Really?" She brightened.

"Yeah, honey." There was that blush again. Something was definitely up. "We'll talk it over later." He pulled into Walter's driveway. "Time to get ready."

"Think we have enough time to play in the shower?" she teased.

He turned redder. "I think they can live without us if we show up a little late."

Bear's hands covered Ellie's body as water coursed down her skin.

"I love your freckles," he murmured against her skin. "My own private constellations." He ran his finger from one freckle to the next, tracing patterns only he could make out. She had always been self-conscious about her freckles, but with Bear, she felt beautiful and accepted.

She moved against him as his hands caressed her body in gentle circles. The warm water flowed over them, enveloping them in warmth. Her heart raced as his lips brushed against her neck, sending shivers all the way to her toes. His kisses grew more passionate. She closed her eyes and let out a soft moan as he continued to explore her body with his hands and lips. With each touch, she felt more alive and free in his arms.

"God, Bear," she whispered. "I want you."

"Ellie," Bear groaned, leaning his forehead against hers. "I want you more."

He lifted Ellie up. Her legs wrapped around his waist. He pressed her against the shower wall as he entered her in one swift motion. Ellie cried out as the sensation of him filling her completely overwhelmed her.

Bear began to move, his thrusts slow and deliberate, each one hitting her in just the right spot.

"I love you, Bear."

"Love you, Ellie."

Ellie's body began to tremble. Bear reached down to rub between her legs, slowly, then faster, perfectly matching her heat and giving her exactly what she wanted.

"Now, honey," Bear groaned. "Take it now."

He sent her over the edge as she cried out his name. Ellie felt weightless, like she was lost among the stars. Moments later, Bear followed her, his release filling her up as he shouted her name.

Breathless and sated, Ellie leaned her head on Bear's shoulder.

"I could stay here forever," she murmured, then kissed his warm, wet skin.

Bear smiled and kissed her forehead. "Forever sounds good." He kissed her one last time, then turned off the water and carried her out of the shower. He set her down carefully on the tiled floor, grabbed a towel, and wrapped her up.

As they got ready for the evening, Ellie watched Bear do

something new. He grabbed a bottle out of the medicine cabinet and poured oil into his hand. Bear smoothed down his beard in the mirror. The oil made the hair shine and it smelled good, like sandalwood and cedar. Like him.

"I didn't know you cared what you looked like," she teased.

"I don't know about the other guys tonight, but when you and me are out together, I want you to feel proud and happy walking beside me, so that means I gotta not look like a slob." He turned away from the mirror.

She looked at herself in the mirror, at her jeans and her oatmeal-colored Henley shirt with the waffle weave. "You don't have to do that. I'm not girly, Bear. I'm not that pretty. I'm plain and small and dull."

"Hey, now, where's this coming from? You're beautiful. You're so damn beautiful you put every other woman to shame every time you smile."

"But they're so...I don't know. They know how to dress up and look really good. I don't. I'm not fancy like that. And sometimes I worry that you'll look at me, then look at one of them, and I won't even come close."

Bear laid his hands on her shoulders and stroked down her arms.

"Baby, I'd never. I don't need some girly-girl, you know? You don't need to be all dressed up for me. When I look at you, I can hardly breathe sometimes, thinking that you want to be with me." He gestured down his body. "I'm not fancy like that, either. I'm rough and shaggy. Some guys clean up good, but I'm not one of them." He tugged his beard. "I didn't know you were supposed to oil these things up until recently."

She covered her mouth—really, she covered the smile trying to turn her lips up. "Who told you that, anyway?"

"Gabe and Shane. They took me aside and said I was

gonna rough your skin up if I didn't put some oil in my beard to soften it up." He pulled his fingers through the coarse black hair. "Said I needed some nice shirts, too, if I wanted to not embarrass you when we went out."

Ellie rolled her eyes. "But, you've never embarrassed me, Bear. I think you're handsome. I always have, from the moment I laid eyes on you."

His eyes softened. "You weren't ever scared of me." At least now, he wasn't asking her, but confirming the truth.

"No, never, Bear. Not for a second was I scared of you."

He opened his arms, a look of wonder on his face. She stepped into them and their warm embrace.

"As a matter of fact, you make me feel brave," she said against his chest. "And strong. Not afraid of anything."

E ventually, Ellie and Bear caught up with everyone else. Ellie laughed when she saw the sign over the building on the outskirts of Lyons.

"Seriously?" she laughed. The sign depicted a chicken and rooster dancing in neon.

"Yeah. This place has been here forever. We used to try and sneak in after their restaurant hours when we were in high school. They just laughed at our fake IDs and sent us home. It's just twenty-one and up after nine at night."

Ellie read the sign aloud. "Chicken Strips and Cocktails. Gosh, what do they serve, I wonder?" She laughed.

"Steak and beer," Bear said with such a straight face Ellie thought he was serious for a minute. She was still getting used to Bear joking around. She had a feeling he was still getting used to it too. She laughed again as he got out of the truck and went around to open her door and help her down.

"They must serve some good steak and beer, judging from the parking lot." It was nearly full. She recognized some of the vehicles as belonging to their friends. The air smelled heavenly of fried chicken though, and made her mouth water. Bear laid his big paw across the small of her back and led her across the parking lot. The air was downright chilly but inside the restaurant-turned-dancehall, it was near sweltering. The music hit them along with the heat. Ellie realized the place was much bigger inside than it looked outside, as she watched people line dancing toward the back. They quickly spotted their friends at a group of tables near the dance floor and wove their way through the crowd.

"Hey! Glad you finally made it," Arden teased as she hugged Ellie. She caught a server's attention across the room, then held up three fingers and pointed to Ellie and Bear. The server nodded and sped off toward the kitchen.

"And that's how you order food," Arden explained. "Because they only serve—"

"Chicken strips," Ellie said.

"Steak," Bear said at the same time as he nudged her.

"What about the cocktails?" Ellie asked. The bar along one wall was beyond well-stocked.

"See, that's why they only serve chicken strips." Arden grabbed what looked like a leather-bound novel off the table. "This monster is the cocktail menu. You'll be too exhausted to figure out what you want to eat after deciding what you want to drink so they made it easy."

"Wow." Ellie opened the menu. It was drinks all the way down. "Where do I even start?"

"Depends on what you want. It's divided up like chapters. "There's speakeasy drinks, Tiki drinks, bourbon cocktails, martinis. Anything you're in the mood for." Arden pointed to her glass. "I'm feeling Tiki tonight, so I'm drinking a Coconut Knockout."

"Yeah, I think I'll have that, too," Ellie said, closing the menu. What are you getting, Bear?"

"Same," he answered quickly.

Ellie did a double take. "You're getting a Tiki drink?"

"Yeah. Surprised?"

"Very."

"Best drink here, from what I remember. I can have a beer anywhere. There are still like a hundred beers to choose from anyway and I got better things to think about," Bear said. He bent to kiss Ellie.

The server returned with three baskets of chicken strips and set them down—two for Bear and one for Ellie. She took their drink orders and sped off again. Bear grabbed one of many bottles of sauces from the center of the table. Ellie read the label—hot honey. No surprise there. Ellie grabbed another one that sounded tasty—sweet barbeque. The drinks came and they were good. Ellie shrugged off all her worries.

"You wanna dance?" Bear asked. Arden had already joined Kyle on the dancefloor.

"You dance?" she asked.

Bear only nodded.

Ellie grinned. Bear was full of surprises tonight.

"Then let's do it."

She laid her hand in his and he led her to their friends who had already lined up for the next line dance. Ellie hoped she knew this one—she hadn't been given many chances to dance growing up but she'd watched videos and practiced steps in her room.

The music started and Ellie quickly caught on. What surprised her was how good Bear was at dancing. He was downright graceful. His friends cheered him on. Ellie couldn't remember the last time she'd had so much fun.

The next dance was a slow one, and Bear bent close to her ear.

"Can I have this dance?"

"Of course." She took his offered hand and he pulled her in close. She'd always been told to 'leave room for Jesus' during a slow dance, but she figured Jesus would understand if he got squeezed out a little. As they danced, Bear led her off to the side where the floor wasn't quite so crowded. The music ended and he bent to kiss her.

So Ellie thought.

She was surprised when Bear kept dropping. Until he was down on one knee.

Ellie covered her mouth. "Bear, what are you doing?" she asked through her fingers. She was vaguely aware of other people gathering around them in a circle. The music had stopped or was that her imagination?

Bear gripped her hand and looked up into her eyes. "Ellie," he said, and his voice cracked on her name. "I'm not romantic. I'm rough, I'm shaggy, I'm sometimes kinda gruff. But I love you. I love you so much, Ellie. You changed my life. I wanna settle down with you. I want to live with you up in the mountains, and stargaze with you, and fish and hunt and..." She watched the color creep into his cheeks. "I want to have a family with you. I promise I'll do everything I can to make you happy. So, will you marry me?"

She couldn't speak. The room blurred and then her tears fell. Bear reached up and brushed them away.

"Didn't mean to make you cry, honey."

"Happy tears only," she said. And then, "Yes, Bear. I would love to marry you."

Bear's eyes looked glassy as he blinked quickly. Then they

widened. "Damn, almost forgot." He reached into his pocket and pulled out a little box. He opened it and gave Ellie the most beautiful ring she'd ever seen. When he put it on her finger, their friends cheered. He stood up, and Ellie was vaguely aware of the DJ talking over the speakers. Bear hugged her, and then someone pulled her away from him.

"They made me do it here," Bear said, pointing at Shane, Ben, Gabe and the rest.

Brianna had Ellie by the arm and dragged her to the middle of the dancefloor while every woman in the place circled them.

"It's tradition," Brianna explained, then kissed her cheek and joined the other women in their circle while the DJ continued his announcement.

"Hey, chicks and cocks! Say congratulations to Ellie and Jon on their engagement and clear the way for the fiancée's dance."

Oh, Lord. Please, please, please just tell me I don't have to do the Chicken Dance in front of everyone.

Ellie started laughing with relief when the next song came on. Abba's "Dancing Queen." She continued to laugh-cry as the women danced around her in a circle, everyone singing at the top of their lungs.

"Love you, Ellie!" Arden shouted.

"Love you, too," Brianna added. Then Harper and Jodie. When the dancing was done, everyone converged on her for hugs. Several women introduced themselves and welcomed her to town. Suddenly Ellie had a hundred new friends.

By the time she left with Bear, Ellie could hardly keep her eyes open. She'd never been so exhausted and so happy in her life.

Her engagement ring twinkled on her hand like the North Star.

TWENTY-TWO

A week later, the night brought snow and fall set in for real. Ellie stirred in bed and opened her eyes. They'd stayed in the cabin that night, since Bear had overseen one crew repointing the chimney and another crew working on the well the day before, and both jobs ran late. The good news was, the chimney was done, and the crew working on the well didn't have to dig deeper, just hydrofrack it—whatever that meant—and now the cabin had clean running water in the kitchen again. There was a temporary tank to catch the water until the septic tank installation was finished, probably by early next week.

Through all the renovations, Bear's friends had come up to help or just watch in wonder as the place went from a ramshackle little cabin to a cute and sturdy house. At one point, Ellie took Ben aside to ask how much money he was spending. Bear wouldn't give her a straight answer, just told her not to worry, so she decided she'd ask one of his oldest friends.

"So, does Bear really have the money to do all this, do you think?"

Ben had just grinned, nodded, and walked away, which was about the best conversation she could expect out of the quiet man. And it completely reassured her.

Bear already had most of the new bathroom plumbing in place and the toilet, shower, and sink installed in the former bedroom downstairs. The generator provided the electricity they needed for now and with the new solar array going in soon, they wouldn't need to hook up to the power grid unless they wanted to. Once the septic tank was in, they could move into the cabin full-time.

They'd finally be in their home.

Which was wonderful—except the thought of driving to and from the ranch down the mountain and through the snow all winter for work made her uneasy. She'd shared her worries with Bear a few days ago and he said he had some ideas brewing. Last night, he said they could talk about it today.

Bear stirred, already awake. He gave Ellie a sleepy smile and a kiss on the forehead that led to so many other things, as his kisses almost always did. After they made love, Ellie cooked breakfast. She made an extra batch of biscuits since bear's friends were due within the hour to get a little fishing in before the lake froze over.

While she cooked, Bear checked his phone messages. Ellie still needed to get into that habit. Bear had programmed in the numbers of all his friends as a precaution, with the instructions that if anything happened, to call Ben, Shane, or Waylon first since they lived the closest. She'd added all her new friends to the contacts along with Ellen. She'd been in touch with her cousin, who sent Charlie back to Watchdog after a couple of days. The police didn't know who had broken in and just blamed bored teenagers. Ellen was excited about Ellie's engagement and was sad she missed the night Bear proposed. She was making up for it by helping Ellie plan the wedding for next spring.

"So," Ellie said. "You ready to talk about those ideas that have been brewing, Bruin?"

Bear chuckled at her joke as he put away a plate he'd just dried. "I think I am. Let's go walk in the woods before the pack gets here."

"Brrr," Ellie said, looking out the window above the sink at the snow on the ground around the cabin. She knew despite the cold, the sun would melt it by early afternoon.

"We'll be under the trees. Not much snow there and no wind." He wrapped his arm around her. "If you get cold, just let me know and I'll warm you up."

She kissed him. "Sounds good to me."

Ellie put on her warmest new sweater, leggings, and hiking boots. As she grabbed her coat, Bear handed her something else he didn't let her leave the house without these days —a handgun in a shoulder holster. Bear set the alarm beside the door—the security system had been his priority and was tied in to Watchdog—and they stepped out onto the cold porch.

"You think Spot's okay?" she asked him.

"Spot's sound asleep under the porch," Bear answered. "He's a happy little skunk. They don't quite hibernate but the cold slows 'em down. We'll leave some food out for him."

They walked into the aspens which had dropped most of their leaves and on into the pine tree forest. Bear had been right—there was almost no snow on the ground and the trees blocked any wind, but they also blocked out direct sunlight. The bushes underneath still held most of their leaves. It was darker, but as long as she was with Bear, Ellie felt safe.

"So, I was thinking," Bear started. "Just on the other side of these trees there's a meadow, a big one. It connects to the one around the lake, then on up that ridge on the other side of the stream. It'd be good grazing land."

Ellie cocked her head. "For sheep? Goats?"

Bear grinned. "Naw. Think bigger."

"Um. I'm not buying a herd of cattle."

Bear laughed. "What? You don't wanna be like Arden's great, great grandma Nancy and steal some cattle out of Nebraska?"

Ellie laughed. "Don't let her hear you call her great-great granny a cattle rustler." She was joking—Arden was the first to brag that she was descended from full-time madame and part-time cattle rustler Nancy Satin, who she swore haunted the ranch. "All the same, I'm not raising cattle."

"Not cattle, honey. Buffalo."

Ellie stopped. "Buffalo?"

"Yeah, babe. I've been talking to a cousin of mine back east. He's looking for a place to put some of his money. He's got this romantic idea of the west—coyotes, antelope, buffalo. He's had this idea of buying a herd of buffalo and keeping them somewhere out west. Like, return them to their natural environment."

"So, how often would he want to come and visit them?"

Bear chuckled. "Don't think he's ever been outside of New York City."

"What? They won't let him keep his buffalo in Central Park?"

Bear grinned. "I'm serious, honey. Could be a good deal for you. He'd rent all this land and all we'd have to do is watch them do their thing. I'd put up some barriers so we don't have them grazing up close to the cabin. It'd be real pretty, Ellie. And I could build tiny houses off in the trees near the lake. We could run a little B&B up here, or fishing retreats. Whatever you want. Means we wouldn't have to commute down to town if we didn't feel like it. Just watch the buffalo roam."

How could she resist those gorgeous eyes pleading with her? *He's just an oversized Saint Francis* she thought. And buffalo *would* look really cool grazing by the lake or on the ridge.

"Okay, Bear. Call your—"

Bear raised a finger to his lips and looked around. Ellie's stomach clenched as the rest of her body went on high alert. They'd done this before—gone out for a walk only to have Bear stop and check their surroundings, even in Lyons just last week when they went to dinner one night. She'd started to have dreams of Arnold showing up—dreams she didn't mention to Bear. Why ruin perfection? Each time, Bear's fears proved unfounded. No Arnold, no Tibbs, nothing.

But this somehow felt different. The forest was quiet, she noticed. No birds singing. No squirrels chittering at them.

Bear motioned for Ellie to hold still. He took a step forward, then another, alert. He turned around and motioned for her to head back to the cabin, mouthing the word *run*.

No.

Ellie heard a pop and felt something fly past her cheek. Then Bear was scooping her up and running with her in his arms. They flew past trees. How could he run so fast carrying her?

Another *pop* and Bear flinched, then looked confused.

The world slowed to a crawl as she watched Bear's face.

They shot him they shot him they shot him Arnold and Tibbs shot him and it's all my fault. Her mind raced as Bear kept running. He was hunched over her to protect her, she thought, until his steps slowed and he staggered. Ellie looked around wildly, fighting back tears. She didn't see any blood on Bear but his eyes looked groggy.

Bear set her on the ground.

"Run," he slurred. "Hit the alarm. Call Ben."

"Bear, no! I'm not leaving you. You've been shot."

"Run." He bent his arms back and looked for all the world like he was trying to scratch an unreachable itch between his shoulder blades. Behind them, she heard footsteps. Then Ellie saw Bear's back.

Sticking out between his shoulder blades was a syringe. Ellie grabbed it and pulled it out but it was too late. The tranq was already doing its job.

"Honey, run," Bear panted.

Ellie ran. But not back to the cabin. She ran into the brush and waited. The gun felt heavy in its holster.

I can't.

She pulled out her phone instead. Ben and the others had to be close to the cabin by now. She had to warn him so he could save Bear.

Arnold and Tibbs appeared. Arnold was carrying a baseball bat and Tibbs had the tranq gun slung over one shoulder.

"Elinor!" Arnold yelled. He swung the bat and it made a whistling sound.

Ellie froze when she heard her name. His voice paralyzed her with terror the way it had so many times before. She was nothing but a helpless little girl about to watch her brother torture and kill one more living thing. Ellie fumbled with her phone, trying to call Ben. No way could she steady her fingers enough to text, let alone fire a gun without risking Bear's life. She hit call on Ben's number. At least he'd be able to hear what was happening and he could track Ellie's phone.

"Come out, Elinor!"

Whack. Arnold hit the baseball bat against a sapling beside Bear. The last, loose aspen leaves fell like coins from the sky.

Whack.

"Next one's gonna be for him, you little shit, if I don't see your face. Where are you? You're here somewhere."

Whack.

"I know all this land is yours." Arold turned slowly in a circle, his arms slightly out to his sides, maniacal grin on his face. "Our dear Uncle Walter left it to *you.*"

Whack. More leaves fell.

"I was gonna just tranq you and carry you home, nice and quiet. But you fucked that up. You and this fucker here." Arnold toed Bear's arm. "You belong back home with your family."

Arnold paused and looked around like his head was on a swivel. "Here's what I want, Elinor. I want you to come out where Tibbs and I can see you. You and I will walk calmly back to the cabin and discuss the terms of you signing over the deed to me while Tibbs stands guard over your fuck buddy here. Once you've signed it over, I'll send him a text saying you were a good girl and did what you were told and he'll leave your bear sleeping in the woods. Then the three of us will head back home and I'll sell this place. If not." Arnold put on an exaggerated sad frown and shrugged. "Then I guess Tibbs makes sure this bear never wakes up."

He's crazy. He can't possibly think he can get away with this.

Whack.

"Listen, you're already fucked, Elinor, you know why? They're looking for you. Well, not for you, but for a woman who pulled a gun on a man at a bus station."

Ellie held back a gasp. All her fears were coming true.

"That's right," Arnold scoffed. "That all went on camera. Nobody knows who you are though and they've pretty much given up since you didn't go on a fucking crime spree. But I could tell them something. I could say, yeah, that's my little sister. She's trouble. You might wanna ask about a dead pawn-shop owner back in Illinois. I think you'll find the gun's a match to the one that killed him, officers. She stole it from me along with some shit from the pawnshop and took off."

Oh, God, were the police really looking for her? Of course they were—how else could Arnold know about the man at the bus station and what she did? Her heart was pounding so loudly now that she couldn't believe they didn't know where she was.

Bear needed help right now, he kept trying to lift his head, to get to his hands and knees but couldn't.

"All I have to do is shoot this fucker here where he lies and tell them it was you." Arnold looked at Tibbs. "Can I get a witness?"

Tibbs laughed and nodded.

"Or you want to watch me skin your boyfriend alive? Lay him out like a rug?" Arnold laughed. "Tibbs, you got that hunting knife?"

Nausea threatened to overwhelm her.

Tibbs drew a huge knife out of his jacket. "This'll skin a bear," he said, and handed it over to Arnold. Bear didn't stir. He had to be out cold.

Arnold took the knife and bent down toward Bear's head. She knew he'd do it—cut the skin right off Bear's gorgeous face. He'd laugh the whole time, knowing exactly what he was doing to both Bear and Ellie. Pain was fun for him.

Something in Ellie finally broke.

That was the man she loved.

That was her future husband.

This was her home.

Arnold had destroyed her happiness time and again.

No more.

She wasn't weak.

Or stupid.

She was strong.

And brave.

We aren't afraid of anything, are we, baby?

Oh yes, she was very afraid. Afraid of losing everything. Afraid of losing the most important person in her life.

But she would be brave. For herself. For Bear.

No. More.

Ellie pulled the gun from its holster and aimed just like Bear had taught her.

The first bullet whizzed past Arnold's head. Tibbs dropped to the ground. Both men looked around wildly, trying to find her. Tibbs was already getting back up, a wild look on his face. He'd always wanted her, like he wanted a punching bag. When he found her, he'd never let go and she'd never get away.

There was no sign of Ben or the others.

If she fired again, they'd pinpoint exactly where she was and come after her. She'd have no choice but to shoot them.

But if they came after her, they'd be away from Bear.

Ellie took another shot.

This one hit Tibbs.

He went sprawling back to the ground, clutching his thigh and screaming. Arnold actually laughed.

"My sister couldn't hit the side of a barn. Looks like she's learned something." He wasn't afraid. He needed to be afraid. He needed to run away and leave her and Bear alone.

Ellie aimed again, this time at her brother.

"You won't shoot me," he said, looking at the bushes where she'd hidden. He grabbed Bear's scruffy head. "I'll kill—"

Bear moved and he moved quickly.

He lifted himself up and grabbed Arnold by the back of the head and slammed him down.

"Told you...to...run...Ellie." She could barely understand Bear's slurred speech. She realized that he'd been playing possum to give her a chance to get away and she'd stayed instead. He would have sacrificed his life for hers. He would even now.

Arnold threw Bear's hand off and both men staggered to their feet. Arnold was laughing, making fun of Bear.

"You were a weak little pussy then. You're no better now." He cackled while he pretended to stagger while Bear staggered for real, trying to focus on Arnold as the man swung his knife hand out. He barely missed Bear's torso, toying with him, getting ready to stab him for real.

No.

No. It was her job to take care of Bear, the same way he took care of her.

Ellie stood up, gun pointed at Arnold, and walked out of the bushes.

"No," Bear slurred. "Run." He took a swing at Arnold who easily dodged him.

"Put that down," Arnold said as casually as if he were telling Ellie to set the table.

"Drop the knife and the baseball bat and get away from him." Ellie kept her voice steady, surprised how easy it was. Her fear was seeping out of her and into the ground, as if her home were pulling it from her. She had a job to do, and that job was to protect Bear. Simple.

We're not afraid of anything.

And Arnold was nothing.

"No, Arnold. I won't put it down. Get away from my fiancé and get off my land." She stopped and planted her feet firmly shoulder-length apart like Bear had taught her. She aimed right at the walking grease spot that was her brother and prepared to do anything it took to save Bear's life and her own.

And Arnold saw it. He stopped laughing. The corner of his mouth quivered in uncertainty. Then before she could react, he turned and swung the bat at Bear's head.

A crack rang out through the forest when it made contact with his jaw. Bear stumbled and went to one knee.

Ellie pulled the trigger. Arnold's right shoulder snapped back and he dropped the bat. A dark red spot bloomed on his shirt and he roared.

Ellie took aim again, this time at his heart.

Not. Afraid.

I love you, Bear.

She pulled the trigger again and felt a sting in the side of her neck at the same time. Her shot went wide and her hand went automatically to her neck.

Where she felt the dart.

Ellie turned to look at Tibbs. He lay on the ground, tranq gun in hand, leering up at her.

At that moment, she saw her future. As the forest blurred around her, she saw Tibbs stand up and walk toward her as if he'd never been shot. She saw Arnold finish off Bear with his bat. She saw them pick her up and carry her helpless to a van and toss her in the back. It was the collecting van, the one Tibbs used to transport merchandise.

Like she was now.

At the same time, she was falling in the woods as if her legs had simply disappeared. The trees spun, Bear roared, and when Ellie hit the ground, a sharp pain to her temple was the last thing she felt before the world was swallowed up in a black sky without stars.

TWENTY-THREE

His Ellie was in danger. Nothing else mattered.

Bear stood as the world spun around him, threatening to pull him down into the blackness he fought so hard to resist. She was supposed to run, supposed to leave him behind and save herself.

But not his brave Ellie.

Rage and loathing thundered through his veins. He didn't even feel the pain in his jaw as he charged Arnold, tackling him to the ground. He felt no fear as he took a swing at him, barely missing his head as Arnold dodged the blow and laughed in his face.

No. Bear had to protect Ellie. He had to get her away from these monsters. He grabbed Arnold by the throat and squeezed, making sure he could never hurt Ellie again. Arnold gasped for air and tried to break free, but Bear's grip was too strong.

Bear leaned in close and snarled, "Move and I'll kill you."

Arnold's eyes widened in fear and he nodded. Bear loosened his grip. Arnold smiled.

"You...almost...killed me," he wheezed. "You wanted to.

See me. Die. You're no... better...than me."

Fuck it.

Bear raised his fist and sent it colliding with Arnold's nose. Blood sprayed everywhere.

He looked up in time to see Tibbs stumbling toward Ellie as she lay helpless on the ground. He raised the tranq gun and pointed it at Ellie's chest.

A rage that eclipsed anything he'd ever felt before surged through Bear. Just as Tibbs was about to pull the trigger, Bear lunged at him. His body collided with Tibbs, knocking him away from Ellie. Bear roared and punched him repeatedly in the face and chest. Tibbs' bones cracked under his fists, but he felt no remorse. He wanted to kill the man who had hurt his Ellie.

From somewhere far away he thought he heard Ben's voice shouting for someone to drop their weapon.

A gun went off in a different universe. Something slammed into the back of his left shoulder from behind. Maybe it would hurt later. More guns fired. They weren't Bear's concern. Let Ben handle it. Right now Bear was busy killing a monster.

Well. What was left of a monster.

The world started to blur and Bear could feel his strength ebbing away. But he had done it. He had saved his Ellie.

He staggered towards Ellie, wanting nothing more than to hold her. But his legs gave out and he collapsed by her side. He reached out for her, but the world was darkening and his arm felt like it was made of lead.

"Ellie?" Was that his voice sounding so weak? "Honey? Open your eyes."

He tried to run his hands through her hair but he touched something sticky and wet at the back of her head. Kind of like his arm right now.

Someone was talking to him but they weren't Ellie so they didn't matter. Hands gripped his arms and tried to pull him away from her and that did matter so he tried to fight back but the leaden feeling was spreading from his shoulder and arm to his entire body.

"Jon. Listen to me."

Who the hell was Jon? Ellie always called him Bear. He touched her face. She was so pale and cold. He needed to get her inside, wrap her up in the mink blanket, and set her in front of the fireplace.

"Jon, we called an ambo. We need to get you both to the hospital."

No. We don't need that. We're home.

"You're losing a lot of blood." A blurry face peered into his. "Can you understand what I'm saying?"

"Ben?"

Another man's voice broke in. Shane's face appeared. "Tranq gun, man. They probably got him, that's why he's so extra fucked up. Paramedics are on the way. Elias is directing them in."

"Bear," Ben said.

That's better. She calls me Bear, not Jon. Bear is me.

"I'm going to have to press on your shoulder. You're losing so much blood."

"Ellie," Bear said, his voice sounding rough and ragged like his words were sharp-edged things scraping their way out of his throat.

"I've got her, Bear." Waylon was suddenly hovering over Bear and Ellie. He was touching the side of Ellie's neck and talking into a cell phone. "Patient's pulse is thready, respiration is irregular at about six breaths per minute, head trauma, possible hematoma. Looks like she hit a sharp rock. She's hemorrhaging." Waylon made a fist and rubbed his knuckles against Ellie's chest. "She's non-responsive to sternum rub, could be a concussion." He glanced at Bear. "Could be something worse. What's your ETA?"

"Don't... don't hurt her, Ram," Bear tried to tell Waylon.

"He's helping her, Bear," Ben said. He was pressing against Bear's left shoulder, which was starting to bother him. The world was filling with black dots. Anti-stars. Bear reached for Ellie's hand so they could be together as night fell. The last thing he heard was Ram's voice.

"Aw, shit. Come on, Ellie. Stay with me. Stay..."

———

B ear woke in an unfamiliar bed, grumpy as his name. He felt groggy and disoriented and his mouth was dry as a desert. He smelled disinfectant and institutional food and heard machines beeping.

And then memories of the worst day of his life slammed back into him. Bear sat up and nearly yanked an IV line out of his arm.

"Whoa, Bear." Gabe stood up from a chair across the room. "Easy, man." He reached Bear's side. "You were shot."

"Where's Ellie?" Bear choked out.

Gabe handed him a giant plastic cup with a lid and a straw. "Drink. It'll help."

"I said, where's Ellie?" Fuck, he'd almost added *are you deaf* without thinking. He sipped the water while Gabe watched him. It soothed his throat. "Where is she?"

"Jon, you need to be prepared."

The world stopped.

"She's not dead," Gabe quickly added. "But she's... it's complicated."

"What room is she in?" Bear swung his legs over the side of the bed.

"Hang on. Don't you want to know what's wrong with you?"

"What's wrong with me is that I'm not with her right now, Timberwolf." The old nickname rolled right off Bear's tongue as if no time had passed since they were kids.

Gabe ignored him. "You were shot, Bear. The bullet nicked a big vessel and you almost bled out. Plus you were drugged. You weren't too far from death yourself."

"I don't care. Take me to her. I want to talk to her." He started to fiddle with the IV in his arm. What did he need that stupid thing for when it was only going to slow him down? So was the damn blood pressure cuff going off every few minutes so he ripped that off. The machines beeped louder.

"Kyle and Ben are handling the police right now, but you're gonna have to answer some questions about Arnold."

"So what?" He paused. "And Tibbs?"

Gabe stared blankly at him. "Tibbs wasn't there."

That made Bear pause again. "But, he—"

Gabe put his hand out, silencing Bear. "Tibbs Hackett was never in Colorado. Certainly, they'll never find his body here. Or anywhere. Much to the joy and relief of the women he abused over the years."

Bear nodded. So he'd killed Tibbs and his pack cleaned up the remains. He tried to find a shred of remorse but couldn't.

"What am I gonna have to answer about Arnold?" He vaguely remembered blood flying.

Gabe pursed his lips. "Arnold probably won't make it. He's in a coma. Last conscious thing he did was shoot you while you protected Ellie."

"Am I facing charges?" Bear noticed for the first time how

much Gabe watched his mouth move as he tried to read Bear's lips. Guilt hit him hard.

Gabe shrugged. "Like I said, you'll answer some questions. But in the end, it'll be called self-defense."

"Great. Where's Ellie?"

Gabe sighed. "Jon. Bear. Ellie's...look, here's what happened. When she fell, she hit her head on a rock. Hard."

Her hair was wet and sticky.

"She's in a coma too, Jon."

Bear had been wrong. The world hadn't stopped before. It stopped now.

"How bad?"

"The doctors are still optimistic—"

"How. Fucking. Bad, Gabe?"

He just shook his head.

"I want to see her. Now."

"Your doc said once you woke up she wants you to stay put until she can evaluate you."

Bear ripped the IV out of his arm and stormed toward the door. His head throbbed but he didn't care.

"Fuck! Bear, wait." Gabe came around in front of Bear, blocking the door. "I'll take you, all right? She's in the ICU. No one else can visit her today, but maybe we can sneak you in."

Bear blew out a long breath. Gabe was his friend. He'd help him.

"Okay."

There'd been a mistake. The small, gray-skinned woman in the ICU bed wasn't Ellie. It was some other woman who looked like she didn't have a lot of time left.

Not my Ellie.

"Bear—"

She didn't have Ellie's smile. When Bear leaned in close, she didn't have Ellie's sweet, berry scent.

"It's not her, Gabe."

"Come on, man."

"No." Bear shook his head and backed away from the hospital bed. "It's not. That's not my Ellie."

"Let's get you back to your room." Gabe took Bear's arm and led him out of the glass-walled room. Bear followed without a word or a fight.

"Lay down, brother," Gabe said when they got back to Bear's room. "You need to rest."

Bear didn't lay down. He stood beside the bed.

Goddamn it. Ellie just wanted a little cabin. She just wanted a home. A safe place that was hers that no one could take and no one could break. That's all. She deserved the world and asked for so little, and in the end got nothing but hurt.

"It was her." Bear wiped his hand over his face.

"Yeah, Bear. I'm sorry." Gabe looked away.

"Gabe," Bear said quietly.

He didn't turn back because his friend didn't hear him.

My fault.

"I failed," Bear raised his voice and Gabe turned back quickly.

"What? You didn't fail, Jon. There was nothing—"

"I failed her. Do you understand me? I failed her!"

Bear picked up the plastic water cup and hurled it at the wall. He picked up the nearest chair and threw it across the room. Gabe backed away slowly.

"I had one job and that was to protect her and I fucking blew it. She's lying in that hospital bed because of me. I..."

He staggered and looked around for something, anything, to destroy. When really all he wanted to destroy was himself.

"Jesus Christ, Jon," Gabe said. "You were drugged, outnumbered and overpowered. You didn't fail her. You saved her. Without you, she'd be dead."

"Did you see her? She's as good as dead!" Bear roared. "She still...might...Ellie...oh, God, Ellie."

Bear felt his fury draining out of him. He scrubbed his hands over his face, trying to work himself back up into a rage. He wanted to hate the world enough to tear it apart, wanted to feel so disgusted with himself that he ripped himself in two. Bear didn't want to feel anything but white-hot fury because when it ebbed away it left another feeling behind, a terrible, terrible feeling.

He stopped scrubbing and covered his face. From behind his hands, he whispered, "I'm not. I'm not. I'm *not* afraid. I'm not afraid of anything."

"Jon?"

Bear's useless hands dropped to his sides.

"I'm not afraid of anything. Except losing her."

"Then go back into that hospital room and save her. She needs you right now, right there. No one else can save her but you. You're the only one who can call her up and out of that darkness. So go face your goddamned fear and conquer it. For her."

"Timberwolf?"

"Yeah, Bear?"

"I'm sorry I failed you, too."

Now Gabe's eyes filled with fury. "Don't, Jon. Just fucking don't right now. We're not doing this here." He pointed at the door. "She needs you. I'm fucking *fine*."

There was nothing more to say. Bear left the room to find Ellie.

TWENTY-FOUR

"I f she's awake, she'll be able to hear you, Mr. Behr, even if she doesn't respond."

Who's that? Bear? Bear, where are you?

"Honey? Can you hear me?"

Bear, where are you? I can't find you, Bear. It's so dark.

"Honey, please, open your eyes for me."

Bear? I can't see anything.

"I'm right here. I'll be here through the night, baby. Maybe you're asleep already. Maybe tomorrow, huh? I love you."

I can't find you. I'm tired. I want to sleep but I can't sleep without you.

"Good morning, honey. I was hoping you'd open your eyes for me today."

Bear! Bear, I'm here! I think I was asleep.

"Can you hear me, honey? I'm right here. I'm not leaving you."

Bear, I can't...I can't see you. It's dark. I'm...I'm afraid, Bear.

"I'm squeezing your hand. Can you feel me, honey?"

Bear? I think I fell asleep again. I can't feel you, Bear. Where are you? Come find me, Bear. I know we aren't scared of anything but I'm scared right now. I'm really scared.

"I'm right here, honey. I'm not going anywhere until you come home to me."

I'm trying. I don't know where I am and I'm so tired.

"I need you to find your way home to me."

I can't find you.

"Good morning, honey."

Bear! I think I fell asleep again. But it's dark. What time is it? Where am I? Where are you?

"Any sign, Mr. Behr?"

"No, ma'am. She hasn't opened her eyes or squeezed my hand yet."

"Keep trying. She'll hear you."

"I'm never giving up on her, doc."

Bear. My Bear. Please, please let that be true. I'm trying, Bear. But I'm so tired.

"Good morning, honey."

No. No, please, not another day. Where am I? Bear? You sound hoarse.

"I'm still here, honey. I'm not leaving you. But, babe. I need you to come home to me. It's been too long and...they say that's not good. The longer you're out..."

Bear, Bear don't cry. Please, I love you. I'll always love you. Just come get me.

"So, honey, I hope you can hear me. And I hope you know I love you and you aren't alone in there."

Alone where? Where am I?

"I hope you're dreaming good things. But I also hope you know those are just dreams."

I'm not dreaming anything. Unless this is all a dream. Is this a dream, Bear? Are we in our cabin, safe and warm, and I'm dreaming this darkness?

"I want you to wake up for me, honey. Open your eyes. Squeeze my hand. Anything. Please. Please, don't give up on me. I'm right here."

I love you, Bear. I'm never giving up on you. I'm trying to come home but I can't see anything.

"Come home, baby."

How?

"Honey? Hey. It's a new morning."

No. No. No!

"Rise and shine, huh? Maybe today's the day you'll surprise me."

I'm trying, Bear. It's so hard, but I'm trying. You sound so hoarse.

"I was thinking, honey, and I hate this thought. But...are you in there in the dark?"

Yes! Yes! I'm here! It's dark, Bear. It's so dark. Can you find me now? Do you know where I am?

"If you're in the dark, I want you to try something for me. I want you to try and remember that first night we went out on the boat on the lake."

The boat? I can't...

"Remember the boat? Remember how we were out on the pond watching the stars coming out one by one as it got dark?"

I'm trying to remember. I don't remember a boat, Bear. Why can't I remember a boat? It's making me tired to try.

"...and as it..."

Bear? Tired.

"...dark, but all those..."

Bear.

"...stars. And I taught you..."

"..."

C an't hear you anymore. Love you. Bear.

TWENTY-FIVE

Bear shifted in the chair beside the hospital bed. He thought he'd been dozing but he couldn't be sure. Did Ellie squeeze his hand and wake him?

No. Nothing. Just like the day before. And the day before that. And so on. The week had lasted several years already.

He blinked at the early morning light. The night nurse would do one last check soon with the day shift nurse and fill her in on Ellie. It would be quick, because nothing had changed.

Another day.

He could only hope this one would be different, that this was the day she'd open her eyes. The day he'd get her back.

Yesterday was bad. The doctor was worried, he could tell. She took an extra-long time checking Ellie over. If anything, his Ellie was even less responsive after he tried to get her to open her eyes. They were worried about organ failure, about her brain shutting down.

It wasn't fair. Ellie was safe from Arnold and Tibbs now and she had a home. Bear had seen to that. Ellie was safe, she had a home, and he wanted to spend the rest of his life with her. A simple, happy life. He wanted to expand the cabin next to make room for the family they'd raise together. He wanted to learn how to garden, to raise plants beside Ellie. To keep bees. To teach the kids how to fish and how to clean their catch so their tender-hearted mama would never have to.

Tender-hearted, but fierce when she needed to be. When she was protecting what she loved. She'd shot her Tibbs and her brother to save Bear. Arnold was in a vegetative state, and if he didn't come out of it today then it looked like he'd be in it forever.

Ellie is in the same situation. If she doesn't respond today—

He cut that thought off with a mental machete.

Bear had answered all the cops' questions. Arnold's prints were all over the tranq gun—with a little help from Bear's friends. Both he and Ellie were clearly acting in self-defense and there would be no charges. Turned out, Arnold had OD'ed his dad right before they left for Colorado. They found him in his recliner during the massive drug bust, kicked off by an anonymous tip. Harlan was in jail for half a million reasons and the whole operation was shut down.

They were in the clear. Ellie would never have to worry about her family again.

So Bear needed her to be fierce just one more time. For herself. For him. For their future children and grandchildren and great-grandchildren.

And we'll teach them all. Teach them they don't have to be afraid of anything.

Bear swallowed his fear. It wouldn't do Ellie any good. He squeezed her hand like he did a thousand times a day and felt nothing back. And then he started over with the story he could only trust she could hear. The story he'd told her over and over, every day until he damn near lost his voice telling it, hoping it would get through to her.

Their story. The one that would guide her home.

"Honey? Good morning. This will be our day, I just know it. Listen. Remember the boat? Remember the first night we went out on the lake after sunset and watched it get dark? All those stars, honey. Remember how I pointed out the constellations to you? You knew the Big Dipper, but you didn't know it was also called Ursa Major. The Big Bear. I can still feel you lying against me, looking up at those stars when I showed you how you can use Ursa Major to find the North Star. And once you find the North Star, you can guide yourself anywhere."

He wiped his eyes.

Then he smiled.

"The lake was so still it reflected the stars just perfect. And you looked up at the stars and down at their reflections and do you remember what you said? You said it looked like we were right in the middle of them. It looked like we were in space, and our boat must not be a boat but a spaceship."

He squeezed her hand. Nothing.

"So I taught you how you could navigate by the stars, whether it was by boat or an airplane or even a spaceship."

Squeeze. Nothing.

"Honey, you're in a place right now where I can't bring you home. If I could, I would. You'd already be back and I'd be feeding you ice cream and I'd give you whatever else you want. I can't get to you though. I can't reach into your head and get you out. That's where you are right now. You're trapped in your head.

"But they said you could hear me, so maybe I can get in there to you after all, huh? Is it dark where you are? Baby, if it is, I need you to listen to me. I need you to look hard into that darkness until you see those stars. Look for Ursa Major. Can you see it? Look *hard*, baby. It's there. We just need to believe..." he rubbed his eyes, "we need to believe Ursa

Major's there until you can see it. Find it, and then use it to look for the North Star. When you find that, use it, too. Let it guide you back here, to me. Let its light shine brighter until your eyes are open. I'm right here, honey, just past that star, but you've gotta find it. You've gotta find it and navigate your way home. Because I love you and I don't want to be here without you anymore. I can't..."

His breath hitched.

"Just remember those stars, honey. You can do this. You *will* navigate your way home. I know you aren't afraid. Because we aren't afraid of anything, are we, baby?"

No squeeze. No glimmer of his Ellie.

Bear didn't let go of her hand. He had to believe that she was there in the darkness searching for him. That as long as he held out hope, she would find her way back.

He started the story over and over until hours later he closed his eyes and laid his shaggy head down on the bed next to her pillow.

TWENTY-SIX

Stars.

So many stars, Bear.

TWENTY-SEVEN

Bear was dreaming of stars.

He was dreaming of a dark night on water when the stars were all around them carrying their boat home. He was holding Ellie's hand and she must have been ticklish because it was moving in his. Something about that was very important. It tugged at him, pulling him away from where he wanted to be—with Ellie on their way home. He fought to stay in the dream until he was awake enough to remember...

There. Was that...? Did her hand move?

"Ellie?" Bear whispered as he opened his eyes. He didn't dare move a muscle. He was in the same position he'd been in when he fell asleep—sitting in a chair, his head on the mattress beside her pillow, her hand tucked into his.

"If you can hear me, honey, squeeze my hand."

Bear kept perfectly still until he felt it.

Ellie's finger moved.

It twitched, just a little. But to Bear, it felt like the entire world shook in the palm of his hand.

"Ellie." Bear sat up very slowly, very carefully. "Do you

see the stars? Are you navigating home? Squeeze my hand if you are."

He waited.

This time, two fingers moved.

"Two fingers, honey. That's so good. You're coming home, baby. Don't be afraid of the dark because you're coming home. And I'm waiting here for you. Come home."

Bear hit the call button and summoned Ellie's nurse.

Ellie didn't wake up all at once. That was only for the movies and books, Bear discovered. She didn't sit right up, kiss him on the nose, and order dinner. Instead, she moved her fingers a little more every day. When she finally opened her eyes, it was only for a moment, and then she was gone back down into the black again. But in that moment when Bear gazed into her eyes, he could see her gazing back. Even if she didn't quite see him, she knew he was there.

So little by little, Ellie found her way back to Bear. Every day she was a little more aware of him and of where she was. Every day, he watched her fight harder to stay with him.

Her first word was *stars*.

Bear wept.

The next day, she said, "Love you, Bear."

And by the end of the week, she *was* sitting up and Bear was ordering dinner for her and telling her about the progress on the cabin. He kept talking, filling the space with words, which wasn't like him at all. She needed to talk, needed to work on her language skills, the doctors said. But as soon as she looked like she was about to speak, off he went again, talking, talking, talking. Braying like a complete jackass.

She fell asleep again, and in the quiet of the hospital

room, he realized he was afraid of what she'd tell him about being in the coma. What she would say about the place where he couldn't keep her safe. Afraid that it had been a waking nightmare for her and that hearing about it would kill him.

We're not afraid of anything, are we, baby? Those words slapped him upside the head. Bear was afraid. He was afraid that *she'd* been afraid all that time. Fear like that stayed with a person, sometimes for the rest of their lives. It made them wander from place to place, trying to get away from it. He didn't want that for Ellie. He wanted to bring her home and he wanted her to be at peace there. Because he'd found his peace finally. With her.

Ellie opened her eyes and blinked rapidly. She squeezed his hand, reassuring herself and him that she was there. Bear fought the urge to start talking immediately. He let the silence stay until she was ready to fill it.

"Love you, Bear." She tried to lift his hand to her lips but she was still so weak so he did it for her.

"Love you too, honey. So much."

Stay quiet. No more words. She's still the wild thing you first met coming out of the woods and you have to be quiet and gentle and let her come to you like you did then. Now more than ever.

"Bear?"

"Yeah, honey?"

"You look sad."

He bit his lip. He could lie, smile and tell her how happy he was.

"I've...been afraid, baby."

She smiled. "But we're not afraid of anything."

"I was, Ellie. I was afraid."

"Why?"

"Because I was alone out here without you. And I knew

you were alone in there. That's so much worse, Ellie. That's why I was afraid."

Bear bowed his head, unable to look into her eyes when she told him just how afraid she'd been. He'd failed her and left her alone in the dark.

"I wasn't afraid, Bear."

Bear lifted his head. She was still smiling that calm, soft smile. Her eyes twinkled like stars.

"You weren't?"

She shook her head slowly. "No. Because I wasn't alone. You were there the whole time. Guiding me home."

She squeezed his hand as he held back his grateful tears.

"And I made it, thanks to you."

It took a few more weeks, but finally, Bear was allowed to really bring Ellie *home*.

He worried as they bumped over some of the ruts on their way up the mountain. He didn't want to jostle her around. The truck bed was full of flowers and stuffed animals and gifts that all Ellie's friends brought her when they visited. They'd talked about being there when she got home, but Bear nixed that plan. She still got tired out easily and needed some peace and quiet at first. But Ellie herself made it clear to him that as soon as she was better, he could expect her to start entertaining.

Fine by him. Anything that made her happy.

Plus, he kinda liked having his friends around too.

Ellie practically had her nose pressed to the window the whole drive. The snow she'd seen before had been dustings compared to this one, and she'd gasped at the beauty of the snow-covered mountains as they'd driven toward them.

"Too bright for you, honey?"

"No, not at all." She tapped her sunglasses. "These are good, thank you."

Bear slowed the truck as they approached a bigger bump in the road. He'd memorized them all, since he couldn't see them under the fresh, white blanket of snow. Damn it, he should have prioritized the grading of the new private driveway on the land back behind the cabin. It was this close to being done, almost connected to the newer road behind it. That would make it much easier and faster to get to and from town, and it sure would have made Ellie's trip home smoother.

"You okay, honey?"

She looked away from the window. "For the thousandth time, yes, Bear. I'm fine." She smiled and reached across the cab to take his hand. "Never been better."

"Can't wait to show you everything new."

"Can't wait to see it all."

"Bathroom's done. Solar's in. All the new paint looks good. Got the new refrigerator. Oh, and the women all brought up food so it's stocked."

Bear parked the truck. He'd bring everything in after he got Ellie settled. He jogged around to the other side of the truck and got Ellie out.

"Bear?"

"Yeah, baby?"

"I'm never gonna build my leg muscles back up if you insist on carrying me everywhere."

He chuckled as he carried her through the bare aspens to the cabin.

"Can't help it. I like how you feel curled right up here against my heart."

"You won't feel that way if you throw your back out carrying me all the time."

Bear chuckled as he climbed the steps up the porch and ducked under the *Welcome Home Ellie!* banner her friends had insisted on hanging. "You don't weigh a blessed thing. No more than a feather in my arms." He punched in the security code and opened the cabin door.

"Well then, this feather is going to eat and eat and eat until I'm so heavy you have to put me down."

"Mmm. Food's a good idea. We have to get some meat back on those bones."

"And *then* will you stop carrying me?" she teased.

He tightened his arms around her. "Honey, I'm never gonna stop carrying you. And you want to know a secret?"

"Sure."

"All the time I'm carrying you, you're carrying me right back."

TWENTY-EIGHT

Gabe "Timberwolf" O'Neil

There were times when Gabe O'Neil looked at his hearing loss as a blessing. Riding with his best friend Shane to Riversong Coffee this morning was one of those times. Shane always got this way when they went to Riversong, so Gabe made a show of turning off his hearing aid.

"Dude! Come on, seriously?"

Gabe could still make out Shane's words, so the man must have been shouting.

"You know I'm right," Shane went on. "You need to make your move." He stopped at the light right before the shop and glared at Gabe until he turned his hearing aid back on.

"Yeah, because all that non-stop flirting you're doing with April is getting you so far."

"Hey, at least I'm talking to April instead of just moon dogging at her."

"What the hell does moon dogging even mean?"

"Dude, go look in a mirror while you're thinking about Little Miss Window Seat and you'll know." Shane pulled an exaggerated face—he tilted his head, his mouth slowly dropped open, and his eyes grew wide.

Gabe resisted flipping Shane off and pointed out the windshield instead. "Green means go."

Shane went through the intersection and pulled into Riversong's parking lot. Gabe's chest tightened as he couldn't resist looking at the window to the far right side of the shop.

There she was, same as every day at this time, sitting in the window seat and reading, her back to one of the bookshelves bracketing the padded bench. He knew she'd have a laptop sitting on the table beside her, and the minute he got his coffee and headed for a nearby table, she'd quickly set her book down, open the laptop, and start typing away.

"Why don't you just go introduce yourself and ask her out?"

"Because she always looks busy, that's why," Gabe said.

Pointedly busy the second he got up his nerve to say hi.

They got out of the SUV and walked to the door. April was finishing up with a customer, giving him a smile and a cup of joe. Her smile disappeared when she saw Shane—turning into something a little more snarky—though it reappeared for Gabe.

"Morning," she said, and without waiting, immediately dumped two spoonfuls of sugar in the bottom of a cup. Next she would pour in coffee and one shot of espresso—just the way Gabe liked his coffee.

"Good morning, beautiful," Shane said, leaning on the counter. "I'll have my usual."

"Oh, of course you will. What was that again? I don't keep track."

Gabe tuned out the rest of their banter and glanced over at her. The beautiful woman in the window. Brunette, not too thin, thick eyelashes, cozy cardigan in all kinds of weather. He never knew what she was reading because she wrapped the covers in brown paper. Was she embarrassed about what she read, or was there another reason? Gabe was dying to know.

He was dying to know *anything* about her.

She lifted her pointer finger to her lips and her tongue darted out, wetting it, then she turned the next page. The gesture was completely unselfconscious and at the same time, extremely sexy. Gabe had to turn away before he embarrassed himself.

April had finished making his coffee and was starting on Shane's drink. Gabe pulled out his wallet.

April grinned and put her hand up. "Your money's no good here today, my friend."

What? Did he misunderstand? "Sorry, I don't think I heard you right. It's free?" he ventured. He watched her lips carefully.

She pointed at his coffee. "That one's already been paid for," April said a little louder and slower.

"You don't need to buy me coffee, April," Gabe said as he continued to open his wallet, feeling like maybe he was somehow the butt of a joke Shane was playing.

April reached across the counter and put her hand on his. He looked up. "*I* didn't buy it for you. She did." Then April discreetly pointed over his shoulder. Shane's eyes widened as did his smile, but April's face was dead serious.

Gabe turned to find the woman in the window seat looking shyly up at him through gorgeous black lashes. She set her book aside and this time, she didn't touch her laptop.

Gabe picked up his coffee as he decided on his next move.

Read about Gabe and Rochelle's adventure in Timberwolf on the Mountain!

NOTE ABOUT THE CHARACTERS

The Watchdog Universe is expanding again!

It's always been my plan to write in one world full of interconnected characters and stories. Each of my series—Watchdog Security, Watchdog Protectors, and now Watchdog Mountain Division—has characters that exist in all three series. While each series—and every book—is a stand-alone, they all fit together as well. But, if you're reading this one first and are wondering about some of the characters' backstories, I decided to do a quick rundown of where you can find their stories.

Kyle and Arden—I think of them as my 'center of the universe' couple who connect all the series so far. Their love story can be found in Watchdog Security's book three – *More Than Puppy Love*. Ellen Sanders and her father Walter are in that one, too.

Flint and Harper start the Watchdog Protectors series (written in Susan Stoker's Operation Alpha world) in *Protecting Harper*.

Watchdog Protectors continues with Badger and Brianna

in *Protecting Brianna*. *Protecting Sylvie* tells the other side of that storyline with Alex and Sylvie.

Shane Foti is also in Watchdog Protectors and will have his love story in Mountain Division. So will Gabe, Waylon, Elias, and Benjamin, who make brief appearances in *Protecting Sylvie*. Charlie and Jodie will have their HEAs in the Watchdog Protector series.

AFTERWORD

Sometimes, a book begins with a song.

Lyle Lovett is a great musician and a good person from everything I've heard. But at one point, one of his songs came on the radio when my alarm went off every. Single. Morning. I'd groan and blearily try to turn it off...and usually fail miserably (I'm not a morning person). That song meant I had to get up and go to a job I hated, one that degraded me. It was a good song that showed up at the wrong time in my life and I hated —hated—it for that reason. So, when it finally fell out of favor, I was relieved that I'd never have to listen to it again.

The thing is, a good friend of my loved Lyle Lovett, big hair and all. Adored him. Saw him in concert at every opportunity. Begged me to come along a couple of times, including when the dreaded song was at its peak. And I always said no. Because of that song. That's how scarred I was by that hated job, even after I'd moved on.

Technically, I was escorted from the building by a security guard, but that's a different story for a different day, one that may even end up in some shape or form in one of my books. I regret nothing.

What I *do* regret is not going to see Lyle Lovett with my friend. A few years ago, she and I fought cancer side by side. She fought harder than I did, but in the end she was the one who lost that battle.

Or maybe not. Before she passed, she filled her life with every last bucket list item she could and she lived hard and strong and good. She loved to travel, she loved Jesus, and she loved Lyle Lovett.

It wasn't until after she'd died (First time I've used that word regarding her. I tell myself we just haven't seen each other lately, that she's on a long trip at the moment and I'll catch up with her eventually) that I heard that dreaded song again after literal decades.

What a difference time and life circumstances can make.

I'd had this nebulous idea for a hero back then, one who I'd think about as I'd fall asleep nights after my last surgery, one who was big and strong and quiet, yet gentle and loving. He'd hold me silently as I fell asleep, keeping me safe in that leap between consciousness and sleep where I'd sometimes fall between those dark cracks and wake panicky. When I'd think of him, I'd make it through safely and sleep all night long.

He faded somewhat as I healed and got stronger and could make it to sleep on my own. When I started writing romances in 2020, he never quite made it into the series as a full-blown hero, though I've loaned out his strength, loving-ness, and gentleness over and over to my other heroes.

Then I was writing in my usual place, the corner spot in my library café, working on *More Than Beauty* when that dreaded song came on overhead. But the strangest thing happened. I didn't cringe. I didn't run screaming from the room. I didn't have a bad memory or feeling go through my head. Instead, I listened to the words, and they made me smile. They're simple, good words in a simple good song, and the song reminded me of my friend.

Bess left on her final adventure before she could read my romances, but she knew I wanted to be an author with all my heart and soul. And here I was, living my dream. I immediately brought the song up again on my computer and put my earbuds in.

And there he was—my Bear. That hero who kept me safe through the scary nights when I was afraid I might not wake up the next morning.

I brought up a new document and started writing this book. My fingers flew while a tiny little voice in my head screamed What are you doing? You have another book to finish! You can't go starting a new one!

I shooed that voice away for the rest of the day. And the next day. And the one after that. And I wrote what have become the most important scenes in this book, the beginning ones and the ending chapters. Then, I banked the Bear fires and went back to *More Than Beauty*, promising myself that I'd get back to Bear, that he obviously had a story to tell, and he'd chosen me to tell it, through a song that once brought me pain but now reminded me of love that endures through the dark and the fear and the pain.

I needed that reminder as I wrote Bear. I'd only gotten back to it when I lost another friend suddenly and without warning. Becca and I had just seen each other earlier in the week. We'd shared a hotel room in Los Angeles for an event and talked non-stop the entire time. Her death felt so unfair and so wrong, because dammit, our friendship was just getting started. I still feel cheated. Yet every now and then, I swear I can hear her voice in my head saying hello and giving me advice.

This is a book born of friendships old and new, a book that

reminds me to live well, to never take my friends for granted, and that dreams do come true through lots of hard work and by following your stars. Mine are about to lead me to Iceland and Switzerland to visit more friends. I know both Bess and Becca would approve.

So, if you've got a minute, put on "Bears" by Lyle Lovett while you read this book. Or, if you've got access to Spotify, I have a playlist that I listened to while writing this book (I have one for all my books) that helped me get in touch with Bear and Ellie's story and reminded me of Bess. You can listen to it here:

https://open.spotify.com/playlist/
4pdPGoDwoEmzoNyNXr1ycF

I hope you love this Bear as much as I do.

ACKNOWLEDGMENTS

Thank you, Lovely, for giving me a chance!

As always, thank you Trinity for your eternal cheerleading, lemons, sprints, and reads (and bear memes. So. Many. Bear. Memes.) I couldn't do this without you!

Thanks to my wonderful assistant, Amber Hamilton. Without her, I walk into walls.

Thanks to the amazing and talented Drue Hoffman, who always has my back.

Thanks to my soul sisters, Michelle and Sara.

Thanks to my fellow Protector Romance authors for helping me get the words on the page: Anna Blakely, Riley Edwards, Rayne Lewis, Kris Michaels, Caitlyn O'Leary, and Bella Stone.

Love to you all!

OLIVIA'S LOVELIES

Follow me to catch my latest releases at:

Amazon: https://www.amazon.com/author/oliviamichaelsromance

BookBub: https://www.bookbub.com/authors/olivia-michaels

Facebook: https://www.facebook.com/oliviamichaelsauthor

Instagram: https://www.instagram.com/oliviamichaelsromance/

Newsletter: https://oliviamichaelsromance.com/

Want more? Come be one of Olivia's Lovelies on Facebook. I can always use another ARC reader or two... https://www.facebook.com/groups/639545290309740/

Or talk to me live on Discord! Find me, Riley Edwards, Caitlyn O'Leary, Kris Michaels, Anna Blakely, and Rayne Lewis on the Protector Romance Talk Channel: https://discord.gg/tSBBrfwR

ALSO BY OLIVIA MICHAELS

Romantic Suspense

Watchdog Security Series

More Than Love

More Than Family

More Than Puppy Love

More Than Paradise

More Than Thrills

More Than Words Can Say

More Than Beauty

More Than Rumors

More Than Secrets (Coming Soon)

Watchdog Protectors Series (Ongoing)

Protecting Harper

Protecting Brianna

Protecting Sylvie

Watchdog Mountain Men Series (Ongoing)

Bear on the Mountain

Timberwolf on the Mountain

ABOUT THE AUTHOR

Olivia Michaels is a life-long reader, dog-lover, gardener, and a certified beachaholic. When she's not throwing a Frisbee for her fur-baby, harvesting tomatoes, or writing, you can find her playing in the surf, kayaking, or kicking back on the sand and cracking open a romantic beach read.

www.ingramcontent.com/pod-product-compliance
Lightning Source LLC
Chambersburg PA
CBHW070727280626
47159CB00023B/2850